THE
STORM

THE
STORM

A NOVEL

Rachel Hawkins

ST. MARTIN'S PRESS
NEW YORK

First published in the United States by St. Martin's Press, an imprint of St. Martin's Publishing Group

EU Representative: Macmillan Publishers Ireland Ltd, 1st Floor, The Liffey Trust Centre, 117–126 Sheriff Street Upper, Dublin 1, DO1 YC43

All emojis designed by OpenMoji—the open-source emoji and icon project. License: CC BY-SA 4.0

www.stmartins.com

Library of Congress Cataloging-in-Publication Data is available upon request.

ISBN 978-1-250-34188-4 (hardcover)
ISBN 978-1-250-44252-9 (international, sold outside the U.S., subject to rights availability)

ISBN 978-1-250-34189-1 (ebook)

Our books may be purchased in bulk for specialty retail/wholesale, literacy, corporate/premium, educational, and subscription box use. Please contact MacmillanSpecialMarkets@macmillan.com.

First Edition: 2026
First International Edition: 2026

10 9 8 7 6 5 4 3 2 1

For Sarah Cantin with an ocean's worth of thanks!

THE
STORM

"It's worse when they come at night."

It sounds like a line from a horror movie, but the woman who says those words to me wasn't trying to be ominous or cryptic. If anything, she was very matter-of-fact, talking about the destructive forces that have, over the past few decades, maimed and murdered, stolen and smashed, the same way someone might tell a visitor not to try to turn left at that one light, or that the Walmart one town over is actually better.

Many of the people who make their living in St. Medard's Bay are like this, so I shouldn't have been surprised that Mrs. Beth-Anne Bailey, owner of the town's largest souvenir shop, was so casual when asked about the four fatal hurricanes that have swept through this little jewel on Alabama's Gulf Coast, starting with Hurricane Delphine on the Fourth of July, 1965, and ending—for now—with Hurricane Marie in 1984. The first storm killed Mrs. Bailey's first husband, Dr. Linus Bailey. Marie killed her second, Charles, too, she tells me, before clarifying that he survived the winds and water but had a heart attack three days later while clearing fallen trees.

Natural disasters are like that, claiming lives in the aftermath, one final jump scare.

A monster that never really dies.

Inside Mrs. Bailey's shop, the air-conditioning is blasting, and Jimmy Buffett plays over the speakers. The smell of cheap plastic from the stack of inflated floats and inner tubes that sit in the front window is almost overwhelming, and I watch a family of four flip through a rack of T-shirts, the sunburned dad guffawing as he holds up one that reads ST. MEDARD'S BAY BLEW ME AWAY! and features a cartoon of a big-busted blond trying to hold on to her bikini top, her eyes wide, her hair horizontal in imagined winds.

Hurricanes have claimed the lives of nearly a hundred people in this town, so the joke seems pitch-black to me, and that must show on my face because Mrs. Bailey shrugs and says, "Is what it is."

The tourists don't buy the shirt in the end, leaving the store with some colorful towels, a few beach toys, and a bright green bottle of aloe vera gel, and once they're gone, I ask Mrs. Bailey again about the storms, the ones that come at night.

"Is it worse because it's dark?" I ask. "You can't see what's going on?"

That makes her laugh. "Baby, trust me, noon, midnight, don't matter. I've been in both. When one of those things hits, you can't see shit no matter the time of day. No, it's worse because of the waiting. All day, you're boarding up windows, and you're filling bathtubs with water, and you're checking to make sure you have enough gas for the generator, and it's almost like . . . it's like you're getting ready for company, you know? Like when your family is coming down for Thanksgiving or Christmas and you gotta get things shipshape."

She pauses, her green eyes far away for a second, and I know she must be thinking of all the times she's made those preparations. "And it's worse because you start hoping, you know? 'Maybe it'll turn, maybe I can just go to bed, and when I wake up, I'll see the whole dang thing decided it wanted to check out Mississippi instead. Or went right back out into the ocean where it belongs.'"

Mrs. Bailey shakes her head, sighing as she adjusts a perfectly straight display of postcards showing off St. Medard's Bay's sugar-white sands and clear green water. Looking at the picture, I find it hard to believe water that beautiful, that calm, can wreak so much horror.

"Tornadoes are nasty," she says. "And I ain't never been in one, but I reckon earthquakes are just as bad. But those just *happen*. Oh, I know they got warnings and scientists for those things, but hurricanes? They're different. They make you wait. They make you . . ."

"Dread?" I supply, and she nods.

"That's it. They *play* with you. And they take this thing you love—the water you swim in, take your babies to play in, drink beer looking out at. The wind that you smell and go, 'Shoot, how'd I get so lucky to live at the beach?' Wind that feels so good in your hair when you're driving with the windows down. Hurricanes turn all that into the thing that blows off your roof, sucks away your photo albums and your wedding dress and your grandmamma's china and sometimes your grandmamma herself. Killing you with the things you love? The things that made you feel so blessed to live here in the first place? Tell me that don't feel evil."

The obvious question arises, so I ask it.

"Why not leave, then?"

Beth-Anne Bailey does not suffer fools, and the look she gives me now tells me she definitely thinks I am one.

"Because this is home, honey. St. Medard's Bay is home."

—"Sun, Fun, and a Thirty Percent Chance of Death: A Small Town on Alabama's Gulf Coast and Its Uneasy Truce with Mother Nature" *(GQ magazine, April 1996)*

Bailey Trial Ends in Hung Jury

DA Thad Morrison claims case will be retried, but legal experts skeptical

The signs were there by Wednesday afternoon: deliberating since Thursday of last week, the jury in the Gloria "Lo" Bailey trial asked yet again for photos from Landon Fitzroy's autopsy report as well as transcripts specifically from Lo Bailey's testimony of the events that occurred the night of August 4, 1984. While the prosecution remained confident to the media, privately, a source within the office let it be known that "everyone expected them to come back with a guilty verdict by Monday, so there are definitely some nerves."

Another colleague in the DA's office put it more bluntly: "If they're questioning not 'Did she do it?' but 'Did a crime *even happen here?*' We're [expletive]."

Those words became prophetic yesterday when, a day after informing Judge Simms that they were having trouble reaching a consensus, the jury announced it was "hopelessly deadlocked," leaving the judge no choice but to declare a mistrial.

In his statement outside the Mobile County Courthouse (the trial was moved from neighboring Baldwin County due to its local notoriety), District Attorney Thad Morrison announced, "While a jury of Miss Bailey's peers was not able to come to a clear judgment on this case, rest assured that the state of Alabama has no intention of letting the death of a bright light like Landon Fitzroy go unpunished. We plan to retry this case as quickly as possible."

But Professor Linda Nowak of the University of Alabama School of Law has her doubts. "It's not a surprise to me that this case captured the public imagination the way it did. You've got a dead politician, a gorgeous teenage mistress, a natural disaster that was biblical in scope . . . I mean, of course that sells papers and magazines. But when you get right down to it, you can't even prove that a crime was committed. Yes, Landon Fitzroy was found with a significant, non-survivable head injury, and it's clear that happened before the waters rose because he doesn't have any water in his lungs. On top of that, you have a mistress who by all accounts—except hers—was on the verge of getting tossed aside, and she was *not* taking that well. I can understand why that might scream 'murder' to some people, but as the defense easily proved, the kind of injuries Landon Fitzroy sustained are not unusual in storm deaths. If you ask me, this was about Governor Fitzroy wanting someone to blame for the loss of his son. And I think the jury sensed that—which is why Miss Bailey is currently a free woman, and why, frankly, I suspect she'll remain one."

The governor's office has issued no comment about the mistrial, nor has any member of the sprawling Fitzroy clan, which includes Landon Fitzroy's widow, former Miss Alabama Alison Carleton-Fitzroy. While Mrs. Fitzroy attended the trial every day, she was not in court when the verdict came in, and sources close to her say, "Her only focus is putting this sordid mess behind her."

Miss Bailey, however, does not appear to feel the same.

"If it takes the rest of her life, Lo is going to clear her name," a family member said, wishing to remain anonymous. "And trust me, when that girl puts her mind to something, she's going to do it. God help anyone who gets in her way."

Press-Register, December 2, 1986

TO: JSHarrison@HarrisonLiterary.org
FROM: HowLo@aol.com
SUBJECT: [no subject]
SENT: 11:39PM, April 19, 2025

Jack—

Do people make money from podcasts?

Thanks!!
Lo

TO: HowLo@aol.com
FROM: AFletcher695@gmail.com
SUBJECT: Jack Harrison/Podcast query
SENT: 2:02PM, April 20, 2025

Ms. Bailey,

I hope you don't mind me reaching out unsolicited like this. My name is August Fletcher, and I'm a writer, mostly of long-form nonfiction for magazines (*Esquire, GQ,* etc.). I came across your story a couple of years ago while doing research for an assignment about hurricanes in the Gulf, and a little digging revealed that you had a literary agent, Jack Harrison. I reached out to Mr. Harrison, who told me he'd initially made contact with you about a memoir sometime in the early aughts, but the project never materialized.

If you don't mind me saying so, that's a shame because I think you have a fascinating story to tell. So much so, actually, that I asked Jack to put us in touch. At the time, Jack did not have your current contact information, and Google was no help, so I told him that should you ever resurface, to please let me know so that I could talk to you about maybe reviving this memoir idea.

I understand why you might be interested in a podcast, especially given the current true crime craze, but honestly, those are a dime a dozen these days, and I'd hate to see a narrative with this much potential get lost in the shuffle. I'm happy to send you some samples of my work, or we can hop on the phone to discuss in further detail.

Warmly,
August Fletcher

TO: AFletcher695@gmail.com
FROM: HowLo@aol.com
SUBJECT: RE: Jack Harrison/Podcast query
SENT: 11:43PM, April 20, 2025

August! That's not a name, that's a MONTH! And maybe it's . . . whatever that big word is that means "fate" that that's your name, as August is, obviously, when the Whole Big Fucking Thing happened. August 4, 1984. Hurricane Marie. Landon Fitzroy. All of it.

Anyway, yes, I first met Jack in 1999, back when I was doing QVC for a little bit (selling bathing suits, in case your research didn't tell you that). He reached out because he said he thought I had a "helluva voice," and at first, I thought that meant how I talked, but later he said that no, it wasn't the way I *sounded*, it was how I *said* it. I'm gonna be honest, I still don't know what that really means, but anyway, Jack thought I should try my hand at a memoir, and I said that sounded great, but I didn't realize he meant that I should *write the damn thing*, lol. This girl was lucky to get out of her 12th grade English class alive, so a book was a little beyond me!

But I'll level with you, August. I did okay after the trial with the talk show circuit and QVC, brief as THAT was, and even this weird 900 number thing I did for a little bit around 1988 where people could call me and ask anything they wanted (it was mostly perverts, but perverts have credit cards, too!). And when that cash ran out, I got a bunch of normal jobs—I waitressed for a little bit, worked in this nice boutique in San Diego, I even substitute taught a theater class in La Jolla before some tight-ass put two and two together and realized that Gloria Bailey was the same Lo Bailey accused of murder way back before any of those kids were even fucking *born.*

Anyway, I'm a little down on my luck right now, so I took this job cleaning at a nursing home (BLEAK!!), and one of my coworkers, Cynthia, turned me on to podcasts. It's the only way she gets through the job, she said. Maybe listening to other people go through horrible shit makes scrubbing toilets seem less tragic, I don't know. But I started listening, too, and then it occurred to me that my own story might end up on one sooner rather than later, and if *annnnyoooooonnnne* is gonna get paid off MY LIFE, it oughta be me, right?

So that's why I was asking Jack about them since I still had his email—and book or no book, it's not like he ever "fired" me from being a client.

But I like this idea of doing a memoir WITH someone. I tell you what happened, you write it down, and we split the money, right?

Xoxoxo!!
Lo

TO: HowLo@aol.com
FROM: AFletcher695@gmail.com
SUBJECT: RE: RE: Jack Harrison/podcast query
SENT: 5:02AM, April 21, 2025

Well, I certainly see what Jack meant about you having "voice"! I absolutely agree that you should tell your own story in your own voice, your own words. And yes, that would be exactly how it worked—all you'd really have to do is submit to a few interviews, maybe some recordings, and of course the words would all be yours, but I would help you organize your thoughts and structure them into a narrative.

And what a narrative it is. There you were, a small-town girl accused of murder, and not just any murder, but the murder of *your governor's son.* A man who was being groomed not just for local politics, but for national. I mean, if things had turned out differently, who's to say you wouldn't have been our First Lady at some point? Instead, you were vilified and slandered, a 20th-century Hester Prynne in a Duran Duran T-shirt.

Like I said, podcasts come and go, and it's a fire hose of content right now. But how many accused murderesses tell their own story in their own words? There's value in that.

There's value in *you.*

Sincerely,
August

TO: AFletcher695@gmail.com
FROM: HowLo@aol.com
SUBJECT: RE: RE: RE: Jack Harrison/podcast query
SENT: 1:09AM, April 22, 2025

August-

When do we start?

Xoxoxo!!
Lo

CHAPTER ONE

June 21, 2025

43 Days Left

A/C is out in 217. Again.

It's not the best text to get before six o'clock in the morning, but I've woken up to worse.

So I just realized that the smoked tuna dip we had last night had expired. SORRY!!! ☹

Hi, it's Nicole from the salon. Doooooon't think you meant to send this text to me, lol.

Gen, I'm fucking tired of talking about this. It's done. Don't contact me again.

I haven't deleted that one yet, and out of habit, I pull it up again, the words incongruous with my ex-boyfriend's smiling face under his contact info. Chris sent that text more than eight months ago, and I've honored his wishes, but for whatever reason, as I sit on the edge of my bed this morning, the sunrise tinting my curtains pink, the waves softly shushing just outside, I find my thumbs moving across the screen.

About to go to battle with the A/C again. 217 remains cursed.

My thumb hovers over the send arrow even though I have no clue what this text might accomplish or even what I *want* it to accomplish.

Okay.

That's not true.

I can already feel the summer bearing down on me, the weight getting heavier and heavier along with the heat and the humidity, and I want Chris to feel it, too.

We were supposed to do this together. This was our *dream.*

The phone buzzes in my hand, and for one heart-jolting second, I think he's somehow sensed me on the other end, that he's in his bed on the opposite side of the country, missing me, missing the Rosalie Inn, remembering the first night it had been officially ours. How we'd drunk champagne from plastic cups sitting on the front steps, our toes buried in the warm sugar-white sand.

But no, it's just a follow-up text from Edie, my best friend and right-hand woman at the Rosalie.

Geneva, I have very sweaty guests in front of me, and it's not even 7AM. Whatshisface at the HVAC place isn't picking up, and I can only bullshit these people for so long. Come save me or I quit!

Another buzz.

And not "quiet" quit or whatever that bullcrap is, I will FOR REAL QUIT. Loudly and dramatically.

I smile at that, some of the heaviness lifting as I take one last sip of coffee. The sun may just be rising, but I've been awake for a while, my brain doing its usual spin cycle: *How do we get more guests, does our Instagram suck, should I hire a social media person, and if I do, how exactly am I supposed to pay them, and why is more money going out than coming in, and would it*

*be so bad to just put a huge fucking For Sale sign on this thing
and walk away, and if I do that, what exactly am I supposed to
do next given that I've maxed out every credit card I own trying
to keep this thing afloat, and why why why why WHY did I let
Chris talk me into selling everything I owned and taking on the
inn after everything with Mom, even with the massive mortgage
on it, and God, how nice it must be to be Chris, washing his
hands of the whole thing and walking away because for him,
this was just a bad investment, not an entire fucking family legacy to uphold.*

Sighing, I open my front door and step out, humid, salty air
settling over me like a physical weight. Every other owner of
the Rosalie had called the inn home, including my parents and
grandparents, but when Chris and I had taken over, he'd been
creeped out by the idea of actually *living* in a hotel.

I've seen The Shining, *I'm good* had been his line, and it had
always irritated me because it wasn't even a good joke. A rambling beach motel was hardly a terrifying fortress high up in the
snow-covered Rockies. We weren't going to get *trapped* in it.
Besides, I'd grown up there, and I'd survived.

Still, we'd ended up buying an Airstream and set it up just
a little ways down the beach, a handful of short, scraggly pines
between us and the inn.

Well, now just *me* and the inn.

The distance is more mental than physical, to be honest.
The inn is big and painted pink, for fuck's sake, so it would
take more than a few sad little pines to block the view. But
it makes me feel better, this little "walk to work" I do every
morning, the Gulf on my right, sand dunes gently undulating
on my left. The water is calm today, smooth and glassy as a
lake, and I watch a pelican dive, the splash overly loud in the
quiet near-dawn.

This stretch of beach outside the Rosalie is public—my mom and her dad before her never wanted to fight that, knowing the last thing you should do in a tourist town is piss off the locals— but this time of day, it's almost always empty.

Today, there's one lone figure on the beach, an old guy in salt-stained khaki shorts, his skinny chest bare and slightly concave, his skin so tanned he looks like he's been carved out of wood. He's got a fishing pole in his bony hands, the surf splashing against his calves, and when he catches sight of me, he lifts a few fingers in a barely-there wave.

"Hey, Cap!"

He has an actual name, I'm sure, but he's been "Cap" as long as I can remember, even if no one in town knows if he actually was a captain at some point in his life.

"Or maybe he just wore a funny cap one time back in 1973, and that's why it stuck," Edie had once suggested over a couple of beers in the inn's courtyard. "This is the South, after all. I once knew a sixty-four-year-old man who went by 'Scoop,' because he was on a newspaper staff. *In middle school.*"

In any case, Cap is a frequent visitor to this beach even though I've never actually seen him catch anything. He's a reminder of what I love about this place and that, like it or not, it's always been home.

You didn't just do this for Chris, remember? You grew up on this beach, you've got roots here, you know the people, the places, the weird little bits of lore that make up every small town. This was your dream, too.

And when I turn and step onto the low wooden boardwalk that leads to the inn, my sandals gritting over the sand that always dusts the boards, I think the Rosalie Inn *does* look like a dream.

If I were anybody else, I could stop and admire it, the charm of its color—somewhere between coral and Pepto-Bismol—and how the white gingerbread trim glows against it. I could smile at the rocking chairs on the front porch, the big baskets of begonias waving gently in the sea air, the morning sun sparkling on all the wide windows facing the Gulf. I could think what a miracle it is that this building has stood here for almost a hundred years despite storms that flattened other, newer dwellings.

But I'm not anybody. I'm her current steward and the woman who signs all the checks, which means that, rather than stand here on this gorgeous June morning, drinking in the sight of my family's legacy, I'm noticing that the third step leading up to the porch is loose, and that the paint is already flaking off the shutters nearest the door even though we just painted those last winter. I'm thinking that we should probably replace said door after this summer, and wondering if there's room in the budget for another housekeeper.

"Girl, if that frown gets much frownier, there will not be enough Botox in all of Alabama to help you."

I'd been so focused on the never-ending tally of things that make up running a place like this that I hadn't even noticed Edie on the front porch, one hip cocked against the railing, a thermal mug in hand.

I hurry up the steps, and she hands me a second mug of coffee that was sitting on the railing before saying, "No need to rush. Whatshisface finally picked up his phone and should be over here in ten minutes or so, and I had a few of those certificates for a free dinner at Shrimp 'N' Shells still hidden in the front desk, so our overheated guests have chilled out in spirit if not in body."

"They're still going to want a refund, watch," I say with a sigh as the shell wind chimes just overhead smack together, their delicate strings tangling.

"If they do, send them my way," she tells me, lifting a pierced eyebrow.

Edie is what people down here would call "a character." She turned up in St. Medard's Bay about three years ago, originally from Natchez, Mississippi, one of those women who could've been thirty-five or sixty-five, it was nearly impossible to tell. And even in a town as quirky as St. Medard's Bay, she stood out with her brightly colored hair—purple at the moment, after a turquoise phase back in the winter—that eyebrow ring, and her tendency to wear flannel shirts and jeans even when it's hotter than hell outside.

I'd met Edie when she was working at Grindz, the subpar coffee shop on St. Medard's main drag, and liked her immediately. So much so that I'd found myself hanging out an extra ten, fifteen minutes every time I got coffee there, and when she'd told me she was hoping to find something a little more challenging than making eight thousand iced lattes for people in Salt Life T-shirts, I'd offered her a job at the inn.

Her official title is "assistant manager," but like everyone who worked here, she did a little bit of everything. She'd work the front desk, handle bookings, pick up the coffee and pastries we put out every morning for the guests. She's even scrubbed a toilet or twelve, and honestly, I don't know what I'd do without her.

"Any other fires need putting out?" I ask her. "Was Carla able to get that red wine stain out in Room 121? Oh, and did the Bakers ever email back? I know we always hold 211 for them for the Fourth of July, but I'd really love to go ahead and get that on the books officially."

"They did," Edie tells me, and something in her voice makes the sip of coffee I just took—delicious and rich mere seconds ago—go bitter in my mouth.

"And?"

"*And* they regret to tell us their daughter booked the whole family an Airbnb in Orange Beach for the Fourth this year, but they're going to try and swing by to say hello."

My stomach drops, my skin turning cold despite the balmy morning. The Bakers always booked the whole week of the Fourth. Even with the loyalty discount I gave them, that was nearly two thousand dollars that I'd been counting on this summer. Two thousand dollars I've already spent, if I'm being honest.

"Fuck," I mutter, and Edie leans over, clinking her mug against mine.

"Before you get too down about that, another email came in last night, too. Check it out."

She reaches for the iPad that's sitting in a nearby rocking chair, its cheap plastic case cracking, the PROPERTY OF THE RO-SALIE INN label peeling off the back.

I open the email app, my eyes briefly snagging on the Bakers' reply—*Hi, Geneva! So sorry not to have replied earlier*—before seeing another message with the subject *Long-term stay, July–?*

I scan the email quickly, almost afraid to hope.

August Fletcher, a writer from California; interested in an open-ended stay starting the first of July; not sure how long, definitely a month, but possibly until September.

September.

Even with a long-term stay discount—my dad had been big on discounts, I'm sadly learning—that would be a significant bit of money. Enough to pay down at least one of the credit cards, secure a couple more months for Mom at Hope House, get a little breathing room.

My mind is still running numbers as I half read the rest of the message.

This guy, August, is working on a book; would love to learn more about local history while here; wants to talk about the inn, and the hurricanes—specifically, Hurricane Marie in 1984.

That part pulls me out of my "once again having a credit score over 500" fantasies.

Lots of hurricanes have hit St. Medard's Bay over the years. It's practically what we're famous for, and the Rosalie Inn is a big part of that: the only beachfront building to survive the wind and waves for decades, the freak structure that's somehow always standing when the water recedes. Maybe it's missing a chunk of roof or a bunch of windows, but it's whole and upright when other, seemingly sturdier buildings are piles of flattened lumber.

We even have pictures in the lobby, framed shots of the hotel in the aftermath of the storms, little placards on the bottom reading *Hurricane Delphine—1965, Hurricane Audrey—1977,* that kind of thing.

Hurricane Marie, though . . .

That's the one that nearly got us. I don't remember it, of course—I was born in March of '85, months after it hit—but Dad talked about it a lot. How a small sailboat ended up in the courtyard, its mast jutting through an upstairs window. How the whole front porch was ripped cleanly off, like some giant fish had swallowed it and taken it back out to sea.

How they'd been struggling to put the inn and their lives back together while reporters invaded the town because one of the victims was a politician's son, and it turned out he'd been in St. Medard's Bay visiting his teenage mistress, a local girl. They'd been without power for nearly a month, Mom had said, no running water for nearly as long, but all anyone had been able to talk about was Mrs. Bailey's gorgeous daughter, Gloria, and the governor's son—and how that governor was saying he wasn't so sure his son had actually died in the hurricane at all.

I didn't know any of that until I was thirteen. There hadn't been another big storm to hit St. Medard's Bay since Marie, so I'd never had any real reason to think about the various hurricanes that had roared in before. Hell, I'd walked past the squat stone monument in the middle of the grassy square we call a "park" downtown thousands of times and had no idea it was a memorial for all the people we'd lost to rising waters and falling houses over the years.

But for whatever reason, one April day in 1998, as I cut through the park on my way to the used bookstore, I stopped at the monument to tie my shoe, and the words in tarnished bronze caught my eye.

"Thou dost rule the raging of the sea; when its waves rise, thou stillest them."—Psalm 89:9.

Under that, there were years at first—1927, 1934, 1946— and lists of the deceased, and then, in 1965, the first named hurricane, Hurricane Delphine. Later, I learned that's because they didn't start giving hurricanes names until the '50s, but at the time, I was mostly fascinated by how every storm listed was a woman's name.

Delphine.

Audrey.

Velma.

Marie.

I was a dramatic kid, the first in my class to discover Ann Rule paperbacks and Dean Koontz hardcovers, and there had been something eerie about those storms, those long lists of names under each one.

I'd gone home from the bookstore still thinking about it, walking along the beach and looking out at the ocean, so glassy and calm you'd never believe it could "rage" like that Bible verse had said.

But rage it had—and rage it did again just a few months later in September of 1998. Hurricane Peggy didn't kill anyone in St. Medard's Bay, but it did destroy that used bookstore I loved so much and blew out the front windows at the Rosalie, soaking all the lobby furniture in a noxious mix of salt water and God knows what else.

Suddenly, those pictures on the lobby wall that I'd walked past every day of my life had new meaning for me, and I studied them intently, matching them up with the names of the storms from the monument.

They'd all been there.

My grandparents holding massive garbage bags but still smiling for the camera once Delphine was done in 1965.

My mom, a gangly tween shading her eyes from the sun on the front porch, the Rosalie basically pristine except for a few missing shingles, courtesy of Audrey in 1977.

Every window broken out in the wake of Velma.

And then nothing. No more pictures.

That's when I'd asked Dad about Hurricane Marie and gotten the story of the sailboat and the porch, of Gloria Bailey and the governor's son.

"We were living in a disaster movie, but everyone acted like we were in an episode of *Dynasty*," Dad had joked at dinner that night, but Mom had only shaken her head, her lips pressed tightly together before she said, "I still have nightmares about that storm. I didn't need any reminders on the wall."

I'd assumed Hurricane Marie had been so rough on Mom because she'd been pregnant with me, and that had to have been fucking terrifying. She and Dad were barely more than teenagers, newly engaged, learning to take over the business from her family because her parents planned to retire to Vermont—some kind of reverse snowbird situation—and then the whole place nearly came down around their ears. I didn't blame her for not wanting to be confronted daily with memories of it.

Which was why the cache of newspapers and magazines I found in the back of her closet when we moved her to Hope House had been such a surprise. Articles from the *Press-Register* and *USA Today*, spreads from *People* and the *National Enquirer*. All ostensibly about the destruction Marie had wrought, but most were much more intent on Landon Fitzroy's death— and on the local girl whom Landon's father was blaming for it. Her photo was always featured alongside those articles: Gloria "Lo" Bailey, glossy and beautiful in the way women were in the '80s, almost painfully blond. The captions always made a point of highlighting her age, too—just nineteen years old—her big, innocent smile giving no hint that she was in the center of a different kind of storm, but one that was no less deadly.

Mom's collection filled up a whole box, and I would have given anything to ask why she'd kept such a detailed account of an event that she never spoke about. But of course, by then, there was no asking Mom anything at all. So it had gone up in the attic with all the other things that had made up Mom's life, things that had belonged to Ellen Chambers Corliss, a person who might still be here in body but is no longer here in mind or spirit. I'd filed the contents of that box away as just one more item on the list of things I didn't understand about my mother.

That list is long.

I'm about to hit reply, not even bothering to finish the rest of the email because this August Fletcher could say he was coming to St. Medard's Bay to write a book on how best to sacrifice virgins under the blood moon and I would've happily taken his money, but then I see a couple of lines near the bottom.

Due to the short notice, I'm willing to pay twice your regular rates, which, if I'm honest, seem too low for such a gorgeous place in such a picturesque location!

Our rates *are* low, much lower than what other places nearby charge—lower than what we charged even a few years ago—but it was the only thing I could think of to keep the inn at least half full during the summer. We're at $200 a night when other places start around $500 during the high season. Four hundred a night for an open-ended stay?

My heart starts beating a little faster as I take in the final line of the email.

Full disclosure: I'm also willing to pay a little more because there's a chance my presence there might spook the locals; I'll be looking into the death of Landon Fitzroy, so there's a true crime element to this book (in case you find such things distasteful!).

I almost laugh. My phone is currently loaded up with podcasts with titles like *And Then They Were Gone* or *Two Girls, One Murder. Dateline* is in heavy rotation on the tiny TV in my Airstream. Immediately, I can see that the death of this Landon Fitzroy would make for a good story. The storm, the mystery surrounding his injuries, the scandal with the teenage mistress . . .

Hell, that might be more than a book. That might be a Net-flix series that launches a thousand Reddit theories. And where there are true crime nerds, there might just be money.

So no, I don't find true crime distasteful, but I do wonder: Do I want my family business to become famous for its connection to a notorious death?

I nearly snort at myself. Worrying about the morality of the whole thing is for people who *don't* have three maxed-out credit cards and a repayment plan with the IRS.

And even if the book comes to fuck all, the money he's of-fering for his stay might just help keep us afloat through the offseason.

So yeah. After months—years, really—of bad news, even this little glimmer is shiny enough for me, and as I reply to August Fletcher's email, I realize I'm smiling.

EXCLUSIVE!!!
HOW "LO" CAN YOU GO?

Dixieland Delight Lo Bailey's OWN WORDS on the night she met Governor's Son (and MARRIED MAN) Landon Fitzroy in a Gulf Coast DIVE BAR.

The blond beauty was BARELY LEGAL when she took up with beloved heir to Alabama political dynasty.

Fitzroy was nearly TWICE HER AGE and married to former MISS ALABAMA, Alison Carleton-Fitzroy.

Acquitted of his murder, LO-LITA is still St. Medard's Bay's SCARLET WOMAN.

Mrs. Carleton-Fitzroy "devastated, HUMILIATED, and in seclusion at this time," say friends.

Read Lo Bailey's SHAMELESS ACCOUNT of how the torrid affair began from her OWN DIARIES.

National Enquirer, January 13, 1985

I can't tell you about meeting Landon Fitzroy until I tell you what it was like to grow up as the prettiest girl in a very small town.

You're rolling your eyes, aren't you?

That's fine, I get it. No one wants to hear a rich person bitch about a goddamn thing, and no one wants a pretty girl whining about how hard it is to have heads turn when she walks by. It's that whole "Oh no, my diamond shoes are too dang tight!" thing, right? So I'm not complaining—this face is the reason I'm here, doing this book. But you need to understand that when I was growing up, it was . . . well, lonely, I guess.

Actually, you know what? Let me tell you a little story.

I went to my school's homecoming dance in the ninth grade—this would've been around '79—and I didn't even go with a date. Just a couple of girlfriends because the thing about being the Prettiest Girl in Your Small Town is that boys your age are scared plum to *death* of you, and you're scared plum to death of the men—and they were always *men*, baby, believe that—who *are* interested in you. So I didn't actually get asked on dates, at least not ones I'd want to go on.

But I was happy going to the dance with Ellen and Frieda since they were two of the only girls in town who genuinely seemed to like me. Ellen's family ran the Sand Dollar Inn, St. Medard's Bay's only hotel, and while I now know that the place was almost always in the red, back then it seemed so respectable to me. My own mom ran a fucking souvenir shop selling *the* tackiest plastic shit you've ever seen, and Frieda's family lived in a trailer off a sandy bit of road just outside town, so trust me, Ellen Chambers was high-class as far as we were concerned.

Anyway, we'll talk more about them later. Right now I want to tell you about how at that dance, Tim Murphy, this jackass senior, tried to pull me into the boys' bathroom. I can still hear the song that was playing faintly from the gym—"Love Will Keep Us Together."

I still hate that fucking song.

Anyway, I was just getting water from the fountain outside the gym when he was there all of a sudden, his hands surprisingly strong, chin bristled, mouth tasting like fucking corn chips as he tried to kiss me, his voice in my ear saying, *It's just a kiss, come on . . .*

The whole thing lasted maybe thirty seconds. I got a knee up fast, plus a couple of kids came spilling out of the gym, shouting along with the music, and that distracted him enough to let me pull away.

And right now you're probably thinking, *Some pimply-faced teenager tried to kiss you, and I'm supposed to feel sorry for you?*

Maybe you do, maybe you don't—I don't really care either way. But I need you to understand that it wasn't fucking Tim Murphy and his marauding tongue that made me understand that looking the way I did might not always be a good thing.

It was after, when I went to tell a teacher.

That's what you're supposed to do when shit happens, right? Tell an adult. So, I went to the chemistry teacher, Mr. Oudine. He'd been chaperoning that dance, and man, I made a *beeline* for him, telling him what had happened. His smile made my stomach turn as he said, *That's just boys, sweetheart. Especially boys all riled up at their first school dance. You look fine to me, so why don't you just go dance with your friends for a little bit, okay?*

Shitty enough, but what was worse was how his eyes had dropped to my chest as he said it.

I'd picked out the dress with my mom in Mobile. It was

one of the rare times she'd torn herself away from the store long enough to leave town, and we'd had a good time, driving over the causeway, the radio loud in our crappy Ford Pinto. We'd even gotten lunch somewhere downtown, the two of us giggling over crab cakes, Mama with her glass of Chablis, me with a Shirley Temple.

The dress I'd chosen was the same pink as that drink, I remember that. Dotted Swiss, very big back then, and a scalloped neckline. Frothy ruffles hitting me right at the knee. It was a little girl's idea of what a Fancy Dress might look like, but when Mr. Oudine had looked at me, it had suddenly felt too low-cut, too short, too much.

I hadn't asked for a face that looked older than it was.

I hadn't asked to need a bra by the time I was eleven.

I *definitely* hadn't asked to be a 32C by seventh grade.

It was all just some fluke of nature, right? Neither of my parents had been super attractive people, but through some weird twist of genetics, I was beautiful. Worse than that, I was *sexy*, never mind that I hadn't even kissed a boy before Tim Murphy attempted to shove his tongue down my throat.

But I saw what was in Mr. Oudine's eyes as they swept over me that night—*What does she expect, walking around like that?*

He died in a car accident five years later, by the way. Mr. Oudine. On the same causeway that Mama and I drove over so happily that day we bought my dress.

Is it gonna make you hate me if I say not only was I not sad about that, baby, I was downright *gleeful*? Well, even if it does, I can't really give a shit. I learned a long time ago that you have to value honesty over everything else. Can't worry if people are going to hate you, can't give a fuck what people might say, because trust me, they're gonna hate you if they wanna, and they're gonna say what they wanna, and once people have an *idea* of you, of the person you are, they won't let it go. I guess that's why it was so easy for people to believe I was a murderer on top of being a slut. If you've broken one of the Ten Commandments, why not another?

Thing is, though, I'm neither. Not a murderer, not a slut.

In fact, when Landon Fitzroy showed up at The Line that windy September night in 1983, I'd only recently shed my virginity, giving it up to this sweet guy I was dating at the time. He was a busboy at The Line, and I wish I could remember his name, but it's one of those things that just got blotted out in the supernova that was Landon.

I still feel bad about it, actually. Forgetting that boy's name. We dated for almost six months, and he had the kindest smile and the reddest hair, and when I finally decided that we could indeed go All the Way, he was sweet as sweet can be about the whole thing. Asking if I was sure I wanted to do it (I was), asking if I enjoyed it (I didn't, but I still appreciated him trying). I guess I broke his heart, and he deserved better than that. So if you're out there, Red-Headed Boy, let me apologize about forty fucking years too late. You were a good guy, and you might have made me happy, but then fate blew Landon through my door, and that was that.

Now, I know if you ask certain people in St. Medard's Bay, they'd tell you I'd had my eye on Landon Fitzroy for years. The Fitzroys were Alabama royalty, after all. Landon's daddy, Beau Fitzroy, was the governor, and *his* daddy, L. B. Fitzroy, had been a senator. L. B.'s daddy had been the richest man in Mobile once upon a time, and there were people in the state who followed the entire family's lives like they were characters in a soap opera.

But I wasn't one of them, scout's honor (yes, I was a Girl Scout, and fuck you if that makes you smirk—I have the sash to prove it!). I knew *of* Landon, of course. The governor had a big mansion over in Gulf Shores, and the family kept their boat docked in St. Medard's, so I was aware of him, but probably in the same way people who lived in Hollywood were "aware" of Marilyn Monroe back in the day. We might have occasionally shared the same air, but we were basically on different planets.

My best friend, Ellen Chambers, was the one who always knew when Landon was in town, who'd breathlessly report that she'd seen him driving around in that Chrysler LeBaron, the one he'd had custom-painted Crimson Tide maroon in honor of his alma mater, the interior a buttery soft cream leather that I can still feel under my fingertips if I think about it.

Ellen's parents ran what was then known as the Ship Wreck Inn because there was a shipwreck just about a half a mile offshore, almost directly in front of the inn. The boat that had sunk there in the '20s had been called the *Rosalie*, and according to Landon, it had belonged to a relative of his, a bootlegger who was the black sheep of the Fitzroy family. He loved that story for some reason, and whenever he was in town, he'd stop by the inn to have a beer with Ellen's dad and talk local history.

I can still see Ellen, her dark ponytail hanging down to the seafoam-green carpet of my bedroom as she draped herself across my bed, her hands resting on her chest, her neck and cheeks flushed.

"He's just so *interesting*, Lo," she said with a sigh one afternoon, about a week or so before Landon came into The Line to change—and ruin—my life. "He's been everywhere, he knows everyone . . . I don't know why he'd want to keep coming back to St. Medard's Bay, but I'm glad that he does."

Ellen had a boyfriend by then, Tim Corliss. He was cute and, more important, he was *tall*, but Ellen certainly never described him as "*interesting*." Tim was "sweet" and "funny," and "super good at basketball," but that was about as effusive as her compliments got.

That was Ellen, though. I was the Wild One, Frieda was the Smart One, and Ellen was the Nice One.

But even Ellen's sighs and pink cheeks didn't make me all that curious about Landon Fitzroy because, in my mind, he was *old*.

And to be fair, to a nineteen-year-old, thirty does seem pretty ancient. Or at least too old to think about as a boyfriend. Plus, he was married, and married to a former beauty queen at that. Alison Carleton-Fitzroy, Miss Alabama 1974. Mama and I had watched her compete in Miss America that year, and I had never coveted anything as much as I'd coveted her sparkly green evening gown as she'd pounded out Rachmaninoff on the piano, her bright red hair practically glowing under the stage lights.

Well, that's not true. After Alison's performance, Mama had sighed and said, "What a *lady*," and I'd envied that.

To be thought of as a *lady*.

(The irony of all this is not lost on me, just so you know.)

Anyway, I'm not trying to make excuses here. I'm not trying to make you like me, or see me as some innocent swept up in circumstances beyond my control. But I do want you to know that there was no planning on my part, no scheme to pry a rich man away from his beautiful and accomplished wife. Other than a few glimpses here and there over the years—and almost always from a distance, when he was either in his car or at the harbor—I hadn't really seen Landon Fitzroy until the night of September 3, 1983.

It was Labor Day weekend, but St. Medard's Bay hadn't had too many visitors that year. We never got the big beach traffic the other towns around us did. We were too small, there wasn't enough to do, and honestly, I think the history of the place creeped people out. Too many storms, too many dead. Hard to sing along without a care in the world to "Margaritaville" when there's a big ol' monument to dozens of drowned people in the middle of town.

But The Line has always existed in its own separate universe. Maybe because it's literally between states, maybe because it's the opposite of something like *Cheers*. Sometimes you wanna go where *nobody* knows your name, and The Line was good for that.

I think that's what brought Landon there that night.

Later, he told me he'd heard people talking about how the prettiest girl in all of Alabama was waiting tables there, so he'd naturally had to come in and see for himself.

(And no, I didn't remind him that he was married to a onetime Prettiest Girl in Alabama. I mean, men liked looking at me, but no one had ever commemorated that shit with a tiara, you know?)

Anyway, I think Landon was there because he wanted to shrug off being Landon Parkes Fitzroy for a night.

I didn't know it at the time, but Landon's father, Governor Fitzroy, had given him an ultimatum that year. I'm sure he said it all fancy and stern, doing that thing rich people do where they talk so calmly that you don't realize you're being threatened until it's too late, but the gist of it was that Landon had fucked around enough, and it was time to Get Serious.

And to the Fitzroys, "Getting Serious" meant getting into politics.

Landon was a lawyer at his uncle's firm in Mobile, and a successful one at that, but no son of Beau Fitzroy was going to be allowed to be "just" a lawyer.

"He won't be happy until I'm the fucking president," Landon told me in one of the last conversations we ever had. "The Alabama Kennedys, that's what he wants."

"Which makes me Marilyn," I remember joking.

He didn't laugh.

But that was all ahead of us. The fights, the lies, the accusations.

The storm.

Still, it's important you know where Landon's head was that night we met. He knew the walls were closing in, that the future that had been practically written into his DNA was barreling toward him. But it hadn't arrived just yet.

Not fucking yet.

That warm and sticky September night, he was walking into a dive bar after a deep-sea fishing trip with some old fraternity brothers, looking for nothing more than a few beers and a band that *didn't* play Lynyrd Skynyrd (he'd be disappointed there—I used to think the bands that played at The Line must've assumed they'd be shot on sight if they didn't give the crowd "Sweet Home Alabama" once every couple of hours).

He wasn't looking for me.

I wasn't looking for him.

But we found each other all the same.

I think about that a lot. How random it all was in the end. Him showing up that night, me being there. I was about to quit working at The Line because the tips were shitty, and I was sick of having my ass groped every time I walked too close to the wrong table.

I was jealous of Frieda, who'd gotten a scholarship to go to college in Tennessee, and damn near pea-fuckin'-green with envy that Ellen's parents had saved up enough to send her to Spring Hill in Mobile. I missed them both and was pissed off that they had somehow managed to escape when I hadn't. My own fault, if I'm honest. I'd gotten it into my head that I was too special for anything as boring as college, and I had been sending off pictures of myself—not headshots, mind you, just goddamn *Polaroids* I made Mama take, I was *that* naïve—to the big modeling agencies that I read about in *Cosmopolitan* and *Mademoiselle*.

Shocking that Eileen Ford wasn't beating down my door, right?

But I hadn't quit The Line just yet, so I was there when Landon and his friends walked in. The bar they'd wanted to go to, the classier place just over the border in Florida, had closed early for some reason, so they'd wound up at The Line, probably more as a joke than anything else. Guys like them didn't frequent places like that as a rule.

I spotted them right away, a group of about five or six guys, all of whom were dressed casually. Khaki shorts, white button-downs with the sleeves rolled up, boat shoes. They looked like a million other guys who showed up at The Line when they were on vacation, red-faced and laughing too loud, feeling a little wild because hey, maybe in a bar like this, they weren't boring-ass Herbert from Accounting but someone cool, someone laid-back, someone Jimmy Buffett would probably want to have a beer with.

But Landon stood out.

It wasn't just that he was, to quote Lori, one of the waitresses at The Line, "sooooooo fine," even though he was definitely that. His hair was dark and curly, a little too long for a lawyer, probably, and while he wasn't as tall as Ellen's boyfriend, Tim, he had a way of holding himself that made him look bigger than he was.

And his eyes . . .

They were so dark brown they were nearly black, and when he looked at you, it was like you were the only thing he could see, the only thing he ever *wanted* to see.

It was the look that got me. Before I ever heard him speak, before our hands brushed as I was handing him a cold and sweating bottle of beer, before we were pressed together on the dance floor, the band playing "Gloria" at his request.

Before he murmured in my ear, "Christ almighty, where have they been hiding you, gorgeous?"

Landon Fitzroy was the first person who ever looked at me not like I was *hot* or *sexy* or *a fine piece of ass* but like I was . . . special. Interesting.

Someone worth their full attention.

Someone worth getting to know.

Maybe that's not what you were hoping for when you picked up this little memoir of mine. Maybe you wanted to hear that this dashing older man swept into the shitty bar where I was working, and next thing you knew, the governor's married son and the nubile teenage waitress were banging against a chipped sink in a filthy bathroom.

I get it. That's way more fun, and honestly, everything with Landon would've been a lot easier if that had been the truth.

But sorry to disappoint you perverts: No banging that night. Not even a kiss—unless you count the one he pressed against my cheek before his friends dragged him out to a waiting car.

In fact, I didn't sleep with Landon until six weeks *after* we met, and it was on expensive sheets in the bedroom of his yacht. (Don't worry, I'll give you enough details on that night to make Jackie Collins blush.)

Honestly, I sometimes wish it had just been sex between us. That would've been a lot easier, a lot simpler.

But no, I actually fell in love with the guy. And I think he was in love with me.

And in the end, I guess that's why he's dead.

Pages of unfinished manuscript titled
"Be a Good Girl: Lo Bailey, Landon Fitzroy, and
the Scandal That Brought Down a Dynasty."
Found among possessions of August Fletcher, 8/3/2025

St. Medard's Bay had seen its share of deadly storms before, including one in 1965 that killed Lo Bailey's own father, but from the start, everyone agreed that there was something suspicious about the death of Landon Fitzroy.

For one thing, unlike most of the bodies found in the aftermath of a hurricane, Landon hadn't drowned. Though he was discovered face down in the surf near a local nature preserve, his lungs were free of water, according to the autopsy.

It was initially suspected that Landon's death hadn't come from the raging surf, but instead from the wind. It appeared that he had been struck by something heavy in the back of the head, an object that had fractured his skull and driven fragments of bone into his brain.

It would not have been an abnormal cause of death in a storm, especially given the magnitude of Hurricane Marie, but something unusual caught the attention of Buddy Byrd, the coroner and owner of St. Medard's Bay's only funeral home (something that might be seen as a conflict in some places, but not Alabama). According to Byrd, Landon appeared to have sustained *multiple* blows to the head, as opposed to a single fatal strike, as you'd expect to see in a storm death.

There was also the odd positioning of the body when it was recovered. Landon was face down, his arms stretched out straight over his head—almost as though someone had pulled him down the beach. Abrasions on his chest were consistent with being dragged through sand, while the otherwise intact nature of his body and his clothing suggested that the fatal injury had occurred on dry land. Even his wristwatch was still tight around one wrist.

But the truly odd discovery was found snagged on the

inner lining of Landon's tuxedo jacket: the jagged tip of a hot pink fingernail.

The chaos and destruction of a storm could explain many of these details. And if Landon Fitzroy had been anyone but Beau Fitzroy's son, his death probably would have been classified, at most, as "undetermined."

But Governor Fitzroy knew there was something odd about his boy being in St. Medard's Bay at all that night. Landon had actually been in Birmingham earlier that evening, a solid five-hour drive away, set to attend a glitzy gala that was meant to be the soft launch of his own political career.

Instead, Landon had vanished from his own coronation only to show up dead on a beach less than twenty-four hours later.

Why?

The answer, Beau decided, was Lo Bailey, and when he put that bug in the ear of Buddy Byrd and the local police chief, Ron Steensland, Lo was hauled down to the station for questioning.

Right from the beginning, there were clear inconsistencies in her story. She claimed to have called Landon's office once the day he died but that she'd talked only to his secretary, Linda Green, as Landon wasn't in. But Miss Green countered that Landon had received *two* phone calls that day, both of which were from Lo, and that the second time, Landon Fitzroy had taken the call. Miss Green said she heard him talking to someone in his office, making promises that he would see whoever it was "as soon as I can."

Phone records later confirmed Miss Green's version of events, but Lo never changed her story.

And then there were her bruises.

Lo showed up at the station in, according to Steensland, a tight T-shirt advertising a local seafood spot.

"Who goes to see the police in a shirt that says, 'Shuck 'em, suck 'em, eat 'em raw'?" Steensland later said on the local news, his beady eyes widening as much as they could in disbelief. "I knew right then that Governor Fitzroy was right to tell us we needed to talk to that little girl."

But it wasn't the shirt that Steensland focused on initially. No, what struck him was the cardigan she was wearing over it.

A sweater.

In Alabama.

In August.

When Steensland asked her to remove it, she apparently refused.

"Gave me some real lip, called me a dirty old man, whole thing," he remembered a few years later. "But she took it off in the end."

And when she did, Steensland noticed the fading bruises on her arms, bruises that looked very much like fingerprints. She claimed she'd gotten them helping her mother, Beth-Anne Bailey, cover some windows at her souvenir shop, but that didn't make any sense to Steensland. When he later confirmed she had in fact called Landon the day of his death, that made two lies he'd caught her in.

And, of course, that nail. Steensland had looked closely at Lo's hands when she came in, and while several of her nails were cracked and broken—more damage from storm prep, according to Lo—the paint that remained was the same hot pink.

It wasn't much, not at first. Circumstantial at best, flimsy at worst.

But that was before one of Lo's friends came forward with a story about seeing Lo and Landon together in the hours before the storm made landfall, about Lo's near-rabid jealousy and determination to hold on to Landon at all costs.

And that was before Landon's own friends told police

about Landon's wandering eye and his growing frustration with his teenage mistress.

Murder is a chaotic thing. It's a violation of the natural order, an event that should never happen to any of us, an act none of us should ever commit, and yet every year, the impossible happens over and over and over again. What do we do with that?

More often than not, we try to make it make sense.

We tell ourselves a story.

And the story that was beginning to twist itself around Lo Bailey made a lot of sense to a lot of people.

By the time she went to trial in the spring of 1985, that story had sharpened and refined itself like a blade.

It went like this.

Lo, realizing that she's losing her grip on her married lover, makes a desperate play, begging him to come to St. Medard's Bay. Is it a test? That's the prosecution's angle, another example of how manipulative Lo is: "Prove you love me by racing toward me as a hurricane approaches."

We'll never know the reason Landon agreed, but he does. He meets Lo at their bungalow on the beach, as is confirmed by Lo's best friend, who sees the two together.

They argue.

Landon is tired of Lo's demands, tired of her petulance, ready to put an end to it all, but Lo is not going easily.

The fight moves down the beach, the prosecution speculating that Lo makes dramatic threats. Maybe she's heading toward the ocean, threatening to walk in and drown herself if he leaves her, to refuse to take shelter as the storm comes in.

They struggle, resulting in Lo's bruises and the broken fingernail found inside Landon's jacket.

And here is where the story falters, just the littlest bit.

Lo strikes him, they claim, but with what? No weapon is ever found, and the best the coroner can say is that the wounds are consistent with that of a "heavy object with sharp edges, possibly a lightweight anchor."

It makes enough sense——that stretch of beach between the Rosalie Inn and the nature preserve is often littered with debris from a handful of shipwrecks just off the coast. Maybe it was an anchor, maybe it was some other piece of metal, but in any case, the prosecution alleges that Lo strikes him again and again, until the back of his skull caves in and he drops to the sand.

Now? Panic. What to do?

Here's where the prosecution really leans in. Lo, they say, grabs Landon's wrists and starts tugging him toward the water. She's banking on the fact that the storm will cover up what she's done, hoping that the ocean of her childhood will wash him out to sea and this whole thing can be chalked up to a bad dream.

But Landon is now deadweight, and Lo Bailey is a petite woman. She can't move him very far, and the storm is only building, and before long she's forced to give up, no doubt assuming that the surging seas will take care of the rest.

Unfortunately for her, they don't. Landon's body is found the very next day, in a condition that can't be fully explained. A young woman's small lies make no sense unless they're covering up a much bigger one, and just like that, Lo Bailey goes from mistress to murderess.

Deadly Waters, Deadly Love
by J. Anthony Marsh, Pocket Books, 1988

LANDON P. FITZROY, ESQ.

9/4/83

Lo,

Forgive the formal stationery, but it's all I had handy, and the way I see it, my choices were either not to write to you as soon as possible (unthinkable, idiotic, not to be borne, etc. etc. etc.) or to write to you on this, and have you think I might be kind of an asshole.

And maybe I *am* an asshole because you probably aren't interested in a letter from some thirty-year-old lawyer who has maybe five years before his hairline gives up the ghost and his love of bourbon and barbecue finally catches up with his waistline, but on the offhand chance that you *are* happy to get such a letter, I'm leaving this for you at The Line. The bartender there is probably used to having moony-eyed guys such as myself passing you notes because I can't imagine who could walk into that place, see you, and *not* want to know everything there is to know about you.

And you *are* probably used to men telling you you're a knockout. Which you are, make no mistake, but I wanted you to know that that's not why I'm writing. I've seen a lot of pretty girls in my life, Lo. "Pretty" isn't what has me awake at four in the morning, writing this with hands that, if I'm honest, are shaking a little bit.

It's going to sound stupid, but when I walked into The Line tonight and saw you there by the bar, I swear to God, it was like you just . . . glowed. Like there was a life force inside you that couldn't help but shine out.

Like you swallowed starlight.

I just reread that, and I'm going to be very honest, Lo, there's a part of me that wants to cross it out because you'll probably think it's A) a line and/or B) almost unbearably cheesy.

If you want to show this letter to your friends and make fun of it, I wouldn't blame you one bit.

But I couldn't sleep until I let you know that even if I never see you again, I'm pretty sure you're going to haunt me for a long, long time.

(But I really hope to see you again.)

LPF

CHAPTER TWO

July 1, 2025

33 Days Left

The afternoon Lo Bailey comes back to St. Medard's Bay, it's raining.

The rain is not a surprise. It's summer in Alabama, summer at the *beach* in Alabama, and that comes with afternoon storms more often than not. It's practically a ritual at the Rosalie Inn this time of year, watching the families gather on the beach under clear morning skies only to scuttle back to the safety of cars or the front porch of the inn—whether they're guests here or not—as thick dark clouds roll out along the horizon. For about twenty minutes, it'll rain so hard you can hardly hear yourself think, the drops hitting the ground so violently they can't even soak into the parched plants and sandy soil.

And then, as suddenly as it comes on, it stops. The clouds smooth out into gray wisps, the sun reemerges with such force that sometimes you can see literal steam rising from the grass, and the families head back out to their chairs and their towels, telling one another that the rain "cooled things off" even as the humidity feels like a second skin.

Still, it feels ominous, the clap of thunder that shakes the inn as I watch a nondescript white rental car pull into the narrow parking lot on the back side of the Rosalie. I'm up on the second floor, standing at the big bay window that looks out on that side of the inn, matching the one across the landing that has a much prettier view of the Gulf. The rooms on the back side are obviously the cheaper ones, but as Mom always said, not every room can look out at the ocean, and some people are happy to pay lower prices just to be near the water, who cares if they can look at it.

This summer, our ocean-view rooms aren't even fully booked, and there's no one on what we optimistically called the "Gull Wing." Probably for the best since two out of the ten rooms up here smell vaguely mildewed no matter how much we clean, or how much I've spent replacing furniture and bedding.

August Fletcher isn't staying on this side, of course. He paid for one of the best rooms we have, a big corner room down-stairs with French doors opening onto a private piece of the front porch, windows facing all that sand and sea.

The driver's side door opens, and an arm darts out, a navy umbrella popping open and nearly hiding the driver from view. I catch a glimpse of one long, tanned, and hairy leg beneath a pair of khaki shorts, a brief flash of white T-shirt, and then he's hurrying around the front of the car and opening the passenger door.

Nowhere in his email did he mention he might have a com-panion, but as soon as I see her—the swirl of floral skirt, a gleam of jeweled sandal, a cloud of blond hair—somehow, I just *know* it's Lo Bailey in that car with him.

My pulse jumps up a notch, curiosity making me want to

press my face to the window like a little kid, but the umbrella blocks my view, and all I can really see clearly is my own wavering reflection in the rainy window.

I'm still not quite used to it, seeing my mother's face reflected back at me. It happened around the same time I turned forty, earlier this year. I always knew we looked alike, but age has made the resemblance even more pronounced, and I can't think about it too much because it reminds me that when my mother was forty—when she seemed *old* to me—I was already twenty. When Mom was the age that I am now, she had a decades-long marriage, a college-aged daughter, and a thriving family business.

What do I have? A shitty ex-boyfriend who wasted twelve years of my life, a spider plant that is on death's doorstep, and a hotel that I alternately fantasize about burning down and also somehow seeing on the cover of *Coastal Living*.

I hear the door open and wait for Edie's usual "Welcome to the Rosalie Inn!," a cheerful cry so loud I sometimes tease her that they can hear it in Orange Beach, but there's nothing, just the sound of the rain and their footsteps on the wooden floors.

Time to play the Charming Innkeeper, I guess.

They're both at the front desk as I enter the lobby, the rain easing up now outside the wide glass doors that lead out onto the beach. A tanned little boy stands just next to the railing, bright blue inner tube in hand, watching the waves, no doubt waiting for the moment his mom tells him he can head back out there.

Not a guest, I'm pretty sure, probably someone staying at the condos farther down the beach and just using the Rosalie Inn's porch for shelter.

I hate how angry that makes me. It's not this little boy's fault that his parents have enough money *not* to book an old hotel for their summer vacation. I can't pretend that it's not probably a fuck-ton nicer, having a whole condo to yourself—a kitchen, a door you can close between you and your family members. If it were me, that's what I'd want.

And still, I feel heat rising up my chest, the urge to tell him that the porch is only for paying customers bitter on my tongue.

Another crack of thunder rattles the windows, and the boy on the porch cringes, but I'm already turning away from him because Lo Bailey is walking toward me.

I've seen her picture on the internet and in the magazines that Mom had hidden away, so I'd known how gorgeous she was when she was younger, but I'm not prepared for how beautiful she still is. Her hair is long and thick, curling a little from the rain, and while calling it "blond" is technically true, it doesn't really do justice to the color. It's a riot of different shades, caramel and gold, platinum and ash, the kind of hair that would cost a fortune in a salon, but I feel like in her case, it's all natural. Her eyes are the same clear green as the water just outside the door, and even though I know she's got to be at least sixty—she was in the same grade as my mom—she could easily pass for ten years younger, maybe even fifteen.

I almost want to laugh at it, how stupidly, almost obscenely pretty she is, a true freak of nature—because *of course* lives got ruined over this woman.

Of course she was a scandal.

Of course a man was left dead in her wake.

"Hi," I say. "You must be August." I turn to the woman next to him. "And I'm guessing you're Lo Bailey?"

"And you must be Geneva."

My attention had been so focused on Lo, this woman who has loomed so large over my hometown, that I'd barely clocked August. But as he steps forward, I realize Lo is probably not the only one used to turning heads. August Fletcher is tall and lean, his black hair a little too long, threaded with gray at the temples, and his teeth are very white in his very tanned face.

When I take his hand to shake it, his skin is warm, his grip is tight, and I'm surprised by the shiver of lust that shoots up my spine. Since Chris left, I've barely looked at men at all, too consumed with saving the hotel and too pissed off at the entire XY contingent to even think about dating, much less sex.

But that part of me definitely wakes up a little when he smiles at me and says, "Hope it's not an issue that Lo decided to tag along. If you've got another room free, that would be great, but we can share if needed."

"As you can see, we're completely swamped," I joke in reply, spreading my hands wide to take in the empty lobby before I remember that sometimes self-deprecation can sound a lot like bitterness.

"Great," August replies, his teeth flashing in a quick grin, then he adds, "And of course I'll pay our agreed-upon rate for Lo's room as well."

That's *eight hundred dollars a night*. For who knows how many nights. I almost feel lightheaded as I nod and say, "Sounds good!," like this man isn't offering a whole fucking lifeline just as I'd felt the waves start to crash over my head.

I'm still reeling when Lo says, "It's still such a pretty spot." She sounds dreamy, like she's talking to herself, not to me. "I forgot how pretty it was."

"You've been here before?" I ask, wondering when she would have stayed at the Rosalie, given that she grew up just down the road.

"Aren't you Ellen Chambers's little girl?" she asks, and I find myself smiling. Only in Alabama can you be forty years old and still be referred to as anyone's "little girl."

"I am," I say. "Well, Ellen Corliss's."

Lo nods at that, still a little distracted, like she's not quite in the same room with us. "Right, right. Well, she'll always be Ellen Chambers to me."

She turns then, and her green eyes get a little sharper, a little clearer. "You knew my mama? Beth-Anne Bailey?"

"Everyone knew Miss Beth-Anne," I say, thinking of the friendly woman who ran the Greedy Pelican, a souvenir shop on Main famous mostly for the giant acrylic pelican on its roof, its beak stuffed with a fake surfboard, beach chairs, and sunglasses. It's hard to believe a woman this stunning came from such a plain, down-to-earth shopkeeper, but genetics are weird that way.

"I'm sorry for your loss," I add. Miss Beth-Anne didn't make it through Covid, and it had been a big blow for the whole town. Thinking about it now, I'm surprised Lo didn't come home for the funeral. I wonder if they had still been on speaking terms.

Lo barely acknowledges my condolences, her gaze still turned toward the sea, and August looks back and forth between us before saying, "I technically understand the words you're both saying, but it still feels like code somehow."

That brings Lo back to the present, and she turns a sly grin on August before winking at me. "August here is from *Ohiiiiiiio-oooooo*, Ellen Corliss's Little Girl. He's not used to an Alabama Greeting. You know, establishing 'your people,' where they're from, how you all know each other."

"Do all people from Alabama know each other?" August asks, and Lo and I both chorus, "Yes."

The laugh that comes out of me is a surprise, and Lo grins, a little moment of camaraderie between us. It shouldn't feel as intimate as it does, given that she's a stranger. Then again, I have a feeling Lo Bailey has never met a stranger.

"Sorry, I was trying to figure out why the phone in 132 wasn't working!" Edie calls out, coming from the back hallway. "Turns out it wasn't plugged in, which is a pretty standard requirement, so—"

"Come say hi to Mr. Fletcher and Ms. Bailey," I call back as she enters the lobby, her hair spiky with sweat.

Edie stops by the staircase, her eyes blinking behind her glasses as she takes in Lo and August standing there.

"August Fletcher," August tells her, stepping forward with an outstretched hand.

Edie is frozen, and there's an awkward beat while August stands there, his arm extended. Edie merely stares at it like she's never even heard of a handshake before.

August gives a bemused chuckle, and Edie finally shakes herself a little, slapping her palm into his. "Edie Vargas. Sorry about that. Still thinking about that stupid phone. Welcome to the Rosalie."

She looks at Lo then, and Lo smiles at her, giving a little wave. "Hi!" she says brightly, and after another one of those weird pauses, Edie raises her own hand.

"Ms. Bailey, was it?" she asks, and Lo tilts her head to one side, a hand on her hip.

"Honey, the last people to call me 'Ms. Bailey' were lawyers at my trial. I'm Lo to everyone else."

"Edie's not from St. Medard's Bay," I say apologetically. I don't understand her sudden social awkwardness, but I know it has nothing to do with Lo or her past. Edie couldn't care less about true crime, always grimaces when she overhears one of my podcasts as I'm working, and while she's lived in St. Medard's for several years now, she mostly keeps to herself. Decades-old gossip wouldn't have reached her.

"Nope, Natchez," Edie confirms, then points toward the front desk. "If y'all will excuse me—"

"Edie, can you get Lo booked into the room next to the Bayview Suite?" I turn to Lo and add, "It's just as nice as August's room, though the view is not *quite* as good. It's funny, I only call it the 'Bayview Suite' because that's what someone else called it—my granddad, probably—even though we're actually facing a gulf, not a bay."

I'm rambling, but suddenly, with the two of them standing in front of me, all of this seems very . . . real.

And exciting.

Hope is the thing that kills. But I'm still damn near giddy thinking about how much money this one stay is going to make for the inn.

The other thing about hope, though? It isn't just fatal, it's contagious.

It starts spilling out of me, and suddenly I'm imagining a gorgeous hardcover book with the Rosalie on the front, our reservation site suddenly filling up, me in one of those talking head interviews, smiling at Lester Holt or—be still my heart—Keith Morrison as I detail the fascinating history of the Rosalie Inn, the one place St. Medard's Bay's storms had never been able to kill.

Is it a little grubby, hoping to become some true crime hot spot?

Probably.

Is it what my great-grandparents would've envisioned when they built this place in the '20s?

Absolutely not.

But I owe it to them to keep the inn open and running in any way I can, and if August Fletcher and Lo Bailey will make that happen, my dead ancestors will have to get over it.

"Got it," Edie calls now from the desk, and I pull out the plastic key card for the Bayview Suite, nodding down the hall.

"I'll show you to your rooms. Lo, I can let you in with the master key, and Edie can drop off the actual key once she's got you all situated."

"Just use my card," August says, handing over an American Express that I dutifully pass to Edie before saying, "This way."

Lo and August pick up the two bags at their feet, following me out of the lobby and into the hallway as I continue my little lecture. I've never been that good at this part of the job, the chatting up guests, the local history, all of that.

"Like I said, St. Medard's Bay *itself* isn't actually a bay, which makes the name kind of a misnomer."

"Not really," Lo replies, startling me and, I think, August, too.

We stop just outside their rooms, and I turn to face both of them.

Lo's sunglasses hold her hair back from her face, and as the sun pours in from one of the second-story windows, I can make out the faint lines on her clear skin, the crease at the corner of her eyes, the only things that give her real age away. It makes me feel better, those reminders, because earlier, in the lobby, it was more like those pictures I'd seen had come to life, like time had passed for everyone else but somehow not for Lo Bailey.

"St. Medard's Bay," she says, waving a hand in the general direction of the town, "might not have a bay, but it *is* named af-ter St. Medard, patron saint of hurricanes. Can't think of a more fitting name than that."

It's funny, but never once in all my years here did it occur to me to wonder who St. Medard was, or why the town might be named after him. I think—not for the first time—how odd it is that I've ended up back in this place that I couldn't wait to escape.

I hand August his key card, then use my master to unlock the room next door for Lo. As she sweeps past me, my eyes follow her, those plastic jewels on her sandals glinting as she walks across the pale wooden floors.

While Lo moves to open the balcony doors, August turns back to me.

"Thank you again," he says. "I really think this is gonna be just the thing."

Before he retreats into his room, I work up my courage and say, "You mentioned in your email you were writing a book?"

August nods, reaching into his back pocket for his phone.

"We are."

We.

"About that guy who died in Hurricane Marie?"

"Landon Fitzroy," he supplies even though I knew the name.

"Right. Well, I'm thrilled y'all are here, and especially excited you wanted to stay at the Rosalie. Surprised, honestly. Most people choose the condos these days, the ones on Airbnb, Vrbo . . . probably some other acronym I haven't even heard of yet."

August finally lifts his gaze from his phone, frowning at me in confusion.

"Of course we'd stay here. I mean . . . this is the place. Where it all happened."

Now I'm the one who's confused. "The storm?" I say. "Marie got us pretty good, but—"

"No," August says, shaking his head. "I mean this is the place Landon Fitzroy died. This is where they found his body."

The name *Fitzroy* is an old one, dating at least as far back as the medieval era. Often given to the illegitimate children of noblemen, the name literally means "son of a king," and if Landon Parkes Fitzroy was not born into royalty exactly, he was pretty damn close.

His family was the kind of rich you only become when previous generations have committed themselves to being as thoroughly evil as possible, and the Fitzroy family tree is full of these types. A war profiteer here, a plantation owner there. A Fitzroy in the 1920s who managed to somehow be both Alabama's attorney general *and* one of the biggest bootleggers for miles. (It goes without saying that one of the reasons he was so successful at this endeavor was that he'd used his political and legal power to drive out the competition.)

Landon's father, the formidable Beau Fitzroy, had risen higher than any of his ancestors, becoming governor of Alabama in 1982, just two years before his only son and heir was killed in a storm off the coast of a little town called St. Medard's Bay.

The reason Landon had been in St. Medard's Bay at all that summer?

The affair he was having with a nineteen-year-old, Gloria "Lo" Bailey.

Before Hurricane Marie swept Landon Fitzroy into memory, the Governor's Son and the Smalltown Tramp was nothing more than local gossip, the story barely making its way past Montgomery, much less to the rest of the country. People whispered about it, gave one another knowing looks when the rumble of a private jet engine was heard overhead or a yacht three times the size of any other ship in St. Medard's Bay Harbor made anchor. But powerful men—even married ones with bright political futures ahead of them—have always been drawn to beauty, and Lo Bailey had that to spare.

Still, it was a shock when Landon's body was found among the wreckage of Hurricane Marie, and even more stunning when the coroner ruled that he had not died as a result of the storm at all, but had instead been murdered.

By none other than Lo Bailey. Or so the state claimed.

Rumors flew with the speed of hurricane-force winds: Landon had been lured to his death by a teenage temptress who knew her time was running out, who knew that once Landon got serious about his future, there would be no room for her in it. As a lifelong resident of a town that had seen its share of deadly storms—one of which had killed her own father before she was even born—Lo, the story went, would've known that the chaotic aftermath of a hurricane would cover her tracks, make the death seem like just another storm-related tragedy.

But there were other rumors.

That Beau Fitzroy had pulled every string at his disposal to see his son's death classified as a homicide, that he intended to see someone punished for what had happened to Landon, and Lo was the perfect target. It was her fault his son had even been in St. Medard's Bay, her fault that he was in danger of careening headfirst into scandal, her fault that Beau Fitzroy's most cherished dream—to build a political dynasty the likes of which the South had never seen—was as dead as his heir.

And it wasn't like the case was without merit.

Lo was caught in two lies that cost her her credibility. She claimed she never asked Landon to come to St. Medard's Bay as the storm approached, but the prosecution had phone records that showed two calls, made several hours apart, from the beach house Landon had purchased for Lo Bailey the year before.

As for the bruises on Lo's arms in the days following the storm? She claimed she fell while trying to secure a window at her mother's store, but the purple marks encircling her biceps didn't look like the sort of thing you'd get in a fall. They *did*, however, look very much like someone's fingers gripping her. Maybe someone trying to push her away or hold her back before she could deliver a killing blow?

Then there was the testimony from one of Lo's closest friends, who swore she saw Lo in the vicinity near where Landon Fitzroy's body was eventually found, and that she had heard Lo threaten that if Landon were ever to leave her, she'd make sure it was the last thing he ever did.

But while it didn't paint a favorable picture of Lo, in the end it was all apparently just too circumstantial for some members of the jury. Whatever the truth of the matter, a mistrial and a DA surprisingly reluctant to retry the case meant that while Lo Bailey was tainted by scandal, she was not, in the end, branded a murderess.

At least not in the legal sense.

In the hearts and minds of the American public?

That was another story.

> "After the Storm: A Golden Boy, A Small-town Girl,
> and the Murder That Maybe Never Was."
> *Vanity Fair*, October 1991

CHAPTER THREE

July 3, 2025

31 Days Left

I don't see much of August or Lo for two days after their arrival. It seems like they're mostly keeping to their rooms and the beach, but I'm also busier than usual around the hotel. We're nowhere near full occupancy—which was once a given during a holiday week—but we still have more guests than we've had so far this summer, and getting them checked in, making sure the rooms are clean, chasing down extra phone chargers, extra blankets, "better" towels . . . it all means I'm running around like a chicken with its head cut off, as Mom would've said.

Still, I've found time in the evenings to look up everything I can about Landon Fitzroy's death, including going through Mom's box of clippings, and—just as I'd thought—I can't find any reference to the Rosalie Inn being the place where Landon's body was found. Over and over again, it's just *the beach near a nature preserve,* or *a lonely stretch of coastline.* There's no mention of the Rosalie at all as far as I can tell, and neither Mom's name nor my grandparents' comes up in any of the things I see online or in the articles Mom kept.

Which makes me wonder—how does August know something I don't?

It's only July 3, but as I step out into the early evening, heading for my trailer down the beach, I'm surprised at how heavy the air feels this early in the season. It rained earlier today, and heavy clouds still hang low over the horizon, deep purple against the pink and orange of the sunset.

August is when the heat starts to feel like a sweaty fist smacking into the sand. September can be that way, too—and every kid who grew up in St. Medard's has a sad story about the Halloween It Was Too Hot to Wear My Costume. That's the kind of heat that drives people crazy, makes them feel like they're walking through hot Jell-O just getting to their cars in the grocery store parking lot.

Edie is obsessed with weather and has told me more than once that this year's hurricane season is predicted to be bad. "They're already on the 'J's, and we've got what? Four more months to go?" she'd said just this morning, pointing at a swirl of red and yellow somewhere out over the Atlantic.

I'd nodded and looked worried and we'd talked about climate change, about rising ocean temperatures, and I hadn't told her that there's a dark, secret place in my heart that longs for one of those storms to come howling out of the Gulf and finally smash the Rosalie Inn to pieces.

A small place, I should add. Most of my heart loves the Rosalie Inn with the kind of passion that can come only when a business has been in your family for generations, when every board, every window, every doorway holds a memory.

But each time I put another charge on my Visa and hold my breath that it will be approved, I'm reminded that sometimes even places we love can become weights around our necks.

Now, as the warm wind blows my sweaty hair back from my face, the sand underfoot squeaking slightly against the soles of my sandals, I wonder if the air really does feel charged somehow or if it is just the doom-and-gloom thinking I find myself engaged in more and more these days.

I'm almost to the Airstream when I hear someone calling my name. I turn, figuring it's Mr. Peters from Room 202—that man never met an amenity or perk he didn't want to wheedle out of me or Edie—or maybe the handyman who's supposed to be figuring out why the shower in 114 keeps leaking. But it's not either of them.

It's August, standing on the boardwalk that leads to the inn, the setting sun limning him in gold. He's wearing loose linen pants and a fitted gray T-shirt tonight, his Tevas held in one hand, Lo's sparkly sandals in the other.

She's just behind him, but her gaze is directed to the clouds on the horizon. Once again, I'm stunned to think that she's sixty. In this light, she looks almost unchanged from those pictures taken when she was twenty years old. Only the delicate thin skin of her neck and upper chest give her away. She's got on a white sundress, and it billows around her legs as the breeze picks up.

"Hi!" I say with forced cheer, retracing my steps to stand in front of them. "Have y'all been settling in okay? Do you need anything?"

"A beer," August says, smiling at me, and I'm about to tell him we don't have a restaurant on-site—Dad closed that up a few years before he died, saying it wasn't worth the expense or headache to run it anymore. But before I can, August adds, "Apparently there's a famous bar around here?"

"Oh, The Line," I reply. Famous is one word for it, but *in*-famous is probably closer to the truth. It started out as a beach shack sometime in the sixties, built right on the state line between Florida and Alabama, hence the name. Now it's a jumble of buildings that regularly attracts hundreds of people a night, thousands during spring break and summer holidays. The night before the Fourth of July? It's going to be a madhouse.

"It's just down the highway," I tell August, pointing in that direction. "Take a right out of the parking lot, and—"

He laughs and shakes his head, curls flopping over his forehead. "No, I didn't want directions. I wondered if you wanted to come with us."

"Why?" I blurt out, almost without thinking. He laughs again, shrugging this time.

"Always nice to have a local on hand, and I was going to ask you some questions about the hotel at some point anyway. Thought I might as well do it somewhere with some ambience, you know?"

Now I'm the one who laughs. "Oh man, if you're after ambience, I have . . . some not-great news about The Line."

"I used to wait tables there," Lo says, almost dreamy as she keeps looking out over the ocean. "And some nights, they let me sing with the band. 'I've Been Loving You Too Long.' That was my signature song. Do you know it?"

When I shake my head, Lo just smiles, fluffing out her long blond hair. "Too young, I guess. How old are you, Ellen's Little Girl?"

"Forty," I reply, and she tips her head back with a sigh.

"A baby. Like August here."

"I don't know about that. Just the other day, I realized I not only have a favorite heating pad, I have a *second* favorite heating pad."

Lo's laugh is a high, bright thing, and when she steps closer, a wave of her perfume engulfs me. It's too sweet, and there's a chemical tang to it, like the kind of drugstore body spray a teenage girl would wear. "You're funny," she says, and then surprises me by reaching out and tucking a strand of my hair behind my ear. It's the kind of easy touch you'd give to a close friend or a family member, not someone you've spent only fifteen minutes with. It makes me miss my mom with a sudden fierceness that has my throat going tight.

Not that Mom was ever particularly free with those easy, affectionate gestures, so maybe it just makes me miss the idea of a mom. Or maybe I just wish that things with mine hadn't been so complicated.

"Your mama was funny, too," Lo says, almost like she'd read my mind. I wait for her to ask about Mom, bracing myself to explain the whole sad thing to her, but instead, she just makes a shooing motion at me and says, "Now, go get changed. I need some quality time on memory lane tonight."

Twenty minutes later, I'm in a hot, crowded room with what seems to be the entire population of Baldwin County, Alabama, plus a few hundred vacationers, some of whom are going to regret anything and everything that happens tonight. That's the kind of place The Line is. Paradise for some—a freewheeling honky-tonk where the band is loud, the beer is cold, and everybody will be your best friend for at least an hour or two. For others—namely me—it's hell. Too many people, too much noise, too much . . . everything. The floor underfoot is sticky with spilled drinks and who knows what else, and there's a constant haze of smoke that stings my eyes. Smoking is still allowed indoors here, and I know from experience it will take at least three showers to fully get the smell out of my hair.

As I sit at a scarred picnic table on the edge of the dance floor,

August throws a long leg over the bench next to me, his eyes narrowed in the dim light.

"People actually like this?" he yells over the band's third performance of "Sweet Home Alabama."

Nodding, I tip my beer to my mouth, grateful that it's cold sliding down my throat. Big fans circulate overhead, and there's a breeze coming in through all the open doors that lead out to the beach, but that can do only so much against a July night and a bunch of people crowded in one space. I'd changed out of the clothes I'd worn all day before climbing in the backseat of Lo and August's rental car, and I'm glad I chose a simple, light-weight shift dress, but there's already sweat dripping down my back and dotting August's temples.

Lo, seated on the other side of the table from us, looks only a little wilted in the heat, her eyes wide as she looks around her. "God, it's exactly the same," she says. I can barely hear her over the band, and I lean in closer.

"Hurricane Peggy did a lot of damage back in ninety-eight, but they rebuilt it exactly like it was. Had to go to junkyards to find signs the appropriate amount of rusted."

Using my beer bottle, I point to one such metal sign, advertising Crown Royal, and she shakes her head, smiling as she rests her chin in her hand. "I didn't think I missed St. Medard's Bay, I really didn't. But Christ, I did."

I believe her. She's practically glowing in the red light from the beer signs, her white dress a beacon in the gloom, and for as dingy as The Line is, it's like none of it is touching her. Like she alone is going to leave this place without a sweat stain under her arms, without the smell of Marlboros clinging to her hair.

"How long did you live here?" I ask, and she slants me a look, tipping her head to the side.

"Ellen Chambers's Little Girl, are you really going to pretend you don't already know my whole damn story?"

"She knows you, Lo," August says, his knee bumping mine—accidentally?—under the table. "Remember, she knew your mom. Sorry, your 'mama.'"

"That's not what I'm talking about, and she knows it," Lo replies, pointing a finger at me. Her nails are short, clean of polish. "I'm asking her if she knows why I left. Landon and all that."

Again, I see that box hidden at the back of Mom's closet, picture after picture of a handsome man with thick dark hair and an honest-to-God dimple in his chin. "I do," I tell her. "Or I guess, the tabloid version of it?" I pause, because it all seems so improbable and silly now. "You were accused of killing the governor's son?"

"Mm-hmm." Lo nods, smiling like I've aced my first test. "Apparently, he was going to dump me, and I decided the appropriate reaction was smashing his head in and hoping everyone blamed it on the storm? Honestly, it sounds like something I *might've* done if Landon *had* been about to dump me—which, trust me, baby, he was *not*."

She says it so lightly, with a little gleam in her eye, like she's *trying* to shock me with her nonchalance. Again, I'm struck by the idea that we've time-traveled somehow, that the Lo Bailey in front of me isn't from 2025 at all, but frozen in amber from 1984. Still young, still beautiful, still full of more sass than her mama knew what to do with.

The band has shifted into a new song, something fast, and I can feel the bass line in my chest, in the soles of my feet. I have to raise my voice louder than I'd like as I say, "August said his body was found at the Rosalie. But the papers never mentioned that, and my mom never—"

"Let's maybe save any talk about all that for when we're

back at the inn," August cuts in, glancing around us. He's smiling, but his lips are tight, his shoulders tense, and Lo waves a careless hand, the bangle on her wrist sliding down her forearm.

"Auggie has so many weird rules about this book, Geneva. Doesn't like to talk about its specifics in public, wants as few people as possible to know that we're even writing the damn thing, so that when he talks to them, he'll get their . . . what was it? Oh, right. 'Their authentic selves.'"

Lo makes air quotes around that, and August's smile tightens. "Just trying to keep things unbiased."

She gives another one of those big laughs, and I see several heads turn in her direction. I wonder if anyone recognizes the former mistress to Alabama's Golden Son. Then again, even if she weren't an infamous figure in these parts, it's hard *not* to look at her.

"Baby, this is the South. No one is *unbiased* about anything. They make up their minds lickety-split, and the better the story seems, the more inclined they are to believe it. Tell him, Geneva. Tell him what it's like around here."

"Well," I start slowly, "I guess I'm actually a good example of that myself."

The beer is sweaty in my hands, and I absently pick at the label with my thumbnail. "I mean, I grew up here, obviously, graduated high school in 2003, then immediately struck out for college in Savannah with these big dreams of being an interior decorator."

"I can see that," Lo says, tilting her head. "Everything in the inn is so pretty. So fresh, and . . . unique. In a good way."

The compliment warms me, and I nod in acknowledgment. "I mean, I'd like to do a lot more, but the environment is already so hard on everything. Any beachside place, you end up replacing stuff every five to seven years, so I can't really justify—"

Stopping myself, I shake my head and laugh. "Sorry. Not the point of the story. I just can't turn Innkeeper Brain off lately."

"Sounds like you might need another drink," August replies, signaling a passing waitress, and once August and I have our beers and Lo has her Bushwacker, I continue.

"Anyway, after school, I stayed in Savannah, got a job with a local firm. I came back to St. Medard's Bay to visit my parents but had zero plans of ever moving back here."

I've had just enough to drink that I almost tell them how lonely I always felt growing up at the inn, how weird it was to feel like everything that was *nice* in your house wasn't even for you, but for strangers. How I wished I had siblings because at least then there would've been other people to *share* that weirdness with. Mom and Dad didn't seem to feel the same way I did.

Instead, I just say, "Then a bunch of things happened." I count them off on my fingers. "One, I met a guy. Chris. He was . . ."

Trailing off, I try to remember the good things about Chris, but every memory still stings, so I push them away and shrug. "He was a guy. Doesn't matter."

"Oooh, *He Was a Guy, Doesn't Matter* might make a good title if *you* ever write your memoir, Auggie," Lo interjects, and August shoots her a look.

"Noted."

Then August nudges me with his beer, folding his arms on the table and leaning in closer because the band has just launched into "Have You Ever Seen the Rain?"

"Okay, so you were never coming back to St. Medard's Bay, and Chris was Just a Guy. Then what?"

"Then," I say with a sigh, "well, then my dad died. Aneurysm in his sleep. And a couple of years after that . . ."

A couple of years after that, my mom was diagnosed with early-onset Alzheimer's. She'd called me, her voice oddly calm as she'd told me the news. She'd been researching the disease, she had a specialist in Mobile, and she was already working on granting me power of attorney over everything.

And, of course, I'll need to put the inn up for sale.

It was the one time in that conversation that her voice had broken, and that in turn had broken me.

I'd cried in Chris's arms that night, in the apartment we were sharing in Atlanta at the time. That's when he'd said that we should take on the inn ourselves.

Keep it in the family, he'd said.

Magic words.

My dad was gone, my mom was going, and I didn't have siblings. My dad's sister moved to England back in the '80s, my mom's brother, Adam, died in a car accident the year I graduated high school, my grandparents were long gone, and here Chris was, offering to be my family.

Or at least, that's what I thought he was offering. After all, we'd been dating ten years at that point. A whole decade. My friends, both in Atlanta and in Savannah, had thought it was insane that we weren't talking marriage, but I always said that we just weren't ready yet, never admitting that there was no *we* in that. *Chris* wasn't ready, but I'd convinced myself he would be. One day.

I don't tell Lo and August any of that, though. I don't need anyone feeling sorry for me.

Instead, I say, "My mom decided she wasn't really up to running the inn anymore, so me and Chris came down here to take it on. It was Chris's idea, actually. He worked at this digital marketing firm, absolutely hated it. I think he thought living in St. Medard's Bay would be an escape from the rat race or something, this quaint small-town life as the local innkeeper. Instead, it's people calling at 2 AM because the Wi-Fi is down, or a toilet is clogged, and oh yeah, we need to replace every lamp in the place, and do you know how much lamps cost these days?"

I laugh, but it sounds more bitter than I intended.

"So he lasted just over a year here before he fucked off. Dumped me *and* the inn in one fell swoop."

August sucks in a breath, leaning back. "Ouch."

"Asshole," Lo offers, suddenly fierce, and it feels good, telling this story and not seeing pity in their eyes, just empathy and righteous anger.

My second beer is now empty, and I'm a little buzzed. I hardly ever have time for a drink, much less two, and the only thing I managed to eat today was a banana and some peanut butter crackers. But it feels nice, the warm, loopy sensation spreading through me, and the heat and the crowd and the noise don't seem so bad now.

"*Allllllllll* of that to say that at the end of the day, mine is the most basic, boring, and sadly fucking *typical* story in the world. Aging parents, a boyfriend who couldn't commit, the hell that is being a small-business owner. Nothing juicy, nothing even *interesting*. But!"

I sit up straighter, pointing one finger in the air, and okay, I might be a little *past* buzzed, but Lo is watching me with avid eyes, and I'm very aware of August's hot, dark gaze on the side of my face, and for the first time in years, I feel . . . lighter.

"To this *day*, there are still about twelve people in this town who would swear up and down that Chris bolted because he caught me in bed with Edie."

"The aging punk behind the desk?" August asks, his mouth curving into a grin.

"Mm-hmm," I hum, nodding. "No idea how that rumor got

started, but Edie thinks it might have been one of the girls who cleans the rooms. Not long before Chris left, he and I got into an argument over replacing one of the beds on the second floor. I was in favor, so was Edie, Chris was not, and best I can figure, they heard Chris raising his voice about a bed and Edie and just went with the *most* salacious version they could dream up."

Lo gives another one of those pealing laughs, her hand slapping the tabletop. "See?" she all but crows to August. "I'm telling you, everybody you're gonna talk to is gonna tell you I murdered Landon Fitzroy and took advantage of the hurricane to cover it up. Some of the details might be different—some might say I killed him because he wouldn't leave his wife for me, or they might say that no, it's because I found out about some *other* girlfriend, or even that he wouldn't buy me some piece of jewelry I wanted. But whatever story they come up with is gonna tell you a lot more about *them* than it will about what really happened that night."

August doesn't answer her but instead pulls his phone out of his pocket and starts tapping away.

Lo rolls her eyes. "He does this all the time," she tells me. "Writes down some silly bullshit I say, acts like it's profound."

It kind of was, though—the fact that the gossip people are willing to believe is more about them than anything else. The thing is, I *get* why people wanted to think Lo had killed Landon Fitzroy because otherwise, he was just a tragic victim of a natural disaster, and that wasn't supposed to happen to men like him. A potential future president wasn't supposed to be dead due to high winds and seas while this beautiful but far too brash girl from some Podunk town somehow managed to survive. A lurid story of murder was so much more fun, so much more satisfying.

But as I watch Lo Bailey sway to the music across from me, even as I see her smile brightly, I find myself surprised to realize I could believe in that story, too.

It's something about the way she'd looked at me when I talked about Chris, the quickness and the intensity with which she'd declared him an asshole. She might be sunshine at first glance, but she's tougher than she lets on, Lo Bailey.

She's already slipped back into happy-go-lucky mode, singing along with the band as they play "Fins," her long-fingered hands drumming along with the beat, her blond hair a reddish pink in the lights. I'm surprised to realize that I'm having fun—a thing as foreign to me lately as hope had been—and I'm considering getting another beer when a man approaches our table.

He's in his seventies, I'd guess, thick white hair swept back from his face, a bright orange Hawaiian shirt straining slightly over his beer belly. A chunky gold Rolex circles his wrist, and a diamond pinky ring winks in the dim light as he bestows a brilliant smile on our table, his catcher's mitt hands spread wide.

"Hey, folks!" he says, all Good Ol' Boy Charm, and I catch myself waving in response. He looks familiar, but he's also definitely a type we see a lot of down here, so I can't say if I know him or not.

August clearly doesn't, but Lo is squinting at the man like she might be trying to place him.

"Hey!" she answers back. "Do I know you?"

"Oh, probably not," the man says, still grinning as he puts his hands in his pockets. "Don't think you and me would've ever run in the same circles. But I know who *you* are. Took me a few minutes, but I figured it out."

He shakes his finger at her like she's a naughty child, and something about that makes the beer in my stomach go sour.

That fun, tipsy feeling is rapidly fading, and the room is once again too hot, too crowded, this man's presence at our table making me feel trapped.

"You still look *mighty* good, Miss Bailey, but even The Line has to have . . . well." He chuckles. "Well, it has to have *a line*, doesn't it?" His smile falls abruptly. "And since I own a ten percent stake in this bar, I'm gonna say the line is trampy little trash like you ordering herself a Bushwacker and having a fine ol' Thursday night in *my* goddamn bar."

"Ten percent your goddamn bar," August says, his voice mild but his eyes hard. I watch as the hand he has lying on the table opens and closes, opens and closes.

Lo isn't smiling anymore, and she looks pale all of a sudden, but she holds the man's eyes as she picks up her Bushwacker and slowly, thoroughly drains the glass.

My stomach once again threatens to rebel—Bushwackers are basically just alcoholic milkshakes, and I'm pretty sure chugging one would kill me—but Lo just sits the glass down on the table with a delicate *tink*.

"Let me guess," she says, raising her voice over the music. "You're one of his fishing buddies. Or maybe you tried a case in front of his daddy back when he was a judge. Or are you a fraternity brother?"

Lo looks him up and down, then shakes her head. "No, Landon always said you could tell a Sigma Chi man with one glance, and I don't think you measure up."

No hint of a smile now, all that false charm slipping off him like oil. "Alison Fitzroy is my cousin, slut," he says, the word somehow sounding worse in that honeyed old-money voice.

August is suddenly on his feet, and I am fully sober now, blinking as I stand up, more than a little unsteady. But Lo only smiles up at the man and reaches over to lay a hand on August's arm. "Don't worry about it, Auggie," she says, then turns those big green eyes on him, winking dramatically. "It'll be a great scene for the book."

With that, she gracefully scoops up her purse from the bench beside her and, head held high, walks out of the bar.

DELPHINE

July 4, 1965

I didn't even want to go to the beach that summer. Linus didn't listen because he never listened, not to anything I had to say in any case, and besides, the Richardsons were going. If Harold Richardson did something, well then, by God, Linus Bailey was going to do it, too.

"Not about to sit and spend the entire goddamn fall listening to him brag to everyone at the hospital that he took his family down there while we sat on our asses here in Nashville, Beth-Anne."

I hated how he said my name. Everyone else sort of slurred it together, pretty, like it was one word. *Bethanne*. But Linus always said it like two separate names.

Beth.

Anne.

It sounded like he was trying to bite something, his teeth clicking around the words.

So we went.

It was a long drive, long enough that we had to stop for the night and stay at a motel halfway there. There were two separate beds in the room, and I'd been relieved to see it, but of course that hadn't meant Linus left me alone. Still, I'd been able to sleep without him there next to me, at least, and that had been enough. I had hoped the room at the Shipwreck Inn might be the same, but it wasn't.

I did like the room, though. It faced the ocean, and there were pretty lace curtains in the window. The sheets were a little stiff from being dried in all that salt air, but the smell was worth it. Every morning, after Linus had left to find coffee, I would linger a little longer, inhaling that fragrance that was nothing like Ajax detergent.

The inn itself was pretty, too. It was painted pink, something that had made Linus grunt when our car had finally pulled up in the sand-and-shell parking lot. It wasn't a good grunt, I knew that, and sure enough, a second later he said, "Wonder if Harold was playing a little joke when he suggested this place."

I guess it's kind of funny looking back. Linus hated women so much that even the color most associated with them offended him.

Wasn't funny at the time, of course. It's only now that he's dead that I can find any of that time in my life amusing.

But I liked the pink. It reminded me of the inside of a seashell. And there was a wide front porch where I could sit and feel the salt air move over my skin, watch the waves crash against the shore. I would sit out there with my book and imagine that maybe I could just stay there forever, stop being Mrs. Dr. Linus Bailey.

Wasn't that what little towns like this were for? Starting over?

I'd barely gotten started at all when I married Linus. Just out of high school, not smart enough to go to college—or so my family said—not pretty enough or good enough at housework to land a real catch. Linus had been a childhood friend of my daddy's, but while Daddy had stayed in Ashburn, Linus had moved up in the world, going to college, then medical school, settling in Nashville. He and Daddy still kept in touch, though, and when Linus's first wife died, my daddy thought marriage to a doctor might be just the thing for me. Linus needed a wife, I needed somewhere to go that wasn't my parents' house, and that was that.

I wasn't forced into it, but I never remembered agreeing to it, either. It was just something that happened, almost like I was sleep-walking. I drifted down the aisle and drifted up over to Nashville and Linus's comfortable house, and I drifted through every day in a kind of numbed fog, and I figured that one day, I just might drift myself down to Shelby Street Bridge and jump off.

He never hit me, never forced me in the marriage bed, but there are other ways for a man to be cruel.

Linus seemed to have studied all of them just as vigorously as he'd studied medicine.

Dinner was never quite right, but my daddy probably drank most of our food money away, so not too surprising that all I could seem to manage was opening cans.

My clothes weren't right, either, but what could you expect from a girl who'd probably never been inside a department store until she was lucky enough to have married him?

Funny how the house never seemed as clean as it should, given that I didn't do anything else all day. Of course, we hadn't had nearly as much to clean when I was growing up, so that must be it.

And wasn't Bernice Wilson looking slim these days? How lucky for Dave, having such an attractive wife. My genes, no doubt. Coming from Robertson County trash like I did, was it any wonder my body wanted to hold on to extra pounds? Never mind that I was a doctor's wife, my body clearly thought I might starve to death at any moment.

He always chuckled when he said that, especially when he said it in front of other people.

But that stay at the Shipwreck Inn was a bit of a reprieve. St. Medard's Bay was a small town, quiet, and there weren't many people for Linus to try to impress. The owners of the place, Mr. and Mrs. Chambers, were nice, too. Mrs. Chambers always brought me a glass of lemonade when I'd settle on the porch, and she always asked about what I was reading and never made fun of it, never called it a "toilet roll someone made the mistake of binding into a book" the way that Linus did. She was pregnant, her belly round beneath the pretty cotton shift dresses she wore, and it always reminded me how lucky I was that no matter how much Linus turned to me in the night, no baby had taken hold.

Mrs. Chambers was excited about her baby. They already had one little boy, Adam. He was only about two, his hair sticking up in dark brown tufts. If this baby was a girl, Mrs. Chambers said, she was going to name her Ellen, and if it was another boy, Thomas. I thought those were real pretty names, and when I told her so, she looked so pleased that it made me want to smile and cry and blush all at the same time.

We were supposed to stay for two weeks, Linus's entire vacation from the hospital, but we'd been there only five days when the weather turned.

I remember the way the air got heavier, the skies darker. The water had been so calm when we first arrived, but in those days leading up to the Fourth of July, it was choppier, the waves higher. I hadn't been out in it since the first day of our vacation when Linus had shoved my face into the water, telling me that I'd never learn to swim if I didn't get over my "prissiness," but I liked watching it.

And even though the ocean scared me, I liked it even more the wilder it got. I liked the way the wind started picking up, that salt scent getting stronger, mingling with another smell, something that reminded me of my mama frying fish on Fridays. The clouds overhead looked swollen, bruised, and if I noticed Mr. and Mrs. Chambers getting more nervous, if I overheard their whispered conversations and the faint drone of a radio, a man's voice crackling through the static, I didn't pay it much mind.

I was a country girl. I knew storms, I thought. I'd seen lightning take down oak trees that had stood before Christopher Columbus showed up over here, and a tornado had once ripped through a field just a few miles away from our place.

I didn't know to be scared until it was too late.

It went on like that for a whole day, rain pouring down, and everyone was disappointed. The inn was full for the Fourth of July, and there had been big plans for the holiday. Fireworks on the beach, grilling in the big courtyard between the two wings of the inn, and someone had brought big galvanized tubs to fill with ice and beer. All that was canceled now, and Linus kept threatening to pack up and head home.

"Might want to wait until this weather clears, buddy," Mr. Chambers told him, and I liked how even though he was smiling, his eyes were hard. Here was someone else who saw Linus for what he was and did not like it, no sir.

I liked it even better when Linus bristled at being called "buddy" like that.

But I should've known that that would only make Linus dig in harder, make him more determined to leave.

The power went out around noon that Fourth of July, and that, Linus said, was the last straw.

He started packing, throwing all his things into his suitcase with angry, jerky movements. "Waste of money," he muttered, "and don't think I won't be telling Harold Richardson that."

The next bit is still a blur. I know I packed my things because I have a vivid memory of watching the powder-blue suitcase my mama had ordered for me for my honeymoon float away in the rising waters later, but all I can remember is the numbness settling over me again.

I'd had five days in St. Medard's Bay, and they had been some of the best of my life, but they were over now.

I think Mr. Chambers tried to stop us. I think he might have even called Linus a "stubborn bastard," and there's a memory in there of Mrs. Chambers standing in the doorway, one hand over her mouth, the other resting on her stomach, as she watched us leave. I hoped her baby would be okay, that this storm wouldn't be too stressful for her, and thinking that I'd never know if she had a Thomas or an Ellen made me so sad for some reason.

The wind was so strong we could barely open the car doors, and even once we were inside, the rain was so heavy, the windshield wipers of our Lincoln Continental were fighting a losing battle.

That was when the fear started. When I realized that all I could see outside the windows was water, water, water, everything gray, and the car slid underneath us, Linus's hands clutching the wheel, sweat popping out on his bald head as he leaned forward and squinted.

And then we were weightless for a sickening moment, the tires losing contact with the road. I screamed, grabbed at the door handle, and even as Linus yelled for me to stop, I shoved the door as hard as I could, tumbling out into the road with a splash.

Whatever road had once stretched out before us had become a lake, and Linus got out of the car, too, then, yelling something at me, but it didn't matter what he was saying. Not when the wind was screaming, when the pine trees on the side of the road were bending, snapping, and the water on the road seemed to be getting deeper.

"Get back in the car, Beth-Anne!" he screamed, but I didn't want to be trapped, didn't want water rushing in as I sat in that burgundy leather tomb. Panic had ahold of me now, and the water was rising, rising, rising.

I remembered coming down this road on the way here, how close the ocean had been, how calm and serene as we'd driven past.

It wasn't calm now. It was a force, pushing in, smelling like salt and sky and death, and my eyes darted around me even as the rain stung, the wind making it hard to stand.

The pines were still swaying, but there, across the road, was another, bigger tree. A magnolia, shivering in the wind but standing.

I ran toward it, and then, as the water moved up my thighs, I slowed down, swinging my arms, pushing myself forward until my hands were pressed against its bark.

I didn't know how to cook, and I didn't know how to dress, and I didn't know how to take care of a house, but guess what?

I sure as shit knew how to climb a tree.

That same body that Linus made fun of, that "Robertson County trash" body, was strong. The bark hurt my hands, and rain meant I could barely open my eyes, but I hauled myself up branch by branch, the wind howling around me.

I didn't know Linus had followed me until I felt his fingers curl around my ankles, and then I looked down to see him below me. The water was high now, already covering him up to the knees, and he'd lost his glasses somewhere in all of this.

For the first time ever, Linus looked afraid.

"Help me!" he screamed, and I hooked an arm around the nearest branch, reaching down, almost out of instinct.

Our fingers brushed, but I wobbled on my perch and jerked my hand back to steady myself.

"Help me!" he yelled again, and I wanted to yell back that I was trying.

His fingers tightened on my ankle—to hold on better, I thought, but then his nails dug in, breaking the skin.

"HELP ME, YOU STUPID COW!" he shouted, lips drawn back in a snarl.

It happened so quickly.

I jerked my foot back out of his grasp, nearly sending him back to the ground and that frothing, angry water.

And then, like I was watching myself from a distance, I saw my foot—my ugly foot, as Linus often reminded me, squat and square, probably why fancy high heels never looked quite right on me—land squarely in the middle of his face.

There was a crunch, and I felt his nose give, the blood shocking red in a world that had turned gray.

His arms pinwheeled, and it reminded me of a cartoon I saw once, Wile E. Coyote, I think, about to fall off a cliff.

Ooh, he'd hate that, I thought. Being told he looks that silly, and then he was falling, the dark waters below closing over him.

Linus bobbed back up a few times. Or at least I think he did. I'd turned my face back to the trunk of that magnolia tree, holding on tight, eyes closed.

So maybe it wasn't him screaming. Maybe that gurgling, shrieking sound was just the storm.

But I don't think so.

Twenty-three people died in that storm. That wasn't that big of a number, really. Just a few months later, Hurricane Greer killed something like seventy people in Louisiana. But for a town as little as St. Medard's Bay, it was a significant blow. Luckily, everybody at the Shipwreck Inn had survived. There was water damage, and nearly every window was broken out, but for whatever reason, she'd stayed safe.

That made me happy to hear.

Hurricane Delphine.

That's what the storm was called, but I didn't learn that until later when I was in the hospital. I was fine for the most part, bruised and scraped up, and I'd broken three toes on my left foot, which the doctor said was probably from climbing the tree, or maybe when I lost my shoes as I ran across that road.

I told him that's what I thought, too.

CHAPTER FOUR

July 7, 2025

27 Days Left

It's ironic that the place where my mom will spend the rest of her days is called "Hope House."

If there ever was hope in a place like this—a long-term care facility off Highway 59, just ten miles or so from the Rosalie Inn—it died a lot faster than its residents tend to. Every time I walk through the front doors, see the burgundy-flecked linoleum, smell the mix of strong disinfectant and whatever vegetable they're boiling to death in the kitchen, I feel like I've suddenly aged fifty years, my shoulders reflexively stooping just a little bit as the weight of this place sinks into my bones.

Callie, the front-desk nurse, smiles when she sees me, raising a hand. She likes me, and since she's always good to Mom, I like her, too.

"She's having a good day today!" Callie calls out, and I smile even though Mom's days are, as far as I can tell, always the same. Not good, not bad, just a kind of limbo that taught me there are a lot of things worse than dying.

When I open the door to her room, I see her sitting in her recliner by the window, her hair, once as dark as mine, now steel gray, her thin hands fluttering in her lap. Her hands are always moving, and I used to wonder if she thought she was still crocheting. She always loved that, making blankets for the babies at her church, sending me socks that were always a little too warm but that I wore anyway because I knew they were her way of telling me she cared—even if the words themselves had never come easily to her.

"Hi, Mom," I say, but as usual, she doesn't answer, just keeps looking out the window, her fingers moving, moving, moving.

She's been here for three years now, and she might be here for five, or ten, or fifteen more. No one really knows. Her body is still in good shape, even if her mind is gone. Hell, she could go on another twenty years like this. Sitting in the sunlight, staring out at nothing.

I putter around her room, straightening bedclothes that don't need straightening, watering plants that are probably fine, talking to her about the inn, telling her what funny thing Edie said last week about the weather. It's the same routine, every time I visit.

Do I do this for her, or do I do it for me?

She doesn't ever acknowledge my presence, and I always leave here sadder, so maybe there's no point in doing it at all.

But it breaks my heart to think of her as one of those patients no one ever visits, so I'll keep coming here every Monday, keep asking her about her day and what she had for breakfast, and telling her gossip about people she doesn't know.

Although now it occurs to me that I *do* have a story about someone she knows.

Someone she *knew*.

"Lo Bailey is back in town, Mama," I say, smoothing the wrinkles out of the blanket on her bed. "She says she knew you when y'all were growing up. She's brought some writer, and they're writing a book about Hurricane Marie. About Landon Fitzroy. I know it sounds silly, but I'm kind of hoping the book is this big ol' hit and then we get people wanting to stay at the inn because of it. Wouldn't that be something? Not exactly how I wanted to put the Rosalie Inn on the map, but beggars can't be choosers, right?"

I turn back to her, and okay, I was wrong. Turns out there must be some hope left in Hope House after all, because as I study her face, I find myself wishing that there will be some awareness in it, a sudden widening of her eyes. That this reminder of her long-ago past might spark something in her.

And for a second, I think it might have. Her fingers stop moving, suddenly going still on her lap, and her lips seem to tremble just the slightest bit.

"Mom?" I ask softly, going to crouch down next to her.

She always had the prettiest eyes, a bright, clear hazel that I sadly didn't inherit—I got my dad's dark brown eyes—but these days, they're dull and glazed over.

Do I see a spark there now? Or maybe I just want there to be one.

"Mama?" My voice is soft as I cover her hand with mine, her skin papery and cool beneath my palm.

And then her fingers start to move again, her lips press tightly together, and I drop my forehead onto the arm of her chair with a sigh.

IT'S PAST NOON by the time I get back to the inn. The families that were staying with us for the Fourth of July have mostly cleared out, leaving just a handful of guests to take care of. The lobby is quiet and still when I walk in, the waves outside sounding unnaturally loud.

Edie is nowhere to be seen, but to my surprise, Lo is there.

She's sitting on the navy-and-white-striped sofa just underneath the biggest window, her blond hair carelessly piled on top of her head, her shoulders a little sunburned under a bright red tank top. There's a magazine in her lap, but she's turned slightly to look out the window, and when she hears me, she glances over, her face breaking out into a smile.

"Afternoon!" she calls brightly. "Haven't seen you around much today."

"I was visiting my mom."

I hadn't meant to tell her that, but as always, the visit has left me feeling raw and hollowed out, and even though Lo is a stranger to me, more or less, she'd known Mom. Known a version of her I never had.

Lo's face crumples in sympathy. "Mama told me about Ellen's . . . troubles . . . before she passed."

Troubles. That's so Southern, to take something as catastrophic as a life-changing—life-*ending*—diagnosis and pretty it up with a vague word.

"It doesn't seem right," Lo goes on, "Ellen being in a nursing home. She's still so young."

"Well, they don't call it early-onset Alzheimer's for nothing," I attempt to joke, but my voice wavers, then cracks.

Lo is up off the sofa in a flash, and I'm suddenly enveloped in a surprisingly strong hug that smells like candy apples and sunscreen. "Oh, honey," Lo says, stroking my hair, and for just a second, I let myself be held.

"I miss her," I hear myself say. "Which sometimes feels ridiculous because she's right there in front of me, but she's not there at the same time."

"Baby girl, baby girl," Lo croons, and she doesn't sound anything like my mom, doesn't feel anything like my mom, but it's still nice, not only having someone call me sweet names, but also being able to say shit like that out loud to someone. I hadn't realized how lonely I've gotten over the past few months, how much the weight of keeping the inn afloat, of making sure Mom is taken care of, has started to drag me under.

After a few more seconds, I gently pull away from Lo's embrace, a little embarrassed as I smile at her. "Sorry about that," I say, "but thank you."

"You've got a lot on your shoulders, don't you, Geneva?" Lo asks, and I give a watery laugh.

"Just your classic twenty-first-century woman, having it all!"

Lo snorts at that.

"Oh honey, they barely let us have *anything*. Why would we ever get to have it *all*?"

She's smiling as she says it, but there's real bite behind the words, and I think back to that man at The Line the other night, the genuine hatred in his eyes as he looked at her.

Lo had handled that encounter like a pro, but what had it been like all those years ago, when she was so much younger, so less calloused by life? How had she stood it back then, knowing that anytime she went anywhere, there was a chance of someone glaring at her or cussing her out or calling her a murderer? She wasn't even twenty when that trial happened, for fuck's sake. I'm twice that age, and I don't think I could have survived it.

"I'm glad you're writing a book," I blurt out, and she raises her eyebrows.

"It's just . . ." I step back from her, my cheeks warm, my

emotions still running high. "I just think you have a valuable story to tell. About what it was like for you back then, about how you were treated. The whole scarlet woman bullshit thing, when you were barely more than a kid, and *he* was the one who was married, with all the power. And *he* was the one who came here of his own free will."

"Man, do you wanna write the pitch for this book once it's done?"

I turn to see August ambling into the lobby, his notebook in hand. He grins at me, and once again, my face flushes.

"I guess I didn't really get it until the other night," I tell both him and Lo. "The way that man spoke to you, the look on his face . . ."

"Oh, he was just a small man with a big mouth," Lo says, waving it away, but August looks at me and says, "That's why I wanted us to come here to work on the book."

"So I'd get yelled at in bars?" Lo asks, putting her hands on her hips in faux outrage, but August ignores her.

"It's been over forty years since Landon Fitzroy died, but some people are still that mad. Like it all happened yesterday."

"Some people around here talk like the Civil War happened yesterday," I tell him, "but I get what you mean." Until the other night, I hadn't understood how large the scandal still loomed for some people. It had been a footnote in my own childhood, after all.

For a moment, the box of articles and clippings that Mom saved, that's been gathering dust in the attic, flashes in my mind.

August gestures at me with his notebook. "I'd actually love to grab an interview with you, if you have some time over the next couple of days."

"With me?" I say, surprised. "I don't really know how much

insight I can offer. I never heard that much about Hurricane Marie growing up, much less Landon Fitzroy."

I'm still picturing that box in the attic. I don't know why I'm reluctant to mention Mom's collection of articles and clippings, only that it feels wrong to tell near strangers about something Mom didn't even share with *me*.

"Right, but you know the town, know the history of the place," August replies. "And the Rosalie Inn is such a fascinating piece of that. Still standing after every storm, for nearly a hundred years now. And named after a shipwreck that killed another Fitzroy."

That's news to me, and in a flash, my true crime fantasies detour into popular history. I knew about the wreck, obviously, but had only ever heard it was "some bootlegger." I had no idea that it had been a Fitzroy.

But I try not to let that intrigue show on my face. Instead, I tell August, "There's usually a lull in the early afternoon when everyone's on the beach. We could try to chat tomorrow?"

"It's a date," he says, and a little frisson shoots through me.

I haven't really dated since Chris. I briefly tried the Dreaded Apps, but after a couple of awkward coffee shop meetups and one dinner date that had *seemed* promising until the end of the meal when he admitted that, okay, maybe *separated* would've been a more accurate term for his relationship, rather than *divorced*, I'd decided that maybe that whole side of my life was just over. I'd be like a nun, only instead of Jesus and the Pope, I'd have the Rosalie Inn and Edie, and that would be fine.

But now I find myself liking how August's hair curls around his earlobes, how strong his fingers look clutching that notebook, the slightly crooked way he smiles at me.

A summer fling might not be the worst thing in the world . . .

I turn back to Lo only to find her watching me with the strangest expression on her face. Just a minute ago, she was joking and smiling, but now she looks . . . worried. Anxious, even.

It's gone in a flash, replaced by another bright smile as she says, "Oh, thank *God*, someone else can take Auggie's five billion questions for an afternoon."

"Kinda hard to ghostwrite a memoir without asking questions, Lo," August says. His tone is light, the words tossed off with a casual shrug, but there's a tightness around his jaw, annoyance in the quick glance he throws at her.

Edie comes downstairs then, her combat boots heavy on the carpeted runner as she calls out, "I swear, that plumber couldn't find his behind with both hands and a flashlight, but the leak in 203 is finally taken care of!"

She falters on the last step when she sees me standing there with Lo and August. She drops her voice and adds, "Um. Anyway, that's one thing off the list. Guess I'll start crossing out the next chore."

"It's Edie, right?"

Lo has stepped forward, studying Edie, her hands braced on her lower back, and I remember they never got much of an introduction on the first day, how stilted Edie was with her.

I step forward. "Edie is *the* right-hand woman here at the Rosalie," I declare with an exaggerated arm wave, like I'm a game show hostess presenting a refrigerator. But when I turn to smile at her, she's already headed down the hall, like she didn't hear Lo's question.

"Okay, that *was* Edie, *the* right-hand woman here at the Rosalie," I say, laughing and hoping I don't look as awkward as I feel.

But Lo isn't fazed. She just pats August's arm before sitting back down on the couch and saying, "Let me finish what I was reading, and then you can interrogate me some more."

"I was planning on going for a walk on the beach anyway," August says, nodding toward the big windows facing the ocean before glancing back at me. "Wanna join?"

"Can't," I tell him, even though it would be nice, walking next to a cute guy on a beautiful day. The sky is ferociously blue this afternoon, and the sun is hot, but there's a breeze off the water. It's the kind of weather that reminds me that St. Medard's Bay isn't all storms and responsibilities. It can be magic in its own way, and I should enjoy that more often. "I took the morning off for some family stuff, so I'm sure I have a ton of emails and bookings to deal with."

I actually have a toilet to unclog in 112, and some mildewed towels that need bleaching, but "emails and bookings" makes me sound more like a serious—and attractive, I hope— businesswoman, less of a scullery maid.

"Gotcha," August says, then gives a little wave before heading for the door.

I glance over at Lo, wondering if she's watching us, wondering if I'll see that same weird expression she wore when August and I were talking a few minutes ago, but she's not looking at us.

She's not looking at her magazine, either.

Instead, her gaze is trained on the hallway that Edie just disappeared down.

I met Landon's daddy only once, and it was by accident.

After that first night, I'd never planned on seeing Landon Fitzroy again, assuming he had a lot better shit to do than hang out in a dive bar in a no-name town, but the next evening, when I'd gone in for my shift at The Line, there'd been a letter waiting for me on the heaviest paper I'd ever felt in my *life*. Seriously, I've had mattresses thinner than that piece of stationery. It had his name at the top, or I guess I should say his *letterhead* because he was the kind of person who had *letterhead*.

It wasn't a very long note, but what was in it made my heart pound, my head swim, my knees get wobbly, alllllll of that.

He just sounded so *sweet* was the thing.

Here he was, a big-deal lawyer, his daddy running the whole state of Alabama, his boat in the St. Medard's Bay harbor bigger than my whole damn house. Bigger than *two* of my whole damn house, seemed like. And there *I* was, a waitress at a bar with a high school diploma and not much else, but you would've thought I was a goddess from the way he was practically begging me just to acknowledge him.

I've kept that letter for the past forty years, the paper so soft it almost feels like fabric from how many times I've folded it and refolded it. I won't quote it, and I'm damn sure not putting it in the book because some things have to stay private, but I will tell you that he told me I looked like I "swallowed starlight," and oh my *God*, that was it for me.

Now, of course, the whole thing seems insane. Writing something like that on his fancy paper with his full fuckin' name on it, walking into The Line in broad daylight to hand that note to Roy the bartender himself, saying out loud that he was leaving it for the barely legal waitress who'd served him and his buddies the night before.

At the time, it was romantic as all get-out, how little he cared about what people might say, how bold he was, how he wanted me so much that he'd risk his whole reputation. All that, combined with how open his letter was, how vulnerable and uncertain he sounded?

Oh, honey.

Show me the teenage girl—shit, show me the *grown-ass woman*—who can resist that, and I'll show you a liar.

Of course, once I *was* a grown-ass woman, all this looked a little less dreamy and a little more reckless, almost purposefully so. I wonder now if he was *trying* to blow it all up, if he wanted to force his father's hand. If the only way Landon could think of to escape the destiny that was waiting for him was to obliterate it as thoroughly as possible.

We had that in common. Not the destiny part, but that need to push, push, push—to see how far we could take something, see how long it took before someone finally said no.

Anyway, he'd scrawled a number on the bottom of that letter, and I called it right then and there from The Line. Do you know to *this day* I still don't know exactly where the phone that number reached was? It wasn't Landon's office, and it *damn* sure wasn't his house. This was before cell phones, but it could've been a car phone, I guess, although it never sounded like one.

He picked up just after the first ring, and baby, we were off to the races.

After Landon was gone, the tabloids made our romance out to be either this epic star-crossed thing or this really tawdry affair where we . . . I don't know, fucked on piles of mink coats and I greeted him at the door wearing nothing but diamonds.

(Okay, actually, I did do that once. The diamonds, not the mink coats. It was just after he bought the little house on the beach in St. Medard's in April of 1984. The papers called it our "hidden love nest," but it was literally like half a mile from Ellen's family's inn, so how "hidden" is that?)

But the truth was, those early days were almost sickeningly normal. We talked on the phone every night during the week, and every weekend, he'd be in St. Medard's with me. At first, our affair was under the radar. People were used to seeing him around town and knew his family had a house nearby, and we were discreet.

For a little while, at least.

Mostly we spent time on his boat, sometimes just anchored at the marina, but we'd also take her out on occasion. Those were my favorite times, the two of us alone surrounded by sea and sky.

"Sometimes when we're like this, I feel like we're the only two people on the planet," Landon said to me one evening as we watched the sun put on a brilliant orange, pink, and purple show as it sunk into the water.

I nodded, wrapped my arms tighter around him, and said, "Me, too," even though I could never feel that way, not on that boat with his wife's name curving along the side in gold paint.

The Miss Alison.

You're gonna wonder if I felt bad about her. Alison. Being "the Other Woman."

I do now. I never met her, never even saw her in person, but if I had, I would've apologized, and if she spat in my face, well, I'd say she fuckin' earned that right.

But at the time, it was more like I just tried *not* to think about her. And because Landon and I had our own little world down there in St. Medard's, and she had her own *big* world of social events and shopping and who knows what else in Mobile, that was kind of easy to do, except for the times when my eyes would drift to the side of the boat, to that swooping "A."

So yeah, at first, it was practically wholesome—other than the whole adultery part.

Then Landon's daddy crashed the party.

Has the governor of *your* home state seen your tits? Because mine has, and I really do not recommend it.

We were on the boat, in the part of the cabin I always thought of as the living room but Landon told me was called the *salon*. It was February, and it was freezing outside, the day damp and gray, the marina practically deserted.

I still had my jeans on when the governor of the Great State of Alabama suddenly appeared on the teak steps that led down from the deck, but my sweater and my bra were long gone, and in the frantic scramble that followed, I ended up clutching a throw pillow that said AHOY! to my chest.

Funny, the things you remember.

Beau Fitzroy had his son's black eyes, and if the way Landon first looked at me had made me feel precious and seen, then Beau's dark gaze made me feel like I was shit he'd just scraped off his shoe.

No one had ever looked at me like that before.

And I never let anyone look at me like that again.

But that cold February morning, I was half naked and shocked and embarrassed and honestly a little afraid. I'd never cared all that much about politics, and up until that moment, I'd always just thought of Landon as . . . Landon. Just a guy. A sweet, smart, sexy man who made *me* feel sweet, smart, and sexy.

But seeing his father there was a real bucket of cold water to the face. Reality crashed into me so hard it took my breath away, and even though Landon and I had been together for six months by then, for the first time, just what it was I was doing—sleeping with a *married man*, a married man who is *eleven years older than me*, a married man whose *father is the goddamned governor*, what the actual *fuck* is wrong with me?—broke through whatever haze I'd been in since I'd picked up that letter and seen Landon's name in embossed letters across the top.

I don't know how long Mr. Fitzroy stood there, silent as the statue they built for him a few years ago, the one that makes him look like a fuckin' *Star Wars* villain. I do remember Landon getting up, fastening his belt while his hair hung over his forehead, his body radiating tension.

"Dad," he started, and faster than a snake, faster than anything I think I've ever seen, Beau Fitzroy reached out and slapped Landon hard across the face.

It sounded like a pistol shot, and I think I might have gasped. Landon just stood there, his head turned to the side, a red mark already appearing on one cheek.

Then he chuckled, but it wasn't a sound I'd ever heard from him before. Landon laughed all the time, and this wasn't that. This was something mean, something dark, and there was another first for me that afternoon.

For the first time, I realized that I might not really know Landon all that well.

"You know, I'm actually old enough to hit back now," he said to his father, but Mr. Fitzroy just glared at him.

Sighing, Landon turned and fished my sweater out from behind one of the sofa cushions, crossing the small space to hand it to me. But taking it would've meant losing my pillow, and Mr. Fitzroy had gotten enough of a show as it was, so I just reached out with my fingertips and snagged the hem, letting the sweater lie limply on the sofa next to me.

"You are determined," Mr. Fitzroy said, his voice deep and so Southern you could smell bourbon and magnolias in every word, "to throw it all away, aren't you? Just plum *determined* to destroy yourself and anyone who loves you."

"Well, you should be fine, then, Daddy," Landon said, one corner of his mouth kicking up.

I loved Landon's smile, but not this version of it. Like his laugh, there was something ugly in it, and I shrank back against the sofa, wanting to be anywhere but on that fucking boat, let me tell you what.

"Don't you dare act like I don't love you, boy," Mr. Fitzroy thundered in reply. "If I didn't, I'd *let* you blow up your entire goddamned life on . . . on boats and beaches and"—he gestured toward me but didn't bother looking in my direction—"whatever this even is. Temporary insanity, one hopes."

Forty years ago, and I remember every word that man said that day. You would, too, if a person you'd seen your whole life on TV, in newspapers, and in a photo on the wall of the DM-fuckin'-V was suddenly standing in front of you, more or less calling you trash.

"Well, you're half right," Landon said, looking a little more like his old self, hands braced on his hips, a faint smile still curving his lips. "I'm absolutely insane about Lo, but there is nothing *temporary* about her."

Now, here is where I have to think.

Because I want to tell you that he then said, "Because I love her."

But did he? I've replayed it over and over again, and I tell myself he must have because I remember sitting there feeling warm all over, *feeling* loved, so much so that it didn't really register what his father said next—not then, at least.

"Like the last one," Mr. Fitzroy said, and now he was smiling one of those ugly smiles. "And the one before her. And the one before *her*, I suppose. When are you going to grow up, huh? When am I going to stop getting phone calls asking if I know where my son is and with whom?"

Now, of course, I could answer that for him.

"August 1984, sir," I'd say. "Just six months from now, and you'll never get those kinds of phone calls again because Landon will be dead, and I'll have turned out to be temporary after all. Are you happy, you son of a bitch?"

But on that day, none of us knew any of that, and Landon just said something about how maybe his dad could stop picking up those phone calls, and his dad blustered something else, and then he was stomping back up the stairs.

He didn't look at me as he left. Other than that first heat-seeking missile of a scowl he'd turned my way when he first showed up, he hadn't looked at me at all. Maybe he was afraid he'd catch another glimpse of my nipples—or, more likely, who I was and what I looked like just didn't fucking matter to him because I wasn't a person, I was just this . . . thing. An inconvenience in his life, a mere tool his son was using to break free from all those expectations, all that *destiny*.

So. You wonder why Beau Fitzroy was so steadfast in his belief that I killed his son? I'll tell you: it's because he felt guilty. Because he knew—that motherfucker *knew*—that if he'd just let Landon live his own life, if he'd just eased up on him for *one damn minute*, Landon might not have been so reckless, so, as he put it himself, *plum determined* to live life on his own terms.

And men like him, men who think they have capital-D Destinies, who think God Himself is personally invested in their success, like He has nothing better to worry about than some politician's stock portfolio, they can't ever lose. It's always gotta be someone else's fault, and if it's a woman they

can blame? Well, hallelujah and pass the biscuits, because
that's even better.

*Pages of unfinished manuscript titled
"Be a Good Girl: Lo Bailey, Landon Fitzroy, and the
Scandal That Brought Down a Dynasty."
Found among possessions of August Fletcher, 8/3/2025*

LANDON P. FITZROY, ESQ.

2/19/84

My Green-Eyed Girl,

Wish I could deliver this to you myself but seemed best to send it through the mail. Don't worry, I'll be back in SMB before you know it, just giving my father some time to cool off. Which, I have to admit, is a slightly humiliating thing for a grown man to confess, but . . . well, you've met my father now.

You probably understand.

I *hope* you understand.

And I am so sorry about that whole fucking scene, Lo, could cut my own heart out over it, honestly. Believe me, if I'd had *any* idea he was going to show up—if I had any idea he even knew where I was—I never would've let that happen to us. To *you*.

Did I mention the sorry part? The cutting my own heart out of it all?

I know you said you were fine after he left, but I saw your face. Tell me how to make this okay, baby. Anything it takes, I'll do. You want to sink the boat? Hell, I'll drill a hole in the bottom myself. Let it sit out there next to the *Rosalie*. You know that was my great-uncle's boat, right? Probably where the Fitzroy legacy truly belongs—not in the halls of power, but at the bottom of the goddamn ocean.

You're the most important person in my life right now, Lo.

Bar none. There's not a single thing I wouldn't do for you. Sink a boat, tell my father to go fuck himself . . . I think I'd probably kill someone if you asked me to.

Who am I kidding?

I *know* I would.

Write back, please. Or call. Your mother has said you've been out both times I called this week, and I really hope that's true, that you're not just avoiding me or . . . Christ, I don't even want to *write* it, but if you're done with me, I wouldn't blame you.

I might not bother saving myself when I sink the boat, but I wouldn't blame you.

Write me, Lo. Call me. Please. I didn't realize just how bright you make every single day of my life until I had to imagine a life without you in it. Too much darkness to contemplate. Even the bottom of the ocean couldn't compare to that.

Put me out of my misery one way or the other, will ya?

Love ∞

L

LANDON P. FITZROY, ESQ.

2/19/84

E—

You said don't call, but you didn't say anything about *writing*. I can already see you rolling those big, beautiful hazel eyes at me, and I probably deserve it, but God, I miss you.

So much.

I know it was for the best that we take a break, and I understand that everything with Lo has been hard on you, which was the absolute last thing I wanted. If I'd had any idea how close the two of you were, I never would've started things up with her, but it didn't even occur to me y'all might be friends, much less best friends. You just seem so different. Night and day, sun and moon.

Anyway. I guess I'd just like a chance to talk to you again, like we used to. Remember that night with the beach bonfire? The two of us must have sat out there until what? One in the morning? Just talking. Talking is so damn *easy* with you, Sunshine Girl, and it's honestly unfair to be both as pretty as you are *and* as smart. Leave some for the rest of us!

I don't blame you if you throw this in the trash, but I really hope you won't. We were friends first, remember? And I think we could be friends again. I *want* us to be friends again.

I could use a friend these days.

In hope,

L

CHAPTER FIVE

July 10, 2025

24 Days Left

One of the hardest parts about owning a hotel is how fucking *nice* you have to be all of the time.

I never realized how much shit my parents must've swallowed over the years, how many tight smiles they'd kept locked on their faces as some sunburned dude on his fifth Coors Light yelled about a room that was too warm, or sheets that were too rough, or—and this one has actually happened to me—that the ocean "didn't have enough waves."

But hey, there's a reason they call this the "hospitality business," so I'm as hospitable as can be when, just a little before sunset, the couple staying in room 104 casually lets me know that they left the two bikes that visitors are allowed to use to explore the area in the little nature preserve about a quarter mile down the beach.

"It was too sandy to ride them, and it was too hot to push

them," the woman—I think her name is Michelle—tells me, her perfectly plucked brows puckered like this is somehow my fault.

I smile back, hoping it doesn't look like a grimace. "Yeah, that's why we advise guests to stick to the roads or, if you're in the nature preserve, the boardwalk."

"Wish we'd known that!" the man replies cheerfully as though I myself had not told them exactly that when they checked the bikes out this morning. Edie had been there, too, and had added to be sure to return the bikes to the porch because the forecast was predicting rain this evening.

I glance toward the front windows now, and while the rain hasn't started falling, the clouds outside are heavy and dark, almost swollen against the few rays of the setting sun. It'll be dark by the time I get the bikes back to the inn, and probably pouring if the rising wind and thick smell of ozone are anything to go by.

I'm tempted to just leave them there, let them rust, let them get stolen, who gives a fuck? These people, Todd and Michelle, are the first to even want to use the bikes in months, and while they hadn't been expensive, every time I saw them sitting on the porch with their cute baskets and jaunty little bells on the handlebars, I thought of me and Chris picking them out at the Walmart over in Gulf Shores, me giggling as I'd attempted to test the bike out in the deserted aisle.

Guests are going to love it, Chris had said. *They can ride into town to grab dinner, ride down the beach where the sand is packed firm enough. It'll be one of those little touches, you know?*

You're really getting into this innkeeper life, I remember saying, and then he'd grabbed the handlebars and kissed me, his lips curving into a smile against mine.

I'm really getting into this innkeeper, he'd replied, and I'd groaned at how cheesy it was, but we'd laughed and bought the bikes and I'd even put stupid little ribbons in the same shade of pink as the Rosalie Inn on the backs of the seats, and then less than a year later, Chris was gone—no longer into innkeeper life *or* this innkeeper—and all I had was a business drowning in debt, a mom who needed expensive care, and these two fucking bikes.

Well, I guess I'd had them up until Todd and Michelle dumped them in the swampy nightmare that is the nature preserve.

So now I smile at the two of them, even giving a stupid little *salute* that immediately makes me want to kill myself.

"No worries!" I tell them brightly. "I'll send someone to go grab them."

The someone is going to be *me*, but let them think I'm above that kind of thing as innkeeper, let them think my "staff" is more than me, Edie, a couple locals who clean the rooms, and Louisa the night shift girl, plus our one maintenance guy, Ray, a man I've seen sober exactly twice in the three years I've been running the inn.

Thunder rumbles somewhere in the distance, and I bite back a sigh as Todd and Michelle blithely turn away, heading back to their room, where they'll probably watch the storm roll in and shiver with delight at being inside to watch it rather than out in it, pushing two fucking bikes over sand for a quarter of a mile.

Edie meets me by the front door as I'm grabbing a Rosalie Inn–branded poncho from the rack, her pierced brow lifting as she nods in Todd and Michelle's direction.

"They didn't bring back the bikes," she says in a low voice, and I give her a tight smile.

"They didn't."

"Gen, leave them."

"Can't" is all I say in reply, which makes Edie frown at me, her hands coming to rest heavily on my shoulders.

"You can, you just won't because you're the most stubborn person on God's green earth."

"Guilty," I say, slipping the poncho over my head, and Edie's eyes dart from me to the door, then over to the coatrack where the other ponchos are hanging.

"I'll come with you," she says, already reaching, but I stop her with a hand on her arm.

"Edie. The bottom is going to fall out any minute. Weather like this always makes you nervous, and you *hate* driving in the rain, so go ahead and get yourself home before it starts. No sense in both of us being wet and miserable."

I don't add that she's already on overtime, and while she'd never, ever insist I pay her that, I'd never, ever *not* do it, so I try not to keep her past her regular hours if I can help it.

"I'm not going to let you drag two bikes up the beach just because I don't like bad weather, Geneva," she says, but another crack of thunder has her flinching, and I pat her shoulder, moving past her.

"Look, if it ends up being too much, I'll abandon them on the beach for some kids to find, okay? More trouble than they're worth anyhow."

Edie doesn't look convinced, but she's going to let me have my way—she always does.

"Ooh, where are we going?"

Both of us turn to see Lo floating into the room, her hair up in a messy bun on top of her head. No sundress tonight. Instead, she's wearing a pair of navy capri pants and a striped top, slip-on sneakers squeaking on the hardwood, and without waiting for me to answer, she crosses the lobby to stand with me and Edie.

Edie steps back a few paces, like Lo is suddenly crowding her in, and her voice is gruff when she replies, "Geneva's dealing with some inn maintenance stuff, not going out for an evening stroll."

I cut my eyes at Edie, silently trying to convey, *Maybe don't snap at a guest?*

But Lo doesn't seem offended. She just nods and reaches past me to grab a poncho for herself. "Well, Auggie is plugged in to his headphones and his laptop working on the book, and I'm bored, so consider me a temporary Rosalie Inn employee."

"Oh, you really don't have to—" I start, but Lo just holds her arms out to her sides, looking down at her now pink vinyl–clad body.

"Too late, already in the poncho," she says, and I can't help but laugh.

"No arguing with that," I say, smiling at her.

I glance over at Edie, expecting her to be smiling as well, but instead, she's still watching Lo, her brows tight together, her lips rolled inward.

This is the second time Edie has been cold to Lo, and while Edie has always had an edge to her, she's never been *cold.*

I make a mental note to talk to her about it later. Maybe Lo was rude to her or something, hard as that is to imagine.

"We've got this," I say to Edie now. "Go on and get home before the rain starts."

Her eyes shift back to me, and I can tell she wants to argue some more, but finally, she just gives a curt nod and says, "Text me once you're back safe."

"Will do," I assure her.

Lo moves past me, opening the door to the porch, and a gust of wind yanks it out of her hand, sending it crashing back against the wall with a thump that rattles the pictures on the wall.

"Ooh!" She laughs, faux stumbling back like the wind has

pushed her, too. Then she lifts her chin, taking a deep breath through her nose as she closes her eyes. "Oh, that smells like *home*."

It smells like salt water and mud and pine and metal, and underlying all of it is the distant stench of rotting fish, but I know what she means. Storms around here always seem to concentrate the various smells of St. Medard's Bay, and I think I'd done the same thing when Chris and I first came back here—stuck my head out the window of our car, breathed deep, and felt the past settle into my bones.

Lo smiles as she looks over at me, and I realize I'm smiling back. "People ask why I came back," I say. "But I sometimes wonder how I ever left."

Something in Lo's face dims just a little bit, her smile drooping before it's replaced with another, even brighter grin. "Well, I don't have to wonder that," she says with a shrug. "I left because everyone thought I was a murderous whore."

And with that, she steps out onto the porch and into the rising storm.

FOR THE FIRST few minutes of our walk down the beach, we're both quiet, lost in our own thoughts. The rain hasn't started, but the sky is getting darker, the air heavier, and the wind blowing off the water is surprisingly cool in the hot July evening. Our pink ponchos flap in the wind, the sound unnaturally loud, and finally, Lo just yanks hers off, balling it up in one hand and throwing over her shoulder, "I'll put it back on if the rain actually starts."

We pass my trailer, but I don't bother mentioning it. To our left, the surf pounds, and ahead of us on the right, the trees grow thicker, signaling the beginning of the preserve. We're about halfway to it when Lo stops, turning to face the ocean.

"It's just out there, you know," she says, pointing. "The *Rosalie*."

Mom and Dad loved telling the story to guests, how some bootlegger had been running liquor in the '20s and got caught in a storm. How his boat—the *Rosalie*, named after his daughter—sank right out from underneath him. Mom's grandfather had apparently gone out into the raging waters himself trying to save the guy, but it was already too late.

Never once did they mention that "some bootlegger" was actually a Fitzroy ancestor—the same Fitzroy who had presided over our statehouse, whose photograph hung on the wall in my kindergarten classroom, next to President George H. W. Bush.

Before I can tell Lo any of that, she adds, "Landon took me out to the wreck once. He wanted us to snorkel around it. It's not down all that deep, you know."

"It is now," I reply, and she turns to me, her eyes widening in surprise.

"What do you mean?"

The wind fades a little bit, my poncho deflating around me as I step closer and point at a spot a little to the right of where Lo was gesturing. "After Hurricane Peggy in ninety-eight. I guess what was left of the wreck was so insubstantial that the waves were able to move it. Some pieces of it even washed up here on the beach, or at least that's what we assumed it was. The rest of it was carried farther out."

It had been eerie, walking along the beach that next day, the sky clear and sparkling after hours and hours of wind and rain, seeing those little flecks of metal, or a tangled and nearly disintegrated piece of rope.

"I told my mom it felt like a threat or something. Like the ocean going, 'Just in case you forgot, I'm a real bitch!'"

Lo throws her head back and laughs at that. "Like anyone who grew up in this town needs that reminder!"

I laugh, too, nodding. "Even people who didn't grow up here know that. When I was at college, my roommate asked me if it was true that St. Medard's Bay was cursed. Apparently, that's the story all along the coastline—from Gulf Shores to Orange Beach, even Mobile."

"And did you tell her it was true?"

I look over at Lo in the waning light, expecting to see that same teasing grin she flashes at August so often, but am surprised to see that she's looking at me very seriously, her green eyes locked on my face.

I give a nervous sort of chuckle and start walking back down the beach. "No, I think I just told her climate change was a thing, and St. Medard's Bay sometimes bore the brunt of that."

Out over the ocean, the clouds are moving faster now, and I can see a thick sheet of rain blurring out the horizon. The wind picks up again, but I have a sense that this particular storm is going to miss us as it blows itself farther out into the Gulf.

"But if that were the case, why do we get hit so much?" Lo counters, coming up next to me and linking her arm in mine with a casual intimacy that startles me. "How else could this one town have so many deaths, suffer so much destruction?" Her hip bumps mine. "And why is the Rosalie Inn always still standing when the storms pass?"

There's a tightness in my chest, but I try to keep my voice light as I reply. "It's funny you say it like that. My mom used to joke that if the town was cursed, then maybe the inn could be blessed. Protected."

Lo gives me a satisfied smile before her expression grows

dreamy and far-off. "The Witches of St. Medard's Bay," she murmurs, and I glance over at her.

"What?"

"That's what we used to call ourselves, your mom and me. And Frieda. We were too old to believe in that kind of thing, but it was the seventies. Witches were very, very groovy."

I laugh along with Lo, but I can't quite imagine my mother being that playful, that . . . innocent.

Why had Mom never once mentioned Lo to me if they used to be that close? Was it because of the murder trial, the scandal? Did Mom think Lo had killed the governor's son, and cut off their friendship as a result?

I've spent much of the past few years wishing I could talk to Mom, ask her questions and have her answer them, but now I find myself longing for it with a fierceness that almost brings tears to my eyes. We'd never been as close as I would have liked, but I hadn't realized there was so much *more* I didn't know about her.

So many wasted years—years I spent living hundreds of miles away, with a guy who would leave the second things got hard. Years when I could have been here, helping her and Dad. Years when I could have been making an effort to have the kind of relationship with my mother that I'd seen other girls grow into with their moms, as the angst and stress of the teenage years faded and they were finally able to just be . . . friends.

And now next to me is a woman who actually knew Mom—who probably knew her better than I ever had.

"What was she like back then?" I find myself asking.

Lo sighs, hugging herself as she looks up at the night sky. "Lordy," she says, thinking. Then, "She was quiet, at least compared to me. She kept her own counsel. But smart, *so* smart. I think that's why she was so funny."

"You mentioned that before," I say as I scratch at a bug bite near my elbow. "But I never thought of her that way? She wasn't, like, super serious or anything, but my dad was the one always trying to crack jokes with the guests, charm them with something witty or clever. Mom was . . . well, like you said. Quiet. Smart. She did all the financial stuff for the inn, handled the taxes, all of it. I never realized just how big of a job that was until I had to take it over. I promptly hired a guy to do it for me."

Lo looks over, the wind blowing a strand of hair across her eyes. She pushes it back before saying, "Were you close? With your mom?"

I don't know why I tell her the truth, but it slips out anyway.

"No."

I wait for her to look shocked, or to rush in to assure me that no, no, maybe it felt like that, but she's just *sure* Ellen Chambers would love the *fire* out of her little girl!

But instead, she just nods and looks sad. "I'm sorry," she says, her voice soft.

"So am I," I reply on a long breath.

"Me and my mama were close until we weren't," Lo says. "No big falling-out or anything, not even after I darkened the family name like it was my damn *job*. But I kept moving around, and . . . I don't know, I guess you think your mama will just always be there. And then Covid happened, and just like that, Mama was gone."

"Why didn't you come back?" I ask her, and Lo gives me a sad smile.

"I don't know. I think it all felt like too much at the time— the shock of losing her, then the idea of coming back to this town that was at the root of so much pain, and when it was already too late to tell Mama I loved her. And with the whole damn world turned upside down . . . I guess I could pretend it wasn't real so long as I stayed away."

We've reached the trees of the nature preserve, and I come to a stop. It's almost full dark now, but the clouds have parted, revealing a full moon, and the sodium lamps the city installed at the entrance of the preserve cast a soft orange glow over both of us as I spot the bikes lying just a few feet away.

I walk over, picking one up by the handlebars, and Lo does the same to the other. As we start wheeling them back toward the beach, I say, "I get that. When Mom first called with her diagnosis, I spent at least a week telling myself she probably just needed a second opinion, and everything would be fine. Magical thinking and all that."

"Ellen was like that, too," Lo says with a nod. "Always hoping for the best."

"You guys were pretty tight, huh?"

She sighs even as she nods. "We were, yeah. I thought we'd be friends forever, the three of us. Me, Ellen, and Frieda. Somewhere in these woods is a tree with *ELF* carved on it, our initials. We thought that was so funny for some reason."

"Did you all just grow apart, or . . ."

I see Lo's fingers tighten around the handlebars for a second. "After I took up with Landon, your grandparents didn't want Ellen spending much time with me. She'd met your daddy by then, so she was all wrapped up in him. And Frieda never really forgave me for what happened during Hurricane Audrey. But she's probably told you all about that."

Confused, I stop in my tracks. It takes Lo a second to realize I'm not wheeling the bike alongside her. "I'm not sure what you mean. I don't know anyone named Frieda," I say. "And Mom never mentioned her." *Or you*, I think but don't say out loud.

Now Lo is the one who looks confused. "But she works for

you," she says, and I can hear the waves crashing on the beach just over the sandy rise, and I know who she must be talking about, but it's still a shock hearing the words that come out of her mouth next.

"The woman at the desk. Edie. That's Frieda."

AUDREY

May 5, 1977

I hate that the last thing I said to my mama was a lie.

And the thing is, I didn't mean for it to be.

When I told her I was going to spend the night at Ellen's house, that was genuinely what I thought I was going to do. It was early May, but the summer heat was already rising. It always felt like our seasons were out of whack down here. Fall was a few weeks at the end of November, winter ended by the middle of wet February, but our spring and our summer stretched out, starting in March, sometimes not ending until October. Maybe some people think that sounds great, but I hated the heat, the sun. Lo always teased me about wearing long-sleeved shirts over my bathing suit, but for one thing, I wasn't tanned and sleek like Lo and Ellen. At twelve, they were already starting to look like women while I just looked like a sad, pale little boy, especially after that stupid haircut. Mama thought it was so pretty on that one figure skater lady, but maybe it was just pretty on her because *she* was pretty.

It made me look like a mushroom.

Lo never teased me about that, though, and when anyone did, she'd be right up in their faces, asking who made them an expert on hair, saying that no one got it because "this is a hick town full of shit-kicking morons who don't understand fashion."

I loved her for that.

And Lo wasn't all that easy to love. She could be mean sometimes, and she would go through these rebellious stages that nearly killed Miss Beth-Anne, who was the sweetest woman alive, sweeter than my mama, much as I hated to admit that.

She was in one of those moods that May. She'd started smoking, preferring Virginia Slims, which always looked too long to me. One time, I told her it looked like she was smoking a tampon, and she stopped talking to me for four days.

Ellen talked her around. Ellen could always do that. Now *that* was somebody who was sweet. Ellen never talked back to her mama or to teachers, never asked why I was dressed like Wednesday Addams on the beach, and the one time she drank, it's because they accidentally gave her the real wine at communion instead of the grape juice they used for the kids.

That wasn't even her fault, but she still felt so bad about it that she told her parents immediately.

We were a funny little trio, I guess. The wild one, the sweet one, and then . . . me. The odd one, the one who didn't quite "match." But we'd been friends since we'd shared the infant and toddler room at the St. Medard's Bay First Baptist Church Day Care, and that was a forever kind of love.

I thought it was, at least.

And then Audrey.

You didn't grow up in St. Medard's Bay without knowing about the hurricanes. Lo's daddy had died in the last big one, Delphine back in '65. Lo hadn't even been born yet. Her mom had climbed a tree, but her daddy had slipped and fallen, drowning "in an instant," Lo always said, even though, privately, Ellen and I sometimes reminded each other that you can't drown instantly.

But I understood why she'd want to think that. It was too awful, imagining him struggling, trying to breathe, only to pull in filthy water, lungs burning, chest like a vise.

The thing is, though, none of us remembered Delphine. We weren't born back then, and our parents didn't talk about it because not talking about anything unpleasant ever is as much a Southern tradition as biscuits and gravy. So even though we grew up hearing these stories, they felt far away. Like a village that had slain a dragon decades ago, and sure, maybe the dragon would come back, maybe the dragon had babies that would grow up and come seeking revenge, but the more time passes without the beating of wings in the sky, the more the villagers start to think maybe the dragon was just a myth.

The day before Audrey hit, she was just a blob far out in the Gulf, barely a Category 1. The news was saying she would swing wide to the west, dumping rain and wind on Louisiana and parts of Texas.

St. Medard's was still watching, though, and they canceled school for that Friday, the sixth, out of "an abundance of caution."

All me, Lo, and Ellen heard was "no school on a Friday."

"We'll do a sleepover Thursday night," Lo declared. She was the Plan Maker. Sometimes the plans were good—the time she somehow convinced the manager down at the Starlite Movie Palace to let us in to see *Jaws*—and sometimes they were bad—last Christmas when she spiked the eggnog at the Shipwreck Inn and one of Ellen's parents' guests got so drunk she took her sparkly reindeer sweater off—but they were always *interesting*, at least.

And a sleepover was, as far as Lo plans went, pretty mild.

It still took some convincing, though. The storm wasn't supposed to hit us, but we'd still get bands of rain, probably some wind, and Mama was not crazy about me not being, as she put it, "in the nest" should the weather change.

"We're staying at Ellen's," I told her. "And it's *extra* safe since it's a hotel, and it has to be because of insurance."

"I mean, of all the places in town I'd want to be if the weather does get a little hairy, the Shipwreck is way up there." Dad had been smiling as he said it, my little brother, Sam, propped on one hip. He was five that summer, and getting too big to be carried, but we all did it anyway because he was such a sweet kid.

So Mama had let me go with a promise to be safe, to come back early Friday morning before the rain had a chance to hit, and I had hugged her and told her I loved her and then said I'd be fine because I'd be at Ellen's and everyone knew Ellen's house was the safest place in St. Medard's. All those hurricanes, and there it still stood. Not even the churches could say that—First Baptist was smashed up in Betsy back in '54, and the Methodists got it in Delphine.

The Shipwreck Inn was just a short walk from my house by the road, but I always cut through the scrubby little woodland behind us and made my way to the inn via the beach.

It was about three o'clock in the afternoon that Thursday, and I remember that the air seemed so clear, the sky marred by only a handful of clouds. Whatever Audrey was doing, it was far away, and I was actually a little disappointed.

It would be cool, I'd thought, if it started raining really hard while we were in Ellen's big bedroom—an actual hotel room she used as a bedroom, which always felt so glamorous to me—all three of us sprawled in Ellen's king-size bed, eating Oreos and drinking Tab, telling the scariest stories we could think of while a big thunderstorm raged outside.

That's really all I'd thought a hurricane was back then. Just a big storm.

I was maybe halfway down the beach to the Shipwreck when I spotted Lo and Ellen walking toward me, duffel bags over their shoulders, Lo wearing a pair of bright purple star-shaped sunglasses.

The three of us ran to one another like we'd been parted for decades, laughing and whooping, throwing our arms around one another, giddy in that way only twelve-year-old girls with a slumber party and a surprise three-day weekend ahead of them can be.

And then Lo had put a hand on each of our shoulders and said, "So. Frieda, your parents think you're at Ellen's. Ellen's parents think Ellen is at *my* house, and Beth-Anne thinks I'm at *your* house, Frieda, so we are free as fucking *biiiiiiiiirds* until tomorrow morning!"

Like I said, Lo went through rebellious phases, and she was in one that May. Hence the calling her mama by her first name, the swearing, and the lying.

I glanced over at Ellen to see if she was as surprised by this as I was, but she was chewing her lip and not quite meeting my eyes. "It's dumb, and we're probably going to get caught," she said in a rush, but then she smiled, a big smile even though she was usually self-conscious about the way her front teeth overlapped just a little bit. Her hazel eyes were shining as she said, "But, like, Lo has a really cool idea."

"I do!" Lo crowed, then turned and faced the sea. It wasn't as placid as it usually was, the waves a little higher, the whitecaps bigger, but there was nothing that suggested there was a monster miles away gathering strength, subtly twisting eastward.

"Okay, fucking ocean, you think we're scared of you?" she cried into the wind.

"Lo," I said, tugging at her shirt. I was giggling, but part of me was embarrassed that she was out here yelling like a lunatic, and another part of me was suddenly a little scared. Like she might actually piss the ocean off or something.

Shit, maybe she did.

"You might have fucked up this town years ago. You might have killed my daddy. But that was before *we* were here."

She reached back for both of our hands without looking, and without hesitating, Ellen and I both clasped an upturned palm and let ourselves be dragged to stand next to her.

"We are the Witches of St. Medard's Bay," Lo went on, "and we protect this town now."

I looked over at her, still giggling because this was still kind of embarrassing, but I had to admit, Lo looked . . . powerful standing there. The wind was blowing her hair, and those sunglasses didn't seem as garish or silly anymore, and whatever new game she was playing, it seemed like it had the potential to be exciting.

Twelve is a weird age for girls. On the one hand, we were starting to like boys, starting to have opinions on lipstick, and we were quick to shun anything "babyish," whether that was Barbie dolls or a T-shirt with a cartoon cat on it. On the other, we were still little girls in a lot of ways. We still *liked* these games of pretend, we just felt embarrassed about it, and afterward, we swore one another to secrecy or pretended that we'd been enjoying it only *ironically*, of course.

But there was no irony now, no affected sophistication as the three of us linked arms and Ellen and I let Lo pull us back down the beach the way I'd come, veering off at the little nature preserve the town had set up for Earth Day back in '72.

There wasn't much to it. A bunch of pine trees, a half-finished boardwalk that meandered over sand, and then, as you got deeper in, marshlands. There weren't any alligators in the preserve, not then, but my dad had sworn he'd seen a bobcat once, so I wasn't exactly thrilled when Lo led us to a spot just inside the trees and pointed at a dark green tent set up underneath some low pine branches.

"You didn't mention camping," Ellen said, frowning, but Lo waved her hand.

"It's not *camping*. It's the secret lair of our coven."

"Looks like camping to me," I replied, and Lo flipped me off while Ellen gave a nervous burst of laughter.

"Okay, fine, it's a secret lair, but what if the weather *does* get bad?" she asked Lo.

"Then we go back to your place. Say Frieda came over, and the three of us decided to stay at the inn instead because you have a TV in your room."

But the thing is, none of us really thought the weather would get bad. We'd never lived through a hurricane, and maybe the twelve years after Delphine let our parents get a little softer. Maybe they trusted the news too easily, maybe they forgot that yes, usually we can predict these things with reasonable accuracy.

Usually.

But hurricanes don't listen to predictions about what they're supposed to do, what the patterns seem to be suggesting.

So all that evening and into the night, while Lo and Ellen and I ate peanut butter sandwiches and came up with fake curses we'd put on various people at school and brewed up a "potion" of pine needles, Coke, and Jean Naté perfume, Audrey got hotter and faster and bigger and hooked hard to the right, St. Medard's Bay in her sights.

We were asleep when it started.

The wind had been picking up before the three of us huddled in the tent to go to bed, but it wasn't anything scary, really. If anything, it just made the tent seem cozier, and it was nice to get a break from the heat that had been squashing St. Medard's Bay in the weeks before.

I'm never sure if it's a real memory or some kind of trauma-induced hallucination, but the rising wind made its way into my dreams that night. I was falling out of a plane, and the engine was right by me, and it was so loud, I thought I'd be sucked in.

But it wasn't the wind that woke me.

It was a crack, sharper than a rifle, louder than anything I'd ever heard, and followed by creaking, rustling, and then a powerful *thwack* as a nearby pine tree hit the ground, shaking the tent and sending the three of us scrambling out into the open.

It was pitch-black, and someone yelled about a flashlight, maybe Ellen, but I couldn't be sure.

Everything that came after that is still a nightmarish blur.

The wind wasn't shrieking or howling because those are sounds that are familiar, sounds you'd recognize, sounds that even humans can make.

This didn't sound like anything I'd ever heard before, and I've never heard anything like it since. It sounded . . . ancient.

That's what I remember telling someone later, how the only thing my brain could process about the sound was "People aren't supposed to hear this."

Like this was some elemental thing rising up out of the earth from a time long, long before Oreos and Tabs and Jean Naté. How could something like this even exist in our world?

It started raining, just a few heavy drops at first, then buckets all of a sudden, drenching us in seconds. My Keds squelched on the muddy ground as the three of us once again linked arms, the tiny orb of Lo's flashlight bobbing and weaving crazily in front of us, but I didn't want to see because all there was was rain and wind and the noise and the terror—the sheer animal *terror*—coursing through my veins.

I'll never know how we made it out that night. I heard other trees falling, felt the rush of air when one fell just a few feet from us. I was jabbering, praying maybe, or I could've been singing Olivia Newton-John, I truly don't know. I just know that it felt right to make my own noise in that cacophony, and I thought Lo and Ellen might have been shouting or singing, too.

It had to have been Ellen who led us out. Later, she and Lo would both say the same thing as me, that they didn't remember much, only that the sand and dirt underfoot gave way to slick road, and we'd miraculously turned right instead of left, leading us onto the main road to the Shipwreck Inn.

It had to have been Ellen.

Lo had led us into the preserve from the beach side, and that would've been her instinct again, to go out the way we came and straight into the ocean.

That fucking ocean that we weren't scared of because we were the Witches of St. Medard's, and we protected this town.

We're not witches, I thought, stumbling up the steps to the door of the Shipwreck Inn, my arms still looped through Lo's and Ellen's. *We're stupid little girls, and we almost died and we're gonna be in so much trouble.*

That still makes me want to laugh. Or cry, I don't know.

I thought that was going to be the worst part—getting in trouble for lying about where we were.

We weren't even all the way up the steps before the door was opening and hands were on us, pulling us inside. It was dim inside the inn, candles flickering on the check-in desk and the big steamer trunk Mrs. Chambers used as a coffee table in the lobby.

I sat down on the floor, took a blanket someone handed to me, and watched as Ellen was lifted off her feet by her dad, his face pale and ghoulish in the candlelight.

"Oh, thank you, God," he kept saying. "Oh, thank you, Lord Jesus, thank you, thank you."

Thank you, I thought alongside him. *Thank you, God, or Jesus or Mother Mary or Olivia Newton-John, thank you, whoever let us not get killed tonight.*

Audrey did her best to take down the Shipwreck Inn that night, but as always, she held. We had to move to the second floor when water started sloshing over the hardwoods in the lobby, but the water didn't rise much further; the sandbags Ellen's dad had placed all around the inn in his own "abundance of caution" had served him well.

I fell asleep around dawn, sitting up in the second-floor hallway, Lo on one side, Ellen on the other.

I go back to that image so often, and my heart breaks for that girl sleeping between her two best friends, exhausted and traumatized and sore but not knowing that when the storm first turned in the wee hours of May 6, phones had started ringing. At Miss Beth-Anne's. At the Shipwreck.

At Frieda Mason's little yellow cottage with the metal awning over the door.

They'd been frantic, our parents, when it became clear that no one had any idea where we were. Miss Beth-Anne had gone out on foot with a flashlight, headed for the big weeping willow that used to be our favorite hideout. She'd gotten only a couple of blocks before downed power lines meant she had to retreat.

Ellen's dad had called a friend in the National Guard in Mobile, asking for advice, only to be told the best he could do right now was wait and "hope the storm wasn't that bad."

And my parents had gotten in our station wagon, buckled Sam into his booster seat, and started searching the rain-soaked streets until they'd made a turn onto Cottonmouth Avenue—an ugly name for a street, I'd always thought—and felt their wheels leave the road beneath them, the current dragging the car inexorably toward the rising waters of Shelton Creek.

It was fast, at least.

Not instant. Drowning never was, just like Ellen and I had always known.

But fast.

Wouldn't have even known what was happening, one of the Red Cross volunteers told me later. They would've been overwhelmed before they even knew it.

I want to believe that.

My mom's sister, Rebekah, moved to St. Medard's to take care of me. She didn't move into that yellow house with the metal awning, though. That was washed away by the same waters that took my family, like we'd never even been a family at all. No home, no evidence of the life we'd shared there. Just me and Aunt Rebekah and a boring brown house on Shell Drive near Lo.

It wasn't Lo's fault, what happened to my family. I know that. It was a freak of nature, literally, a hurricane that zigged when everyone thought it would zag, one that lingered too long in the Caribbean and picked up too much power, and this is the way it goes sometimes, this is the way the world works. She hadn't known, when she came up with her grand plan for the three of us to spend the night in the woods, that she was setting something in motion that would destroy my entire life.

But after that, every impulsive, reckless thing Lo did—and Jesus Christ, did she do a lot—wasn't cool anymore. It wasn't fun or exciting or a chance for adventure. It just felt . . . selfish. Careless.

Because that's what Lo was. Selfish and careless and thoughtless.

There's no malice in her, or at least I don't think there is.

But when someone's left as much destruction in their wake as she has, does it even matter that she doesn't mean to?

CHAPTER SIX

July 11, 2025

23 Days Left

I'm waiting on the front porch when Edie arrives the next morning.

She doesn't see me at first—she's not looking for me, not this early—and when I step out from the shadows, she startles, nearly dropping her keys.

"Lordy, Geneva, did you decide a heart attack would wake me up better than coffee this morning?"

"Why didn't you tell me you knew Lo?" I ask, and then the words start spilling out too fast. "Actually, forget that. Why didn't you tell me you knew my *mom*, Edie? That you grew up here?"

She's very still in the early morning light, the waves making a quiet, rhythmic shushing sound in the background. Finally she sighs, stepping back to rest against the porch railing.

"I don't know, kid," she says, her voice soft enough that I lean forward to hear her better. "This place . . . St. Medard's. When I left, I pretty much had nothing. Your mom had her family, had the inn. Lo had Landon and all these big dreams. Audrey had made sure I didn't have any of that shit. No family, no home, certainly no dreams. I was . . . I was pissed off, and sick of everything, so I left and swore I'd never come back, and then . . ."

Edie sighs again, turning her head to look out at the ocean. Now, for the first time, I can see that she is older than I'd thought. Sixty, like Lo.

Like my mom.

"I don't know. It's like no one can ever leave St. Medard's, not really. Look at Lo. Look at *you*."

She gestures to me, and I fight the urge to squirm as she goes on. "You left here for college, probably thinking you'd visit plenty but never planning on living here again. But it pulled you right back like the town is the moon and you're the tide."

"No, what *pulled me right back* was my mom getting sick," I say, my voice rising along with the anger that's been building up inside me ever since last night. "And never once, at any point in the last *three years* that I've known you, that I've worked along-side you, that I've *cried* in front of you about my mom, did you bother to say, 'Hey, neat thing, Geneva! I actually knew Ellen! I grew up with her and maybe could tell you some stories you've never heard, or—or things about her you never knew—or—'"

There are tears in my eyes now, and I scrub them away with a shaking hand.

"Your mom cried when she got mad, too," Edie says softly. "If that's something you didn't know."

"I did know that, actually," I say, my voice catching on a sob. It's another memory that makes me feel like someone's squeez-ing my chest. I was about fifteen, and Mom was standing behind the front desk in tears after some rude guest chewed her out, stamping her foot and saying, *Oooh, I hate that I do this!*, as she dabbed at her eyes with a Kleenex. *It's like my own body undermines me.*

They're not tears, they're liquid rage, I'd responded, and that had made her laugh, the big, goofy laugh she gave when something had, as she would have put it, "really tickled her."

I don't know if it's the memory or the way Edie is looking at me, her face open, her eyes kind, but the fight suddenly drains out of me, and I sigh, tipping my head back. There's a wasp's nest in the corner of the porch ceiling, and I make a mental note to deal with that as soon as we're done here, the innkeeper part of my brain still chugging along, even now.

"I just wish you would have told me, and I don't understand why you didn't."

"Because I'd spent the last few decades of my life putting Frieda Mason behind me, and I loved that when I came back, no one recognized me. I introduced myself as Edie Vargas because that's who I'd been for the last thirty-something years, and no one remembered sad little Frieda Mason and her dead family."

Lo had told me about Edie's family, what had happened to them during Hurricane Audrey, and now a stab of pity—and a little bit of shame—pierces my heart. "I'm sorry," I tell her now, my voice soft as I reach out and give her arm a squeeze. "I . . . Lo told me."

Edie's jaw is tight as she nods, and she clears her throat before she says, "Thank you. But to be honest, that look on your face right now?" She points at me. "That's what I got so tired of those last years that I lived here. That's what I didn't want to see again. So that's why I didn't tell you initially, because I didn't want anyone else making that connection. But when you asked me to come help out here at the Rosalie, I should have said something. I just—I wanted this job. And I wanted to be able to do something for Ellen's little girl. And yeah, I've felt crappy about it for a while now, but once I really regretted not saying anything, I figured too much time had passed, it was too weird now, and that you'd probably be . . ."

She huffs out a humorless laugh. "Well, you'd be as ticked off and freaked out as you apparently are."

"I'm not 'ticked off,'" I say, then sigh. "Well, I *was*, when I first heard, but I understand a little more now. At least about you keeping it from me. Though I'm still not sure I get why you came back here at all."

"Same reason you did," she says, and I raise my eyebrows at her.

"I came back here to take over the inn."

"Sure," Edie replies, studying me from under her brows. "But it was more than that, wasn't it? You tried city life. You lived in Savannah, Atlanta . . . but did either of those places ever really feel like home?"

I don't answer, but she's right. I know it, and she knows it. Yes, I came back here for Mom and for the Rosalie and Chris's dream of us basically living in a Hallmark movie, but it was more than that. It was the tug I felt every time I visited, the way I sometimes dreamed of green waves and white sand. For all the stress and heartbreak of running the inn, something in my soul had settled when I came back to these shores, and maybe that's another one of St. Medard's Bay's curses.

Or blessings.

In any case, I turn to Edie now and say, "Anyway, I'm not angry, not anymore. It was just a shock, hearing it from Lo."

Edie's expression hardens. "I didn't think she recognized me."

"She said she didn't at first," I reply, leaning back against the railing. Sweat is popping out on my forehead, my upper lip, and I can tell today is going to be another hot one. "But I guess there

was something you did the other day—some phrase you used—
that made her look a little more closely at you."

That's what Lo had told me last night, after we'd brought
the bikes back, the two of us sitting in the rockers on the porch,
drinking lukewarm beers I'd snagged from my Airstream on the
walk back.

*As soon as I heard her say, "Couldn't find his bee-hind with
both hands," I thought, "Hooooooly shit, that's Frieda Mason!" She always said* bee-hind, *like that, never* ass. *Her mama
would've washed her mouth out with soap if she'd ever heard
that girl cussing.*

It hadn't occurred to me until that moment that for all of her
exterior toughness, I'd never heard Edie curse. But it's true, she
doesn't, and the weirdness of the situation—that *Lo* knew *Edie,*
knew her better than I ever had—had washed over me.

Why didn't you say something to her right then? I'd asked.

Well, she hadn't said anything to me, now, had she? Lo had
countered. *So I figured she was happy I hadn't made the connection, and I thought given everything, it was probably best to
let sleeping dogs lie.*

I'd asked her what she'd meant by that, "given everything,"
but she'd only shaken her head and stood from the rocker,
stretching her arms over her head, her shirt riding up to reveal a
sliver of tanned and surprisingly taut stomach.

*Too much reminiscing for one night, and August probably
has a thousand questions for me already,* she'd replied before
heading off to her room, leaving me to stare at the ocean for a
few more hours.

Now I say to Edie, "I noticed how weird you seemed when
she was around, and I couldn't figure out why. I guess you were
afraid of exactly this—that she'd recognize you and tell me."

To my surprise, Edie shakes her head, the multiple silver

hoops in her left ear clinking together. "No, it wasn't that. Or not *just* that. It's this whole thing." She waves her hand in the air with exasperation. "Her, and that guy, August. Writing this book. Dragging up the past. The fact that it's been forty years, but it's still like she'll die if she's not the center of attention." Edie's cheeks have flushed, and her eyes are flashing. "That's why she's doing this, you know. Whatever she's saying about wanting to 'clear her name once and for all,' that's BS. She's just bored and broke, and she's looking for something that might give her one last little turn in the spotlight."

Frowning, I fold my arms over my chest. "That's not the kindest read on the situation, Edie."

She steps closer, resting one hand on my forearm. "Don't let her fool you," she says with a vehemence that startles me. "She's really good at this whole seduction act, I know. She's fun, and sassy and sweet, and she's everyone's best friend. Until she's not. And your mama would've told you the same thing."

I think again about the box in the attic, the articles Mom kept for all those years, every little clipping about Lo Bailey and Landon's murder trial. It all seemed almost lovingly collected and preserved. Once again, I wish I could ask her why.

"Me and Ellen knew Lo better than anyone in this world," Edie continues. Somewhere inside the inn, I hear a door open and shut. Out on the beach, Cap is once again casting his fishing line.

But I'm focused on Edie and only Edie as she says, "And that's why we both knew she was lying back in eighty-four. That's why we knew she killed that man."

At my trial, the prosecution went on and on and *on* about all the stuff Landon had bought me. Clothes, jewels, a cute little Miata that I crashed a month or so after he died . . . *That's* what I stood to lose when Landon dumped me, the prosecution insisted. My mama was a poor widow, and I'd just barely gotten a high school diploma by the skin of my teeth. What future did I have, what luxuries could I look forward to, if Landon was through with me? He was my only ticket out of town, the only chance I had of escaping a life of service jobs and barely making ends meet.

I wanted to tell them that I wasn't with Landon for that shit, nice as it was, nor was I with him for his money, which I had no access to anyway. But okay, even if I *was*, it wasn't like pretty girls have ever had a hard time finding rich men to give them presents in exchange for sex. Come *on*, now. (My lawyer 'bout had a heart attack when I suggested saying that on the stand, but it was the truth, and isn't that what you're supposed to tell when you're up there in that little box? I guess I wouldn't know, because in the end, they didn't let me testify.)

Anyway, the prosecution literally put up a *list* of everything Landon ever bought me, but let me tell you, the biggest bee in their damn bonnets was that little beach house.

Yes, yes: the infamous "hidden love nest" that was really just a two-bedroom bungalow built sometime in the '40s. The front door sagged, and the water from the sink always tasted a little salty, and somehow no matter how well you rinsed your feet before coming inside, there was always sand in the sheets, but we loved it there. Sure, we had a lot of sex in that house, but it was more than that. Landon would fish right off the beach, and I'd attempt to cook even though just about the only thing I knew how to make was spaghetti, but whatever I made he devoured, declaring it was the best thing he'd ever eaten.

Looking back now, I think he loved that place because it let him pretend he was normal, just some Alabama beach bum instead of the governor's son.

Maybe that's who he really wanted to be, but of course, Beau Fitzroy wasn't about to have that. Not for his only son, the blessed Golden Boy born after four useless daughters.

After that little scene on board the *Miss Alison*, Landon's daddy had been even more on his son's ass to get serious about his political future. Landon never wanted to talk about it, but later I learned there had been a real push for him to run for mayor of Mobile in '86. Good ol' Beau had his eye on the presidential election in '88, and if he wanted to bring Landon along for the ride in some way—a cushy cabinet post, something like that—then Landon needed to have at least a little bit of "civic service experience."

Landon and I never talked about any of this shit, probably because the whole point of being with me was to forget all of that, to shake himself free of the weight of family legacy and responsibilities, but of course it was brought up at the trial. A couple of years later, I was living in Myrtle Beach, and while flipping through *Southern Living* at the salon, who do I see but Alison Carleton-Fitzroy herself, looking very beautiful and classy on the grounds of her fancy-ass house in Birmingham. They didn't mention Landon much in the interview, but at one point, she said something like, "Landon always said he'd be a senator by the time he was forty, and I truly believe he would've accomplished that dream. He was so driven to serve."

It made me wonder if she was just saying that because it was the Family Line, or if Landon was someone else entirely when he was with her. Were there different versions of Landon Fitzroy that he slipped into, depending on who he was with?

I can say only that the man I knew was mostly interested in boats, good food, loud music, and very pretty women.

But there was one time, there at the beach house, when family came up. Not his family, but ours. Or our *potential* one, anyway.

We were lying in bed, the windows open, the sound of the surf better than any damn sound machine. It was May, but the summer hadn't fully arrived to kick us all in the teeth yet. The nights were still cool, and I was almost asleep when Landon curled his body around my back, his hand resting on my stomach.

"We would have the prettiest babies," he murmured, his voice dreamy. I'd almost been asleep, but hoo boy, did *those* words wake me the fuck up.

"Pretty bastards," I said, covering his hand with mine and moving it to my hip. "No, thank you."

He raised himself up on one elbow. "You wouldn't want to have my baby?"

I rolled onto my back to look up at him, laughing in disbelief. "For one, I'm nineteen. For another . . ."

His left hand was still lying on top of my hip, and I lifted it, shaking it slightly. In the dim glow of my night-light, his wedding band winked.

"Well, what if those things were different?" he said. "What if it was a few years down the line, and *you* were the one who had put a ring on my finger? What then?"

He'd never mentioned it before, the idea of leaving Alison. I'd wanted him to, of course, had caught myself fantasizing about it, but . . .

God, this sounds so silly. The truth is, I never forced the conversation. And it's because I was trying so hard to be sophisticated, you know? A grown-up who was worldly and way too cool to care about some stuffy institution like marriage. A sexy, independent woman who had no problem being a man's mistress because wasn't that way more fun and glamorous than being a wife?

So I pushed any neediness—and certainly any shame—down as deep as I could and told myself that part of why he loved me was *because* I was so accepting, so free. Because I didn't give him a hard time about what he should or shouldn't do.

It never once occurred to me that part of why he loved me was because I was so *naïve*.

Still, I was being honest when I told him, "I don't know. I never really thought about being a mom, I guess. Beth-Anne always says that I was the only little girl she knew who cried because she *got* a baby doll for her birthday."

(That's true. I'd wanted a Malibu Barbie.)

"I always wanted to be a dad," Landon said, his voice growing a bit wistful. "A good one, obviously. Nothing like mine."

He lay back down, one hand behind his head, his eyes fixed on the small water stain on the ceiling, and I rolled onto my side to face him.

"Why don't you and . . . why don't you two have kids?"

I almost whispered the words, I remember that. It felt dangerous, bringing Alison's specter into our space like this, but there was real longing in his eyes, and I was curious.

He sighed, still looking at the ceiling. "We can't. Or *she* can't. Something about the shape of her uterus, or maybe one of the tubes, something like that."

For the first time since I'd taken up with Landon, I felt sorry for Alison. Not because her husband was cheating on her, not even because she couldn't have kids, but because it didn't seem right, him telling me something so personal in such an offhand way. Like my mom had said, she was a *real lady*, and I knew she'd be mortified.

Worse, she'd be hurt.

"You could adopt?" I suggested, and he looked over at me, his face suddenly very serious.

"If I'm going to have a child, it's going to be *mine*. It has to be a Fitzroy."

That was the first time I had a peek at that other Landon Fitzroy. The Heir, the Future Politician, the Man with a Destiny.

Unfortunately for both of us, it wasn't the last.

Pages of unfinished manuscript titled
"Be a Good Girl: Lo Bailey, Landon Fitzroy, and
the Scandal That Brought Down a Dynasty."
Found among possessions of August Fletcher, 8/3/2025

CHAPTER SEVEN

July 18, 2025

16 Days Left

For the next week, the inn keeps me too busy to think about Lo or Edie or anything but dealing with twenty teenagers spread out over five rooms on the first floor and their two harried (and not particularly observant) chaperones. It's a youth group from Mississippi, ostensibly here to do "acts of service," which means that they spend about fifteen minutes every morning picking up trash along the beach and the next sixteen or so hours tanning, screeching at one another, and running down the inn's hallways so loudly a guest on the second floor called down to see if we were doing construction at 10 PM.

Normally, I'd be so happy about seven rooms booked at once that I wouldn't have cared if they'd all taken up Riverdancing in the lobby at midnight, but they're paying a deeply discounted rate because back in the '80s, when the inn was doing well, my dad had decided to do a kind of "Rosalie Inn Gives Back" promotion for youth groups that want to come to town and do community service.

I've let that fade away for the most part, but apparently the First Baptist Church of Piedmont, Mississippi, hadn't forgotten because they'd booked early this year, and I'm a sucker.

I'm heaving a mighty sigh of relief as their van bumps off down the gravel-and-shell road when August suddenly appears at my side.

"Have to say, until this trip, I never realized that innkeepers should be considered for sainthood, but watching you deal with that crowd? You should probably start polishing the halo now."

I laugh, closing the front door with one hand and pushing my sweaty hair back from my forehead with the other. It doesn't seem to matter that I grew up in this very building—every summer, the heat catches me by surprise. I keep telling myself it's not any worse than usual this year, but each morning, the air feels heavier than the last.

"Oh, that's nothing," I tell him. "We had a bachelorette weekend three years ago that turned my hair completely white. This?" I point to my head. "Very expensive dye job."

Now it's his turn to laugh, his eyes crinkling. He's wearing a white T-shirt this morning, setting off the deeper tan he's acquired since he got to St. Medard's Bay, and my stomach gives a pleasant little swoop.

"Well," he says, putting both hands in his pockets and rocking back on his heels, "I'm sure you want to face-plant into the nearest margarita after all that, but I was wondering if now might be a good time for that interview. And we can multitask and grab lunch while we do it."

Between visiting my mom, the shock of learning Edie's background, and the general chaos of the church group, I'd never gotten around to talking to August like I'd promised, and even though I know there are a million other things I should be doing, I find myself nodding. "Yeah, sure, let me just tell Edie I'll be out for a little bit."

I find her in the office, once again on the NOAA website, studying the two-week forecast. Now that I know about her family, her anxiety over storms makes complete sense. "Anything to report?" I ask, and she frowns, the bright blues of the map reflected in her glasses.

"There's a system I'm keeping an eye on out in the Caribbean. Not loving the look of it. Did you know that the water temps are already higher than they were this time last year? Not loving that, either."

I look over her shoulder at the map. I've been lucky—in the few years since I've taken over the inn, the worst weather we've had was a couple of severe thunderstorms. But that doesn't mean that I don't prep for a hurricane every year. Both Mom and Dad instilled in me early on that a good innkeeper is always prepared. So before June 1—the official start of hurricane season—I make sure the generators have plenty of fuel and are still in good condition, check the storm windows, and load up on bottled water that I store in the office. It's silly, but it always makes me feel like I'm doing some kind of protection ritual, gathering my talismans or something.

The Witches of St. Medard's Bay, I find myself thinking, and almost smile.

Instead, I reach out and pat Edie's back. "Well, forewarned is forearmed, right?"

She only grunts, and I give her shoulder a squeeze before letting her know I'll be off the property for a little while but will have my phone with me.

I don't tell her I'm going with August, or that he's interviewing me for Lo's book. In fact, we haven't talked about Lo at all

since that morning on the porch when Edie told me she was sure
Lo had killed Landon Fitzroy.

It had taken me aback, the certainty of it.

It had surprised me even more to realize that I didn't believe
her.

It's not that I thought Edie was lying to me. I'd seen the look
in her eyes. She absolutely believed that Lo was a murderer.

But I . . . didn't.

The night after I'd confronted Edie, I'd finally gone back to
Mom's box of clippings, staying up way too late reading every
piece, poring over every word.

It didn't do much good.

Some were fawning tabloid puff pieces about what a babe
Lo was, basically, and some were poison-pen "burn the witch"–
style takedowns, but there wasn't much in terms of actual truth
in them. In fact, I realized as I went through all of it that it was
mostly old tabloids or magazines, hardly any newspapers, and
nothing about the trial itself.

She had more pieces about the Fitzroys than I'd realized, too,
including a *Southern Living* article about Landon's wife, Alison,
from years after he died. I studied her pale oval face, her soft
brown hair, and thought how different she was from Lo, almost
like the negative of a photograph.

But nothing in that whole box felt like a smoking gun, like a
clear sign of *Yep, she did that shit.*

Still, Edie has her own reasons for distrusting Lo, and I can't
blame her for those. And her insistence that Lo needs the spotlight to be on her is making me wonder why Lo has suddenly
chosen to publish this book *now.*

August is waiting by the back door that leads to the beach
when I come out of the office, and I'm glad I paid a bit more
attention when I got dressed this morning, pulling out a coral

tank top and long white skirt, pairing it with my favorite pair of sandals.

I slip those sandals off as we step onto the porch, nodding down the beach.

"There's actually a place we can walk to," I tell him, and he slides off his own boat shoes, following my lead.

It's still punishingly hot, but the breeze keeps us cool as we walk the quarter mile or so down the sand toward Shrimpy's. It's only a few steps above The Line in terms of classiness, but it's got great boiled shrimp and fried grouper, and you can walk right up to one of the tables on the deck from the beach, something that seems to delight August.

"Oh, this is the dream for a kid from a landlocked state," he says as we take a seat near the railing, as close to the ocean as we can get.

We both order beers, and then he takes his phone out of his pocket, pulling up something on the screen before laying it on the table between us. "So I'll record this via an app, and I'll send you a copy tonight. If there's anything you realize you've said that you don't want put in the book, let me know and it's gone."

I raise my eyebrows as the waiter drops off our sweating bottles of Corona. "What if I say something really juicy? Something that would make this book a *guaranteed bestseller*? Would you delete *that*?"

"Oh, fuck no, ethics thrown out the window *immediately*," he replies, and I laugh.

"No worries on that front," I say before taking a sip of my beer. "I honestly don't think I know anything that could be all that useful, but I'll give it a shot."

August folds his arms on the table, muscles in his forearms bunching, and leans in. "Can you tell me why Frieda Mason is now going by Edie Vargas?"

I almost choke on my next sip of beer, the bottle wobbling clumsily on the picnic table as I set it down just a little too hard. "Oh. Um. Wow."

His hand shoots out, hovering over the phone. "Want me to start over?"

I shake my head. "No. No, I just . . . how did you know about Edie?"

"Lo told me," he says matter-of-factly. "But she also said you didn't know, until she mentioned it. About Edie, how she grew up here with Lo and your mom."

"I didn't, but Edie had her reasons for not sharing that with me, and I'm fine with it."

Mostly true.

"Anyway," I continue, trying to regain my composure, "I don't really see what any of that has to do with Lo or the book. I mean, they were friends when they were kids, so I guess there's history—"

"Frieda—or Edie, as you know her—was one of the prosecution's star witnesses in Lo's trial," August says, pushing his sunglasses on top of his head and squinting slightly in the glare off the water. "She was, in fact, the *only* person who confirmed seeing Lo and Landon together in the hours before Marie hit. She said she had gone by the bungalow, looking for Lo, and instead saw her and Landon, and it was clear they'd been fighting. She also said that in the weeks prior, she'd heard Lo remark that she'd kill Landon before she'd let him . . . 'throw me away like a fucking gum wrapper,' I think the phrasing was."

I trace a water ring on the table, trying not to show how shaken I am by this news. But August picks up on it anyway, and he presses a button on his phone's screen and sits back in his chair. "I'm sorry," he says. "You thought we'd just be talking about the inn or the town's history, and I throw something like this at you."

"It's fine," I say, even though it definitely isn't, and based on his probing expression, I suspect that he also isn't sorry. That he very much intended to put me on the spot. Why didn't Edie tell me this part? Or, for that matter, why didn't *Lo*? She acted so nonchalant about Edie, like whatever beef there was between them was just silly girlhood stuff, back from when they were kids, not from the trial.

Edie had been one of Lo's closest friends. What would it have felt like, seeing her up on the witness stand, telling everyone that you were a murderer?

Obviously, August wouldn't have an answer for that question, but I ask him another one I hope he *can* shed some light on.

"Why now?" I ask, then clarify, "For the book, I mean. Why is she suddenly wanting to rehash all of this?"

August turns his head, looking out at the ocean. I watch the reflection of waves crashing against the sand in his aviator sunglasses as he says, "There's no telling."

Turning back to me, he flashes a crooked smile. "In case you haven't figured it out yet, Lo's motivations are sometimes a mystery even to herself, I think. When she first reached out to me about this whole project, it seemed pretty clear she was just low on cash and thought a book deal might be an easy meal ticket, especially if someone else was doing the writing. I honestly wasn't sure there was enough to her story *for* a book. But then she suggested coming here, and I thought, okay, I can see a bit of a *Midnight in the Garden of Good and Evil* goes coastal vibe. And then the next thing I knew . . ." He spreads his hands wide, leaning back so that his chair rests on two legs. "It was a fucking book. And, I think, a really good one."

His chair smacks back onto all four legs, and he picks up one of the plastic menus the waitress left with us. "Okay, let's get some food in us before—"

"Do you think Lo did it? Killed Landon?"

The words come out louder than I intend, but the Kenny Chesney song blaring over the speakers means that no one at any of the nearby tables heard me.

August studies me as he scratches the side of his jaw with his thumb before saying, "I honestly don't know. When I started this project, I didn't think so, but there are parts of the story that just . . . okay. For example."

He leans in again, the breeze ruffling his hair. "All of the stuff from the trial—the police interviews, the court transcripts, the autopsy report—literally *all of it* says that Landon's body was found between the inn and the nature preserve. But when Lo first mentioned coming to St. Medard's Bay, specifically to the Rosalie, to work on the book, she said, 'That's where he died. His body was right under the porch.' She said it sort of offhand, and I thought she was either misremembering or it had been kept out of the press so as not to damage the inn's reputation. But when you weren't aware of it, either, it started gnawing at me more."

I nod in agreement, but then, thinking of Mom, add, "Memory is a tricky thing, though, especially when people start aging."

"Don't ever let Lo hear you say she's aging," August says with a laugh before continuing. "Another thing: Lo says that on the day of the hurricane, she called Landon's office in Mobile. She says she never spoke to him, that she had to leave a message with his secretary. And the secretary confirmed that, but she also said that an hour or so after that, she heard Landon on the phone with someone. Someone he was calling 'baby' and 'sweet girl.' And she wasn't the only one. At least three other people at that law firm remember him on the phone, talking to what sounded like a young woman on the other end."

The sun is beating down on my back, but I still feel a shiver go through me.

"And phone records show two phone calls to Landon's office from the beach house he'd bought Lo—one earlier in the day, and again in the early afternoon," August continues. "But Lo insists she called only once, that morning, and that she hadn't been asking him to come to St. Medard's, she'd just been checking on him because of the weather. And sure, it's possible those people at his office were lying, that Beau Fitzroy paid them to say all that and make Lo look guilty, but . . ."

Trailing off, he shakes his head. "She called twice, three hours apart, from the same phone. The second call was placed around the same time that people in the office can confirm he was talking to someone. Now, why would she lie about a small thing like that?" He pauses and shrugs. "Unless, of course, she has something to hide?"

I don't have an answer for that, but August is just warming up, and he goes on.

"Meanwhile, she swears that things with Landon were steady at the time, but according to his friends, he was seeing at least two other women. They didn't know names—Landon was apparently just enough of a gentleman that he didn't kiss and tell—but none of them thought Lo was going to last much longer. Landon was starting to get serious about running for office in a few years, and Alison was reportedly getting fed up with all the girlfriends, and given that the Carletons had nearly as much money and prestige as the Fitzroys, he couldn't risk her asking for a divorce. It would've strangled any political career in the cradle. So . . ."

August blows out a breath, then links his fingers, stacking his hands on top of his dark curls as he leans back. "So, did she do it? I don't know. But *could* she have done it?"

His eyes meet mine. "Abso-fucking-lutely."

WE ABANDON ANY pretense of an interview for the rest of the meal, eating and talking about anything *but* Lo. Instead, he tells me about his family back in Ohio (parents still living, still healthy, one sister practicing family medicine in Chicago) and the various pieces he's written over the years (a profile of some mountaineer for *Esquire*, an exhaustive list of "Sock Trends for Men" for *GQ*), and I tell him a little bit more about Chris, the most demanding clients I had back when I was in interior design, and the three families who are banned from ever darkening the Rosalie Inn's doors again.

It's nice, talking with August, and the time gets away from us. It's after two by the time we make our way back down the beach, and the heat has kicked into high gear. On the horizon, thunderheads are piling up, and I figure we'll get a traditional Afternoon Downpour within the hour.

We're about halfway back to the inn when I see someone walking toward us, the sun making a rainbow out of the sparkling, chunky necklace she's wearing.

It's Lo, decked out in another floral sundress, and she waves both arms over her head as she sees us. "There y'all are!" she calls, and jogs a little to catch up with us. She takes in my outfit, and—I think—how close August is standing to me.

"How did the interview go?" she asks, and I'm about to tell her we pretty much scrapped it when August says, "Great! Got some really good stuff."

I glance over at him, but he's still looking at Lo from behind his sunglasses, and I can't get a read on what he's thinking.

"Yay!" Lo says brightly, but there's something a little brittle about it, and then she moves between us, threading one arm through August's, the other through mine.

"Geneva, do you mind if I go ahead and steal August back?" she asks. "I thought he might like to see where my beach house used to be. It's real close, just a little ways over there," she says, nodding back in the direction we'd been coming from. "Of course, you're welcome to tag along, too, but I'm sure you have lots waiting for you back at the inn!"

All of this is delivered in Lo's usual sweet-as-sugarcane voice, but I don't miss the fact that I'm being dismissed.

I also don't miss the way her hand curls tightly around August's biceps.

It's not a jealousy thing, I don't think. Not in the traditional sense. Lo doesn't want August romantically, but maybe she's gotten used to being the center of attention, his sole priority.

I don't know, but for some reason, looking at the way she's holding on to him, I'm reminded of a line about Lo that I saw in one of the articles that Mom saved.

God help anyone who gets in her way.

CHAPTER EIGHT

July 25, 2025

9 Days Left

The rain starts on a Friday morning, and unlike our usual summer storms, it doesn't peter out after half an hour or so. It begins early, before I've even left my trailer. Not the hard pounding of an afternoon thunderstorm, but a steady *drip-drip-drip*, off the eaves of the inn, pattering on the ocean waves, dimpling the sand and soaking the baskets of begonias on the front porch. It sounds soothing, and a different woman would take it as an invitation to stay in bed, settle in with a good book and mugs of tea until the skies cleared.

Unfortunately, I'm not that kind of woman.

By lunch, the whole first floor of the inn smells like the ocean, and not in a pleasant, sea-breeze kind of way. It's a dank, rotted scent that brings to mind slimy seaweed and dead fish tangled in plastic.

There are only three other groups staying at the inn besides Lo and August: a family of four from Tennessee who spend the afternoon arguing over a game of Monopoly in the lobby, an older couple on their honeymoon who stay in their room, and a pair of girls in their twenties who, as I see when I glance out the big windows, are filming TikTok dances on the beach, rain be damned.

"They shouldn't be out there," Edie says, coming to stand next to me, her arms crossed tightly over her chest. Her fingernails are painted turquoise, and they're bright against her black shirt but ragged and a little raw, like she's been biting them. "Unless getting struck by lightning is some new internet challenge."

"It's not even thundering," I tell her, only to be made a liar literally two seconds later when a boom rattles the windows and makes the girls on the beach shriek.

"Okay, so yeah, they probably should come in," I amend, turning away. "But I'm not their mom, and they're adults, so—"

"GIRLS!"

I flinch as Edie's voice booms out the back door; she has one hand cupped around her mouth. "LIGHTNING!" she shouts, and they wave, gathering up their soaked towels and clear plastic beach bags.

"Whoooo, I forgot the set of lungs you have on you!" Lo says, coming down the stairs.

She and Edie have still barely interacted, but I guess she's decided there's no sense in pretending they don't know each other now that I've been filled in.

I can tell by the way Edie's shoulders tense up that she would've been perfectly fine ignoring Lo and their history forever, but she turns to face Lo now, scowling.

"Yeah, I get loud when people are putting themselves in danger. Learned the hard way on that one."

Now Lo is the one who flinches. Barely, almost imperceptibly, but I see it. Then her customary *ain't we havin' fun* expression reappears, and she continues down the stairs, a pair of leather mules flapping on her heels.

"Maybe if this book doesn't work out, I can do whatever it is those young ladies were doing. Dancing for the internet?"

"When has anything ever not worked out for you?" Edie mutters under her breath, and Lo's head snaps around quickly.

Her smile never wavers, but there's venom in every word as she says, "Oh, I don't know, Frieda. Maybe when I sat in a jail cell for over a year waiting to go to trial for something I *didn't do*? Ooh, or maybe it was when I *got* to that trial and saw the same girl I'd once called a blood sister telling a bunch of fucking lies about me that could've gotten me *the electric chair*. I feel like that's probably a time that things didn't really work out for me."

The girls are up on the porch now, giggling and talking over each other, but in the lobby, all the air seems to have been sucked out of the room, the three of us frozen in place as Edie and Lo stare each other down.

"Everything good?"

August appears at the top of the stairs, and even though he's holding himself loosely, one ankle crossed in front of the other, a casual hand the banister, I see him taking it all in and wonder how much of Lo's outburst he overheard.

"Peachy keen!" Lo singsongs back, and Edie takes a sharp inhale before saying something about checking the weather and vanishing into the office.

"Sorry about that," Lo says as soon as she's gone. "Guess I'd been holding that in for a while."

I'm still too shocked to respond, but luckily, August changes the subject, nodding out the windows.

"Any idea when that's clearing up?"

"Apparently not until this evening, at the earliest," I say. I'd checked the weather report just an hour ago myself. "But that's not unusual for this time of year. And it's supposed to be pretty tomorrow."

"This is how it was back in eighty-four," Lo says, moving closer to the window. "I thought it would never stop raining that July. But then, of course, it turned out that July was just the appetizer. The *real* rain was biding its time way, way out in the ocean, building itself up into Marie."

I follow her gaze out toward the water and think about how even now, miles and miles away, there's a storm churning out in the Caribbean, gathering speed, getting hotter. I saw that in the weather report, too, and I know it's the same system that Edie's been keeping her eye on. It could fizzle away to nothing, or it could build itself into a monster. Either way, there's nothing we can do about it.

Except wait.

THE FAMILY OF four check out later that afternoon, and since the girls went to see what fun could be had in town and the honeymooners seem perfectly content locked away on the second floor, I decide to take the evening to visit Mom.

She looks the same as always. Sometimes I feel like time has stopped at Hope House because nothing there ever seems to change, except the seasonal decorations at the front desk and down the hallways. Same nurses, same faded bulletin boards, same blank expression on Mom's face. Even her outfits blend together, some version of a top, pants, and a sweater, slip-on Keds on her feet.

I stay longer than usual, watching an old episode of *Dateline* with Mom—or at least while I sit next to her, I guess. "I know,

I know," I say, her hand cool and limp in mine. "Me and my 'murder shows.' You always hated this kind of thing, but this TV has like three channels, so it's this, sports, or home shopping."

Once again, I find myself waiting for a reply that isn't going to come, and I sigh, laying my head on her shoulder. "I wish I could talk to you," I tell her softly. "I wish you could tell me what Lo was like, and Edie, too. Frieda. I wish you could tell me why you kept all those articles about Lo, and if you really thought she killed Landon Fitzroy, and—"

Her hand spasms against mine, and I jerk my head up, looking at her face. "Mom?" I ask softly, and she doesn't look at me, but her hand keeps moving, weakly flapping against my palm, and as I watch, a tear spills from the corner of her eye.

"Mom?" I say again, wiping the tear away with my thumb, but in the end, she only sighs once, then twice, and finally her hand goes still again, her expression distant as ever.

It gnaws at me the whole drive home, that shaking hand, that one tear. She's had little reactions to other things before—a tapping finger when I played her a song she used to love, a soft smile once when I kissed her cheek before leaving. But those were all at least a couple of years ago.

I'm still thinking about it as I pull back into the tiny staff parking lot just off the inn's main lot. The rain hasn't stopped— if anything, it's coming down a little heavier now—and I tug the hood of my rain jacket up before opening the car door.

Only to stop short when I see Edie's truck is still in the lot.

I check the time on the dash. It's past eight, and Edie never stays later than six, even if I'm not here. We have a night desk manager, Louisa, who comes in then and handles things until Edie returns at 6 AM, and of course I'm always on call through-out the night just in case.

Louisa's little red Mazda is in its usual spot, and as I jog through the puddle-filled parking lot, I wonder if it's the rain that made Edie stay late. She hates driving in it, but she hates not being home by dark even more. It would surprise me if it was enough to keep her here.

The lobby is empty, the inn quiet. Louisa sits behind the desk, playing on her phone, and doesn't even bother looking guilty when I come in. "Been dead," she says, not raising her eyes from the screen.

"Yeah, hardly any guests here right now," I say, then glance around. "Have you seen Edie?"

"Nope," she replies. "Figured she'd already left. I didn't see her when I got here."

"Her truck is still in the lot," I say, but Louisa only shrugs and flips her strawberry-blond braid over her shoulder.

"Didn't see her," she reiterates, and for the first time, something like worry starts tickling the back of my brain. Louisa's been here since six. That's two hours, and if something had gone wrong, something that required Edie staying so long past quitting time, she would have either texted me to let me know or mentioned it to Louisa.

There are no messages on my phone, though, and when I glance over at the walkie-talkies lined up behind the front desk, Edie's is firmly in its cradle. That's always the last thing she does before leaving, putting her radio back.

I shoot her a quick text, and as I wait for a reply, I check the back office, the staff kitchen, even the laundry room despite Edie frequently telling me, "I'll do a lot around here, Geneva, but I ain't doing laundry."

No sign of her.

No reply to my text, either.

Moving back into the lobby, I dial her number. It starts ringing, but after five rings, it goes to voicemail, Edie gruffly saying she'll get back to me while sounding like that's the last thing in the world she intends to do.

I've teased her about that message before, but now it makes my skin feel hot and cold at the same time, because something is wrong. Edie's truck is here, and Edie's radio is here, but Edie doesn't seem to be, and I move to the back door, trying her number again as I pace up and down.

"Maybe she's asleep in one of the rooms," Louisa suggests as Edie's cell starts ringing again. I'm about to tell her that Edie would never do that, that once you've spent as much time in these rooms as we both have, they're the last place you can think of relaxing, but then I hear a noise.

Edie's phone is still droning in my ear, but there's another, tinnier sound somewhere nearby. It's distant and hard to hear over the rain, but then my brain makes sense of the sound, twisting it into something familiar.

"Free Bird."

Edie's ringtone.

My heart leaps, and I end the call, then immediately dial again, opening the back door and stepping out onto the porch.

The song is still faint, but it's louder out here, and I pull my cell phone away from my ear, calling out, "Edie?" over the rain and waves.

There's no answer, and I start moving toward the corner of the porch where the ringtone seems to be coming from.

It gets louder as I turn the corner onto the side porch, narrower and darker than the main one facing the beach, nearly hidden by a row of overgrown azaleas my grandparents planted in the '60s.

"Edie!" I yell out, stepping forward into the darkness only to feel my feet slip out from under me.

I land hard on my hip, my teeth catching my tongue sharply enough to make me gasp, rainwater cold on my bare legs beneath my shorts.

My phone has fallen out of my hand; I reach for it, fingers closing around it as I distantly hear Edie's voicemail message start up again, and I look down at the screen, wanting to turn on the flashlight.

But something's wrong with it, the light dimmer now, the words blurred, and for a second, I think maybe I dropped it too hard, maybe water got in it and that's what's making it look like there's something smeared across the screen.

But then I realize that it's blood—on the screen, on my legs—not rainwater. At first, I think it's my blood, that I cut myself as I fell, cut myself so deep that I can't even feel it.

It's only when the phone's flashlight beam lands on a pale hand with raggedy turquoise nails that I start to scream.

CHAPTER NINE

July 26, 2025

8 Days Left

It's nearly three in the morning by the time I get back from the hospital.

Edie was still alive when the paramedics showed up, but barely. One of them told me that if I'd been just a few minutes later, it would've been too late, but looking at her—pale and motionless as they loaded her into the ambulance—I wasn't sure I had found her in time after all.

Skull fracture, they said. It looked like she'd slipped on the side porch and cracked her head on one of the old stone planters out there, the heavy square base denting a spot just behind her ear before the fall sent her sprawling onto the porch steps, a sharp corner gouging a trench from her temple to the crown of her head. That was where most of the blood came from, the doctor said, but the wound to the back of her head was the serious one.

They'd had to cut a chunk of her skull away to relieve the

pressure, and she was in a medically induced coma in the hopes that it would help with the swelling. They hadn't let me go back to see her since we aren't family, but the doctor, an older man with sad eyes, had told me that he'd call if anything changed, that the next forty-eight hours were critical, and that even if she did pull through, this was a very serious injury, especially for someone her age.

I absorbed all of it numbly, standing there in the St. Medard's Bay emergency room, Edie's blood drying in dark streaks down my legs, on my hands. For a small town, we have a surprisingly big hospital, and I was relieved Edie would get to stay close by instead of being sent to Mobile or Pensacola, but all I could think about was the blood—so much blood—and how could anyone lose that much of it and still be okay?

As I drive home from the hospital, my mind settles on something else, something less urgent but just as troubling: Why the fuck had Edie been out on that porch anyway? There was nothing over there—no furniture that needed moving, no repairs that had to be done. Even if there *had* been, Edie had more sense than to go out in the rain, in the *dark*, to do them.

The weather cleared sometime around midnight, and the air is back to being thick and muggy as I make my way to my trailer. I'm so exhausted, so overwhelmed, that I almost don't see August at first.

He's sitting on the steps leading up to the Airstream, and as soon as he sees me, he jumps up, shoving his hands into his back pockets.

"Is she all right?" he asks nervously.

I have a vague memory of August and Lo waiting in the lobby as the ambulance arrived, of pale faces and wide eyes, but all my focus had been on Edie.

"They don't know," I tell him, my voice dull. "It's . . . it's bad.

Really bad. But she's alive, for now, so that's . . . that's something."

My voice breaks on that last word, and August makes a soft sound low in his throat before coming closer, his arms wrapping around me.

He smells like laundry detergent and sunscreen and sweat, and his chest is warm and hard against mine, and I let him hold me, feeling like I can barely stay upright.

"God, that had to be awful," he says. "I'm so sorry."

I can only nod, then I pull away, gesturing down at myself. "I'm going to get blood on you," I tell him, but he only shrugs.

"Wouldn't be the first time while on the job. I once did an assignment on extreme piercings. I also followed this crazy tattoo artist for a week. A little mess doesn't scare me."

That makes me smile, or at least attempt it. Not so much the anecdote, just the fact that he offered it, that he's trying to make this night seem a little less horrific. And despite my exhaustion, despite my appearance, I find myself asking, "Do you wanna come in for a drink?"

I POUR US each a couple of fingers of bourbon, then take mine into the tiny bathroom so that I can shower.

The blood on my legs and hands is dry now, and it flakes off as I scrub, the water turning pink as it sluices down the drain.

My skin is also pink as I towel off, from both the heat of the water and the brutal scouring I gave myself, but I feel a little more human by the time I emerge from the bathroom in a tank top and pajama shorts, my wet hair dripping over my shoulders.

August is sitting at the little dining area, his glass in one hand, a folder in the other.

Mom's articles. I forgot I left the box sitting right there on the table, and maybe I should be pissed off at him for looking through my things without asking, but I'm too tired for that right now. Besides, he's the one writing a book about Lo. Seems only fair he should have access to this makeshift archive, come to think of it.

"Where did all this come from?" he asks, and I prop my chin on one hand as I reach for the bourbon bottle with the other.

"My mom," I tell him, sloshing more liquor into my glass. "And before you ask, no, I don't know why she had all of it. She never even told me she and Lo were friends."

"Huh" is all August says, and for a little while, I drink, and he reads in silence.

And maybe it's the bourbon, maybe it's the shock, but the one question that has been growing louder and louder in my head for the last few hours finally slips out. "Do you think it was Lo?"

August's dark eyes flick up from the tabloid clipping blaring out HOW "LO" CAN YOU GO?, and he takes a sip of his drink before answering.

"You mean Edie. Tonight."

"God, that makes me feel crazy to say," I groan, scrubbing at my face with both hands before pulling my feet up onto the banquette and wrapping my arms around my knees. "But"—I nod at the box—"I've read those articles. I know what happened to Landon, how his head was all caved in, like someone had hit him with something, and . . . the way the doctor was describing her most serious wound to me tonight, it sounded exactly the same. Besides, Edie never goes out to the side porch. There was literally no reason for her to be out there. And yes, it was raining, and yes, that painted wood can be slippery, but how could one little fall do that much damage?"

It feels simultaneously good and horrible, getting that off my chest. Like when you finally throw up after being nauseated. I feel lighter somehow, but also exhausted and shaky, and I throw back the rest of the bourbon in my glass.

I don't know what I want August to say. No, scratch that—I want him to tell me I'm being crazy, but to do so kindly. To tell me he understands why my mind might go there, but here are all the reasons that it couldn't possibly be true.

Instead, he nods. "Things did get pretty nasty between them today."

That exchange in the lobby had been bothering me, too. Not just what Lo had said, but how she'd said it. The way she'd pretended everything was fine with her and Edie, that there were no grudges held, no scores to settle—only to unleash that vitriol, seemingly with a flick of an internal switch.

But it hadn't just been anger fueling her outburst. It had been deep hurt. A sense of betrayal, nurtured over the decades.

Could they have argued again after I left? Had Edie followed Lo out to that porch in the rain, and had Lo finally seen her chance to get revenge?

"Did Lo say anything to you?" I ask him. "After they took Edie away?"

August lifts one shoulder, taps his fingers against the side of his glass. "Just that she wondered what had happened, she hoped Edie would be all right, and that falls are so tricky when you're as old as Edie."

I frowned. "They're the same age."

"Not in her mind."

We're quiet again, each of us lost in our own thoughts until August says, "I didn't see her tonight. Lo, I mean. We were working in her room for a bit around four, probably until five, but then she said she was going to make a phone call, maybe take the car and grab a quick bite to eat. I didn't see her again until we heard the sirens."

I take that in, my brain feeling slow, sluggish. I shouldn't have had that second glass of bourbon, not when I'm this tired and probably still in shock. My mouth is dry, my head fuzzy, and I stand up to get a bottle of water from the mini fridge.

"Edie definitely believes Lo killed Landon," I tell August, pressing the cold bottle to my warm face. "And she says my mom had always thought the same thing." I briefly fill him in on my mom—her condition, Hope House, all of it. "And both times I've mentioned Lo around my mom, she's had a reaction," I continue. "Not a big one, but it's more than I've gotten out of her in the last year or two. And she had all these clippings hidden away, but she never once mentioned Lo's name to me, ever. I feel like there's some piece of this I'm just not seeing, and if Mom were still herself . . ."

August rises to his feet, coming to stand in front of me, his hands landing on my bare arms. "Hey," he says softly. "You've had a fucking terrible night, you're probably dead on your feet. Whatever is going on here, we don't have to figure it out right now."

That *we* is a balm, sliding over me, clearing some of the panicked static buzzing in my brain. God, I've missed being part of a *we*. I've been doing so much hard shit alone, and it's nice to think that this might be one hard thing I don't have to face by myself.

August's hands are still wrapped around my biceps, the bottle of water icy cold as it presses against my chest, leaving a damp spot on his T-shirt because we're standing so close together.

So it feels natural—inevitable, even—when he lowers his head to kiss me.

His lips are soft and a little dry, and he tastes like bourbon when his tongue finds mine.

The bottle of water tumbles to the floor as I instinctively wrap my arms around him and kiss him back, every touch-starved cell in my body suddenly singing with life again, and his hair is soft against my fingers when I link them at the back of his neck.

It feels so good just to have another body close to mine that I'm able to ignore the distant alarm bell ringing in my head, reminding me of Lo's face when she saw me and August on the beach that day, the way her arm snaked protectively through August's as she stood between us.

God help anyone who gets in her way.

Some clarity breaks through the fog in my head, and I pull away. Things are complicated enough here at the Rosalie without adding whatever this is to the mix.

But August keeps his grip firm on my waist and searches my face. "What is it?"

Gently, I step as far back as I can in this tiny space. "I'm tired and maybe a little drunk, and possibly neither of us are making great decisions right now."

August sighs and ruffles his hair. "You're right. This is . . . yeah, this is not the time, and given the size of that bed, probably not the place."

Turning, he picks up his glass from the table, throwing back the little bit of whiskey left, then sets the glass back down with a thump. "Listen," he says. "If Edie didn't just fall, if Lo was involved somehow, I promise you, we'll get to the bottom of it, okay?"

"Okay," I reply, my voice barely above a whisper.

He nods, then looks back at the table and gestures to the box. "Would it be all right with you if I borrowed these for a while? I promise I'll return them, I just want to see if there's anything in here that might be good for the book."

"Sure," I say. I'm almost tempted to tell him not to bother bringing them back, that I don't want to look at them anymore. It's too painful to wonder why my mom kept something like this from me. To remind myself over and over again that I can wonder all I want, but she'll never be able to explain herself to me.

He hefts the box into one arm and is turning to go when something occurs to me.

"What makes you think any of that stuff would help with the book?" I ask. "I mean, aren't you just helping Lo write her memoir? Her version of what happened? Why would the stuff that was written *about* her be relevant?"

A grimace takes over his face. "That's the book she thinks we're writing, yeah," he says finally, and I see him pull the box a little tighter. "But I don't know if that's the book *I'm* writing anymore."

One of the most interesting things about Lo—and one of the things I had a hard time believing was genuine when I first met her—was that there was zero bitterness in her. This was a woman who'd had her teenage diaries splashed all over America's tabloids, a woman who basically had a scarlet "A" tattooed on her forehead for something that happened when she wasn't even old enough to order her first drink. Sure, people also thought Landon Fitzroy was trash, the married man with a young bride at home and a mistress everywhere else, but death afforded him a dignity no one wanted to give Lo.

And when the attention faded away, what did she have? The money she was paid for her story ran out quickly, and she wasn't educated, wasn't skilled. She moved around, she tried her hand at acting in some epically terrible B movies, and she eventually ended up in the dreaded "Inland Empire" of California, working at a call center, paying too much rent for too small an apartment.

When I first reached out to her about working on a book, I'd expected her to be greedy and grasping, a trunk full of axes to grind at her feet.

I wouldn't have blamed her for that.

But there was no malice in her for any of it—not for the scrutiny, not for the allegations and insinuations.

Not for Landon's powerful family, who did everything in their power to destroy her in the wake of his death.

And, most intriguing to me, not for Landon himself.

You can see it in those diary entries the *National Enquirer* published. She had honestly loved the guy.

In fact, when I went back and listened to our conversations for this book, all those hours and hours of talking, it was clear to me that not only had she loved Landon Fitzroy in

1984, she was still in love with him in 2025. Never mind the various boyfriends she'd had over the decades since Landon's death, never mind the husband she'd briefly picked up in the mid-nineties. Could Dave (who drove Gator boats in Louisiana) or Larry (who sold Buicks in Indiana) or Gary—also known as Skeeter, for reasons no one seems to know (who attempted some sort of "marijuana marshmallows" business in California)—ever hope to live up to the myth that was Landon Fitzroy?

To the outside world, Landon was a typical rich asshole with too much money and too few nos in his life. To her?

~~He was still her knight in shining armor.~~

~~He was still her savior.~~

~~He was still her Prince Fucking Charming.~~

He was [TK].

Listening to her talk about him, it was almost impossible to believe that she'd ever raise a hand to the man, much less kill him.

But there were plenty of people who thought she did, and the more time I spent with her, the more I began to think they might be right.

Pages of unfinished manuscript titled
"Be a Good Girl: Lo Bailey, Landon Fitzroy, and
the Scandal That Brought Down a Dynasty."
Found among possessions of August Fletcher, 8/3/2025

CHAPTER TEN

July 26, 2025

8 Days Left

I get maybe two hours of sleep before my alarm goes off, and it's awful, those few seconds of consciousness when my brain tells me, *Edie's got it, you can sleep a little longer.*

And then I remember that Edie is currently lying in a hospital bed ten miles up the road and once again, it's just me. Alone.

But when I manage to drag myself through the back door of the inn just after six, it turns out I'm not alone.

Lo is sitting on the couch in the lobby, and for the first time since she's shown up in St. Medard's, she looks, if not her age, at least close to it. The early morning sunlight highlights the creases by her eyes, the deeper grooves framing her mouth.

She's wearing a baby-blue satin robe over a white cotton nightgown, and when she sees me, she leaps up. "Oh my God, honey, how are you?" she asks, rushing over to me.

I let her fold me into a hug, but only for a second, hoping she doesn't notice the way I tense up when her arms go around me.

It's easier in the bright light of day to believe that she couldn't have had anything to do with Edie's fall. That it was exactly what it looked like, a simple slip that turned into something more serious. But I can't forget how she'd glared at Edie yesterday, how hard her eyes had been, even as her pink lips stayed curved in a smile.

"I'm fine," I lie, going over to the front desk and wiggling the mouse to wake up the computer monitor. "I mean, I'm tired and I'm worried about Edie, but physically, I'm okay."

"How is she?" Lo asks, her voice smooth like syrup. I look up, searching her face for some clue, for anything that might tell me if she's being sincere right now.

But I don't know her well enough for that, and even if I did, something tells me that Lo got very good at hiding what she might be feeling a long time ago.

I repeat what the doctor told me last night, adding that when I called the hospital earlier this morning, they said there hadn't been any change, good or bad.

"As long as she's not getting worse, that's the main thing," Lo says decisively, then glances out toward the porch, pulling her robe tighter around her. "I can't imagine what she was doing out there. Especially in that weather."

"Neither can I," I reply, but the words come out too flat, too blunt.

Lo's head swivels back to me, and I feel her eyes move over my face as I look back down at the computer. Then she says, "Did you talk to August when you got back?"

I've got nothing to feel guilty about, and yet weirdly, that's the oily emotion that unfurls in my belly at her question. The memory of his mouth on mine is suddenly so vivid that I feel like I'm probably projecting it directly into her brain.

"It's just that I heard him leave his room sometime around

two, and he didn't come back until nearly four. I wondered if he'd decided to wait up for you."

"He did, yeah," I say, letting my gaze flick back down to the computer like it's no big deal, like I'm only half paying attention. "He was worried about Edie."

"And you, I'm sure."

My eyes shoot back up. Lo is still watching me with that faintly appraising gleam, and I can't keep the irritation out of my voice when I say, "He was, yeah. He's a good guy. We've become friends. Or at least friend*ly*."

"Is that all you are?"

There's a sharpness in her tone that I haven't heard directed at me before, and it makes me straighten up to my full height, my arms folded over my chest. The lack of sleep and the worry have left me jagged, an open wound. "Lo, if there's something you want to say about me and August, please just get to it. I have a lot to do this morning."

"I just don't think it's a good idea, is all," she says, almost breezy as she shrugs and fiddles with the belt of her robe. "You and him."

I almost laugh out loud at her frankness. "Wow. Okay. Any particular reason why?"

"For one, I know his type," she says. "He's charming and sweet, and smarter than any man that pretty should be, but at the end of the day, the only person he's ever really gonna love is himself."

"Are you describing August or Landon?" I ask, and she jerks her head back, blinking.

It's the first time I've seen Lo caught off guard, but it doesn't last long. "Ooh, Ellen Chambers's Little Girl has some *bite* to her. Good for you, baby!"

"I'm just saying, I'm not sure you know August as well

as you think you do," I say. "You just met him, what? A few months ago? And only because you wanted someone to write your book. It's not like you've been best friends or . . . or *lovers*, or whatever."

Lo's brow wrinkles in confusion. "I didn't want him to write my book. *He* wanted to write *my* story."

A lie, I know. August told me himself that she was the one to reach out, and why would he make something like that up?

But Lo is already waving it away. "Doesn't matter. Point is, I'm telling you, you don't want anything to do with that boy. I'm just giving you the same advice your mama would—"

"Don't," I say, and my voice doesn't even sound like mine.

Lo blinks again, then steps closer to me, her brow puckering. "Have I done something?" she asks, and it's right there on the tip of my tongue.

Well, Lo, that's what I'm starting to wonder.

Instead, I take a deep breath. "I'm sorry," I tell her. "I'm just really on edge about Edie, I'm running on a couple hours of sleep, and you just surprised me with this August stuff."

I don't know if she fully accepts that explanation. There's something about the way she's watching me, about how she's fiddling with the silver ring on her middle finger. Lo is too self-possessed to fidget, too confident in her own skin, certain that she belongs in any room she walks into.

Finally, she gives me a tight smile, her hands falling to her side. "You must be *exhausted*, honey. I get it. I need a full eight hours and three cups of coffee, or *someone's* head is getting bitten clean off!"

She laughs and pats my shoulder, but the only head I'm thinking of is Edie's, covered in blood—and Landon Fitzroy's, under that same porch, his own skull cratered.

I gesture toward the office. "I . . . need to . . ."

"Go on, go on," she says with a wave, and if it weren't for the way her hand goes back to that ring, twisting and twisting it, I'd think she was every bit as fine as she's trying so hard to appear.

It's weird, flipping on the light in the office, seeing the desk empty. Edie is always here before me; this is her "command center," as she likes to call it. Her *Star Trek* mug still holds cold coffee from yesterday, and my throat goes tight again as I gently push the mug aside and sit down at the desk, robotically running through the usual checklist. Emails first—a couple asking if we do weddings, someone looking to book over Christmas, and then, right in a row, three cancellations, all for next week.

My eyes skate over them, my stomach knotting.

Looking at the weather . . .

With the potential for a bad storm . . .

Probably an overreaction, but better safe than sorry!

I've been so consumed with Lo and my mom, Edie and August, that I haven't paid that much attention to the forecast in the last twenty-four hours. Or rather, I've always left that to Edie since it's her particular obsession, trusting her to tell me when something is—literally—on the horizon.

Sure enough, when I pull up the NOAA website, there it is.

It's far out still, somewhere over Central America, but it's big. Bands spiral out from the eye like tentacles.

I know it's the fear and exhaustion taking its toll, but looking at it—at *her*, Tropical Storm Lizzie—I can't help thinking that she's already reaching out for us, trying to pull herself across land and sea to demand her traditional sacrifice from St. Medard's Bay.

I'm so absorbed that I don't hear August come in, don't even notice him until he's right at the edge of the desk.

"Bad weather headed this way?" he asks, and I startle slightly, glancing up at him. I'd avoided mirrors this morning, but if I look as bad as August does, it's going to take more than an extra cup of coffee to get me passing for human. His skin has a faint grayish pallor, stubble thick on his jaw, and his eyes are bloodshot. His hair is rumpled, a little greasy, and I realize he's still in the same clothes he was wearing last night.

"Yeah," I tell him, turning back to the computer and tapping the screen. "This bitch Lizzie is getting hotter and stronger, and it looks like she might head this way. Hopefully she fizzles out somewhere around Mexico, but if not . . ."

If not, we could just get a lot of rain.

If not, she could swing west and become Mississippi's problem.

Or, *if not*, we find out whether the Rosalie has some luck left in her yet.

I turn off the monitor, those whirls and swirls already making me vaguely motion sick, and rest my elbows on the desk, pinching the bridge of my nose as I take a deep breath.

"Anyway. That's my morning so far. Yours?"

August stands there, one hand flexing at his side, and I can tell he's trying to figure out how to say something. Had he run into Lo on his way here?

"If it's about last night—" I start, but he shakes his head, cutting me off.

"No. Well, yes, but not . . . it's not about . . ." He trails off, looks away. It's like he doesn't want to meet my eyes right now, and that's almost more alarming than those weather maps.

"August, what's going on?"

He does glance over at me now, clearly still weighing something in his mind, and then he steps forward, his shoulders tense.

"I was up all night looking through your mom's . . . collection, clippings, whatever you want to call it. And you were right. There wasn't much in there that I didn't already know, or that wasn't just your usual tabloid crap. But that wasn't why I couldn't sleep. I kept thinking, 'Why?,' you know? 'Why did your mom keep all of this?' You said it yourself, she never really talked about any of this to you when you were growing up."

"She didn't talk about it *at all*," I correct. "I didn't even realize that she and Lo were close."

"Right. And then I thought, 'Maybe she was just into true crime, or maybe she thought it would be interesting for the hotel and its history one day, if she kept a record.' And that made sense to me for a while."

I consider that theory, nodding. "That could make sense to me, too. Though, I know she wasn't into true crime—like, not even *Dateline* or *20/20*, things like that. I've always loved those shows, and she used to tease me about watching them. But she definitely saw herself as . . . the keeper of the flame, I guess. The Rosalie Historian."

August nods, a lank of hair falling over his brow before he impatiently pushes it back.

"Exactly. Solid theory, nothing weird about it, just a record of an extraordinary thing that happened in her town, involving one of her best friends. Especially if it's true that Landon's body was found here. But it still bothered me for some reason, and I kept feeling like I was missing something. So I got out all my research on the case, on Lo, on Landon. And when I didn't find anything there, I went online and I searched for . . ."

He stops himself, reaching into the pocket of his shorts to pull out his cell phone. His fingers move across the screen, and when he sets the phone on the edge of the desk, I see his hand is shaking.

A young woman smiles back at me, her dark hair shiny over her bare shoulders, her skin pale against the black velvet drape. It's a senior portrait, probably from the '70s, if her hair and makeup are anything to go by, but what I'm most struck by is just how much this woman looks like . . . me.

Her eyes are dark, not hazel, and her chin is just a little bit weaker, but for the first time in my life, I look into another face and recognize my thin nose, my upside-down mouth, upper lip fuller than the bottom, my strong brows, the one dimple in my left cheek.

I raise my eyes to August, my mouth dry, my pulse thudding heavily in my chest, my throat, my ears.

"Who is this?"

"Camile Fitzroy," he says, and I know the next words he'll say before they're even out of his mouth.

"Landon Fitzroy's sister."

"Landon," I hear myself nearly whisper, and August nods, his mouth now set in a hard line.

"Geneva, did you really not know Landon Fitzroy was your father?"

VELMA

November 20, 1980

Landon always knew he had a destiny.

From a lot of people, that would probably sound pretentious, but when he said it, it just sounded like a fact.

I think it's the way he was raised. His whole family was like that, all the Fitzroys. Big believers in signs and blessings and fate.

We Chamberses were a little more down to earth than all that. The only "destiny" I ever had was knowing that one day, the Shipwreck Inn would be mine.

Lo used to tell me how lucky that made me. "You're gonna be so *fancy*," she'd say, which was Lo's highest praise. There was nothing better in this world than being *fancy* as far as Lo was concerned, but I'd been working beside my parents at the Rosalie since I was old enough to hand Daddy a wrench, and I knew there was nothing *fancy* about running an inn, not even one that was on the beach.

But then it was the inn that brought me Landon.

I was fifteen the first time he came to St. Medard's Bay. It was November, the offseason, my favorite time of year. For one, it wasn't hotter than Satan's armpit like it was from April all the way to Halloween, and for another, that was the only time the inn ever really felt like a *home*, like our home. When it was just me and my parents, with only the occasional guest to mar the illusion.

And I loved the beach in November. St. Medard's Bay is famous for its clear water and white-sugar sand, but I liked it best when the sky was gray and looming, the water darker, whitecaps frothing. I could walk for hours along the shore in November, the sleeves of my sweatshirt tugged over my hands, my feet bare and numb from the water, the wind blowing my hair back from my face.

Lo was the one with the flair for drama—she was always making up stories for us to act out, and God help you if you'd decided your Barbies should be going to prom when *she* thought they should be attending a royal wedding. I mostly just went along with whatever she said because it was easier, and because, to be honest, her stories and ideas usually *were* better than anything I could come up with.

But out on that beach, my brain ran wild with my own stories. I was a sailor's wife anxiously scanning the horizon for her beloved, or a mermaid who'd been turned into a human against her will and now longed to go back to the sea. I once spent so long imagining that I was a castaway shipwrecked on a deserted island that I ended up walking nearly two miles away without even realizing it. Mom had to send Cap, the guy who did odd jobs around the inn, down the beach to find me.

I never acted these things out. Even when I was little, that kind of thing had been hard for me, shy as I was. But in a way, I liked that, that no one looking at me had any idea of all of the things going on in my head. To them, I just looked like Boring Ellen Chambers, the one who got great grades but never had much to say, the one who let "that little Bailey girl run right over her!"

But inside, there were worlds. Universes. And they were all mine.

Lo was one of the only people who got that about me, actually. Lo, and later, Landon.

Funny when you think about it.

Or awful.

Anyway, like I said, it was November, usually a dead time for the inn, but that year, 1980, we were busy. A group of men had booked a deep-sea fishing trip, and for whatever reason, they'd decided that our inn was the place to stay.

I don't even remember how many of them there were. When they checked in, it seemed like dozens and dozens, there were so many loud, deep voices emanating from the lobby, so many flashing watches on perpetually tanned wrists, so many Hawaiian shirts unbuttoned to reveal chest hair. It was way too much testosterone for me, and I'd planned on mostly staying out of their way. It would've been easy to do—I had school, and they'd be out on the boats all day.

But that year, the weather decided to remind us that hurricane season technically ran all the way past Thanksgiving, thank you very much, and just one day after that herd of men checked in to the Shipwreck, a nasty tropical storm out of the Caribbean started gathering strength and turning our way.

"Velma," Lo announced the day before the storm hit, me, her, and Frieda in our normal spot at the end of the lunch table. It was turkey tetrazzini day, normally Frieda's favorite lunch, but that afternoon, she just picked at it.

"That's what they're calling the storm," Lo went on, pulling one leg up onto the bench next to her and swinging an arm around her knee. As she did, the wide leg of her shorts sagged just enough to flash me and Frieda a glimpse of her bright pink underwear. "Velma. Like in *Scooby-Doo*. Sooooo lame. The one that killed my daddy was called Delphine. Now *that* is a cool as shit name for a storm. Even Audrey was—"

"Hush," I heard myself say, my eyes darting to Frieda.

We hardly ever talked about Audrey, about what had happened to Frieda's family.

About how if we hadn't lied—if we hadn't gone along with Lo's plan—they might never have been out in that storm looking for Frieda, and then they would still be alive.

To be honest, sometimes I could hardly bear to think about it.

But Frieda just shook her head and sighed. "She's right, Velma is a stupid name. But this late in the year, I guess they didn't have many choices left."

"Zelda," Lo offered up. She was in her Zelda Fitzgerald phase at the time. Lo had barely passed English, but that was just because she never turned things in. I knew she'd read *The Great Gatsby* at least three times just for fun, so I wasn't surprised that was the name she picked.

"It's funny, isn't it?" I asked, looking between the two of them. "How the storms that make landfall here are always named after women?"

"Females are deadlier than males!" Lo whooped, sending several heads turning in our direction, but as usual, Lo didn't care if people stared. She just smiled brightly at Tammy Turner, the girl sitting closest to us, then snapped her teeth open and shut hard, once, twice. Like she was biting something's head off.

"Y'all are weird," Tammy muttered, but before Lo could say something that would probably get her another round of after-school detention, the intercom overhead rang out three shrill tones.

Our principal, Mr. McGinnis, came on, his nasally drawl letting us know that, due to the "potential for severe weather," school would be dismissed early today, after fifth period, and that classes were canceled for the next two days, Thursday and Friday.

There were a few claps, a few half-hearted cheers, but Audrey had put the fear of storms back into all of us, and even the promise of a long weekend was nothing to celebrate if it meant St. Medard's Bay was once again in the monster's path.

When I got back to the inn that afternoon, I expected all the deep-sea fishing guys would have left. They'd gone out a few times already, before the weather had turned, and there definitely wouldn't be any more fishing trips until Velma had passed.

But to my surprise, they were still there. Or at least some of them were.

Two were on the beach, filling up sandbags, and I saw another hauling gallon jugs of water around the corner of the porch. A fourth guy was down near the prefab tin building we used as a toolshed, helping Daddy set up a couple of sawhorses. Big slabs of plywood rested against the shed, ready to be sawed into the right size to cover the windows.

When I stepped into the lobby, there were two other men moving the green sofa away from the windows, joking and laughing as they did, their teeth very white in their sunburned faces.

When Mama caught sight of me, she pointed upstairs. "You know the drill!"

That meant filling the tubs with water. When Audrey hit, all of St. Medard's had been without water for over a week. Mama said when Delphine came through, it was nearly a month. The jugs I'd seen that man bringing in would be for drinking, but the bathtubs would be for everything else, and as I walked into Room 202, I wondered if

Frieda's parents had filled their bathtubs before Audrey, and what was the point of doing that at all if the storm just killed you, or blew down your house *and* its bathtubs?

There was a good view of the beach from 202, and I glanced toward it as I closed the door behind me. The sky was gray and cloudy, the water rough, but the awful wind that was seared into my memory from Audrey hadn't picked up yet. I was telling myself that maybe this one was going to just miss us, or at least not be as bad, when a sound from the bathroom nearly sent me jumping out of my skin.

It was the tub running, I realized, and I had a disorienting moment where I thought maybe I'd already done this room on autopilot and forgotten. But then a figure stepped into the doorway, backlit by the lights from the vanity behind him.

"Oh!" he said. "Um. Hi?"

He waved then, awkwardly, and laughed a little before shoving his hands into his back pockets. "Sorry, am I not supposed to be in here?"

Then he took another step forward, and the face that had been shrouded in darkness was suddenly fully visible.

Of the two of us, Landon was the one who believed in destinies, but in that moment, I think I believed in them, too, because my heart—my very *soul*—seemed to lurch inside me.

You're going to say that it's because I was fifteen, and here was the best-looking man I'd ever seen *in my life* smiling at me, almost a little sheepishly. That the frisson I felt, that sudden sense that I was waking up for the very first time, was nothing more than teenage hormones running amok.

And maybe you're right. My inexperience, my naïveté, were definitely part of it. Landon was only twenty-six that year but still a grown man in my eyes, and yet *not* like those other men downstairs. Those men felt like . . . well, dads, honestly, regardless of whether they actually had kids. They felt like capital-M Men in a way that freaked me out at that age.

But Landon seemed somewhere in between them and the boys my age, not coarse and loud and hairy like those guys, not gangly and sweaty and embarrassing like the boys I went to school with. His hair was a little too long, and instead of a Hawaiian shirt and khaki shorts, he was wearing jeans and a Led Zeppelin T-shirt.

He had the prettiest eyes, too. Nearly black, so dark you couldn't see his pupils.

"Like a shark," Lo said later, but that's not what I saw. Not then.

"I was filling up the bathtubs—that's what you're supposed to do in this kind of thing, right?" he went on, and my face felt scorched as I realized I'd been standing there, just staring at him, not saying anything.

"N-no. I mean, yes, yes, that's what you're supposed to do, that's actually what *I* was coming in here to do, but you're not . . . well, you're not *not* supposed to be in here."

"Not not supposed to be in here," he repeated, scratching his jaw and studying the ceiling. "Okay, so I do believe that means I'm allowed in here, then?"

I couldn't tell if he was teasing me or making fun of me—there's a difference, and by fifteen, I was very aware of that, especially where boys were concerned—but then he smiled at me and reached out, gently thumping my arm.

"Sorry if I scared you. Honestly, I was just trying to make myself useful doing something that *wasn't* hard labor."

He winked, and I somehow blushed even hotter, and then he laughed and said, "But if you're here to take over, I guess I'll have to go be manly with power tools or prove I can lift more sandbags than Dave."

Then he tilted his head, squinting at me. "Unless you need an assistant?"

"I do," I blurted out because in that moment, I would've done just about anything to keep talking to Landon Fitzroy.

I didn't know that's who he was until we were out in the hall and he formally introduced himself, but the name didn't mean anything to me back then anyway. Remember, I was fifteen and living in a small town. I barely paid attention to anything that wasn't school or my friends or the inn, so I definitely wasn't well-versed in Alabama politics. Didn't know Landon's father was the state treasurer with an eye on the governor's office. Didn't know Landon had been a big deal in football at the University of Alabama, or that he was finishing up law school in the spring.

And I certainly didn't know he was engaged.

Here was what I knew about Landon after that hour we spent filling bathtubs and sinks:

He loved music, the louder the better, and had seen the Doors play in Miami when he was just fifteen—had snuck out, hitchhiked, scared his poor mama half to death.

He'd hated school but liked history, enough that he'd gotten his degree in it at Alabama.

He'd come to St. Medard's Bay as a kid with his grandparents a few times and loved it, thought it was the most perfect place on God's green earth because it never changed. Every time he came back, it was like everything had been "preserved in amber" waiting for him.

He wanted to buy a boat, his own boat. His family had one, but it was too big, too grand, "like trying to take the fucking QE Two—pardon my French—out in a backyard pool."

He wanted to sail around the world, wanted to spend as much of his life on the water as he could for as long as he could.

The whole time we talked, he never once treated me like a kid. But he also wasn't creepy, either, you know? I was sheltered, but I'd been around older boys, and I knew when they were looking at me in a way they shouldn't. When they were assessing how they could take advantage.

That wasn't Landon. It was more like I was his buddy, just an interesting person he'd decided to pass the time with, and I loved that, loved how often he said my name as we talked, loved how he laughed when I told him that *living* in St. Medard's Bay sometimes felt like being frozen in time, too, but not in a good way.

Later, I realized he never really asked me much about myself, that I wasn't so much "a companion" as I was "an audience."

Another quality that he and Lo had in common.

By the time I went back downstairs to see if Mom needed anything else, I was in the throes of a crush so powerful it was almost painful, but I wasn't in love with Landon Fitzroy.

That happened the next afternoon, when Velma made landfall.

So much of that storm is still a blur. It wasn't as bad as Audrey, thank God. For one, we knew how seriously to take preparations this time, so all of us—me, my parents, Landon and his fishing buddies— were huddled in the kitchen in the back of the inn when the wind started to howl.

There were no windows in there, plus there was a back staircase up to the second floor in case we needed to get higher, so it was the safest place to be.

That didn't stop me from giving a small, panicked cry when the flickering lights finally went out, plunging all of us into pitch-black darkness.

"Fuck," Daddy muttered, the first and only time I ever heard him swear, and I could hear him fumbling around for the big flashlight he'd brought but hadn't wanted to turn on until he absolutely needed it because it went through batteries so fast.

Outside, the wind sounded like it had the night of Audrey, like something human and angry, and panic was a trapped bird in my chest as I squeezed my eyes shut despite the total darkness we were already in.

The air around me moved slightly, and two scents filled my nose— the Irish Spring soap we put in every guest room, and something else, something sweet and floral.

Violet candy, I later learned. A weird, old-fashioned sweet that Landon's grandmother had loved, and she'd passed on that love to him, so he was forever pulling out that bright purple foil tube and popping one, sometimes two into his mouth.

It meant that when you kissed him, he tasted like flowers, but I wouldn't know that for years yet.

In November of 1980, sitting in that dark kitchen while Velma pounded her fury against the walls of my home, I knew only that his hand was warm and sure when it lay against my upraised palm, and that his voice in my ear was gentle as he said, "You're gonna be okay."

I could hear the smile in his voice as he added, "You're with me, and trust me, I'm not going out like this. So no one with me is, either."

Daddy's flashlight blazed on then, but when it landed on us, Landon had already pulled back his hand and subtly moved back a few inches.

Upstairs, I heard something crack, but Landon didn't even flinch. He just sat back with his arms wrapped around his upraised knees and let the storm rage all around him.

Like I said, it was years after that night before we ever kissed, before I knew what his touch felt like elsewhere on my body. And when Lo asked me later—tears on her face, blood on her hands—when it had started, and how, I told her about the letters we wrote back and forth, the secret looks. The time he reached for my hand as we passed each other in the lobby at the Rosalie.

I told her about the night—the one night—on his boat, the one with his wife's name on the side, the one that he'd finally docked in St. Medard's Bay Harbor, just like he'd always wanted.

How he looked at me under the stars, took a deep breath, and said, "Please tell me you've been thinking about this for as long as I have," before kissing me with violets and sugar on his tongue.

And that's the truth, but like many things in life—so, so many things—it's not the whole truth.

What started between me and Landon began on that kitchen floor, his hand in mine, a storm all around us, and Landon offering his destiny like some kind of protective cloak he could drape over anyone he cared about.

"I'm not going out like this," he'd said.

And he was right. But what was waiting for him instead—his real destiny, the path he started down the first time his grandparents drove him into St. Medard's Bay on a sunny Fourth of July the year before I was born—was much, much worse.

CHAPTER ELEVEN

July 27, 2025

7 Days Left

Slowly, the inn starts emptying out.

The few guests who hadn't already canceled decide to leave early. I numbly agree to refunds and hear myself say things like "Always a gamble this time of year!" and "Of course, there's no sense in staying and worrying!" But it's like some other Geneva has taken over, some autopilot system that knows how to walk and talk and say the right thing to guests while the other Geneva—the real one—sits shattered and unmoored and overwhelmed.

I've lived in this kind of split world ever since yesterday morning, ever since August's question—*Geneva, did you really not know Landon Fitzroy was your father?*—ripped my own personal space-time continuum in half.

I didn't know. Didn't even suspect.

That's what I'd told August, or tried to, after I'd gotten past the knee-jerk denial.

There's no way, I would've known, Mom would've told me once I was an adult, my dad would've realized, and he never—

But I hadn't even been able to finish the sentence because I knew it wasn't true, what I'd been about to say. That my father never would've raised another man's child as his own.

My dad was gentle, kind, easier to understand than Mom for so many reasons, and he'd loved my mom fiercely. Devotedly.

He'd loved me the same.

That's the one steadying thought I've been clinging to for the past twenty-four hours, that even if Landon Fitzroy had fathered me, Dad was still *my dad*, and that was a different thing, and in any other world, it would be the only thing that mattered. Except in *my* world, the man who fathered me had maybe been murdered, possibly by the woman currently staying at my inn, a woman who had apparently been very close with my mom but whom Mom had never mentioned.

Does Lo know?

That had been my first question to August, after the denials sputtered out, after my lips, numb with shock, could finally make sounds again.

I'm not sure, he'd replied, but his eyes had been almost feverishly bright as he'd said, *But if she did . . . Geneva, if Lo found out that Landon had also been seeing Ellen, that he'd gotten Ellen* pregnant . . .

He didn't have to finish the thought.

The motive they'd assigned Lo at her trial—that she was on the verge of being dumped and refused to take it—hadn't managed to hold much water. But what if she had learned that her lover, the man she was depending on, had simultaneously been carrying on with one of her closest friends? Was, in fact, having a *baby* with that friend?

Suddenly, murder might make a lot more sense.

I haven't seen Lo since yesterday morning. I figure she's giving me a wide berth after our tense moment in the lobby, and I'm grateful for it because I can't be sure that I won't start throwing questions—accusations—at her like they were grenades.

But at the same time, as I reminded August yesterday, it's just a picture. A picture isn't proof. The likeness is eerie, though, I admit that, and when August and I looked at the dates—when my parents got married, when Landon died, when I was born—they lined up. Landon was dead by August 5. Mom and Dad were engaged later that month, married by September, and I was born March 3.

"Which would've meant you were conceived in late May, early June," August had said, stacking his hands on top of his head as he gazed into the middle distance. "If we can find out if Landon was here around that time . . ."

That's when I'd bailed.

It was too much to process, and I could see that August's journalist brain was already whirring, the book morphing as a new narrative began taking shape in his head.

The book.

Another land mine exploding under my feet. If August was right, this revelation would be going into a book. This sordid secret that my mother had kept for years, not even revealing to her own flesh and blood, would be something strangers would read about on planes and in waiting rooms, or listen to while walking on treadmills, and they'd judge her—they'd judge *us*—and think what trashy people we were. Sure, it might mean more people came to the inn, but it would only be so that they could judge in person.

Those were the thoughts that circled my brain last night, round and round, keeping sleep far away until I'd finally gotten up, determined to look through Mom's clippings again only to

remember I'd given them to August, which had started all of . . .
this.

He wasn't around this morning, and by the time I've checked
out the last guest, my skin is nearly itching with the desire to get
out of the inn.

I go visit Edie first, but there's little change. It'll be a few
more days before they can start bringing her out of the coma,
and I get to see her for only a few minutes at a time, squeez-
ing her chilled hand, telling her the weather is fine and there's
nothing to worry about, even as a TV in the corner of the ICU
waiting room scrolls a banner saying Tropical Storm Lizzie has
officially been upgraded to a hurricane.

On the drive to Hope House, I pass the big Walmart and see
people bringing out cases of bottled water, mountains of toilet
paper, and I grip the steering wheel a little tighter.

There's little change at Hope House, either, but that's always
how it is. Like the whole place is frozen under glass and starts
up again only when someone visits.

Mom is sitting in her usual spot, her recliner turned toward
the windows, and I pause before I walk into the room, looking
at the back of her head.

The truth is in there, somewhere, under that fall of silvering
dark hair, but her disease means that she might as well be a
locked vault. The unfairness of it all washes over me every time
I'm here, but this time, there's a sharper edge to it, honed by
desperation.

*Just five minutes. Just give me five minutes with her so she
can tell me what happened that summer. Who I am, who she
was, because I'm not sure I know anymore.*

I move into her room, cross over to her chair, and crouch
down in front of it.

Her eyes look through me, her lips slightly parted. "Mom,"

I say softly. "Why didn't you tell me? About Landon Fitzroy. I understand why you couldn't when I was younger, but after Dad was gone. When I was an adult . . . I would've understood. Or I want to think I would have. And I wish you had trusted me with it. I wish . . ."

Too many things, really, and none of them are going to come true.

"Everything okay in here?"

I look past Mom to see Opal, my favorite nurse, standing in the doorway, a plastic pitcher in hand.

"Yes," I say, then can't help a bitter laugh. "I mean, no, but—"

"I get you, honey," Opal says, her eyes kind. "And don't you worry about this storm they say might be headed our way. Our director, Ms. Diane, lived through Marie back in eighty-four, and she takes evacuation orders seriously. If it gets bad, we'll get your mama somewhere safe."

Guilt stabs low and deep that I hadn't even been thinking about the storm, what they might need to do with Mom, but I nod at Opal and thank her.

Rising to my feet, my knees protesting, I sigh and lean down to kiss Mom's temple. "I love you. I miss you," I tell her, just like always, but this time, I lean in a little closer and murmur, "And I know whatever lies you told or secrets you kept, you had a good reason."

I glance down at her hands, hoping they might move like they did the other day, that she can give me some kind of sign all of this is getting through.

But they just lie there, limp in her lap.

The sleeve of her cardigan is snagged on something around her wrist, and I go to straighten it, smiling a little as I do. It's one of the things I've always liked about Hope House, that when they get the patients dressed, they'll add little bits of their own jewelry from home, something to help things feel a little more normal, a little less sad. I'd brought up a box of Mom's stuff when we moved her in. Not the fancy pieces like Grandma Eileen's ruby ring or the tennis bracelet Dad got her for their twenty-fifth anniversary, but some of the costume bits she had, things I'd seen her wear occasionally.

Her sweater has gotten caught on the little enamel flowers of a silver bangle, a bracelet Mom actually hadn't worn all that often in my memory, but one I liked for how different it was from anything else in her collection. The silver filigree makes it look like a tiara in miniature, and the flowers are cute and colorful, a now-faded riot of pinks and blues and yellows.

I situate it on her wrist, running my thumb over the silver disk that makes up the center of the bracelet, like a full moon rising over a garden.

For the first time, I realize there's an engraving on the disk, faded with time and wear but still visible.

I lift Mom's wrist up, her arm limp, and tilt the bracelet toward the window.

The light catches on the disk, a brief glare stinging my eyes, but not before I see the letter delicately etched into the surface.

L

LANDON P. FITZROY, ESQ.

5/12/84

E—

Sorry if my handwriting's a little shaky, but that's what seeing your return address on an envelope did to me. Not even two fingers of bourbon could get my heart to stop racing, so I figured I needed to write back to you right away, penmanship be damned!

First of all, you're welcome for the bracelet. I need to come clean and confess I didn't have it made—I actually found it in a flea market on the road between Foley and Daphne. One of those little side-of-the-road things that sells fruit and big bags of boiled peanuts. But I think that makes it more magical, and I hope you do, too. Like it was meant for me to find, meant for me to send to you, meant to open up some kind of path back to each other.

It made me think of you because it was so delicate, so feminine. The filigree, the little enamel flowers, all of those seemed so *you*, so imagine my surprise when I looked more closely and saw there was an "L" engraved on that little silver disk in the center.

Is it awful and chauvinistic of me to like the idea of you wearing my initial?

Maybe. But if this is all I can give you of my name—for now—that's enough.

Ellen, I know there's a chance that you just wrote me that note to be polite, a good Southern girl sending her thank-you notes—even to a bastard like me—but I have to believe it's more. I have to believe you miss me, too.

Lo and I are done. It never should have started, and I'm so sorry for all of the pain it has caused you, but you broke my heart, sweet girl. You stopped talking to me, and I didn't know how else to get your attention. I promise you—I *swear*, yet again—that she doesn't know about us, never even suspected. I haven't even told her I'm planning on coming back to St. Medard's Bay for Memorial Day.

I'm planning to take the boat out to that little cove you showed me. The one my bootlegging great-uncle apparently used to hide out in.

May 28. Early evening for the sunset.

Meet me there?

In hope (as always, forever),

LPF

It's impossible to know just how many words were written about Lo Bailey's trial and the death of Landon Fitzroy, but I'm pretty sure I've read every one of them.

There were at least two books, both the kind of cheap paperback you could buy on a wire rack at the grocery store, each with a contrasting view of what happened. *Sweet Sixteen: Alabama's Deadly Prom Queen* obviously posits that Lo did it, but given how much it gets wrong (Lo was nineteen, she was never prom queen, and at one point, the narrative breaks with reality completely and claims Lo killed Landon to get her hands on incriminating recordings of various political high rollers, apparently because she wanted to blackmail them and start a fancy brothel in Birmingham), it's almost offensive that they ever expected anyone to pay $2.99 for that trash. Adding insult to injury, I had to pay a lot more on eBay, thanks to it being long out of print.

The other one, *Deadly Waters, Deadly Love*, comes down much harder on Landon Fitzroy, who's portrayed as a reckless playboy, seducing a naïve teenager only to get himself killed because he didn't take the storm warnings seriously—and because he was desperate to bed his barely legal mistress after a long separation. It's not well written, either, but at least it mostly sticks to the facts of the case: no blackmail, no Best Little Whorehouse in Alabama flights of fancy. Also, it was less expensive to track down, although when I look at how much money—not to mention *time*—I've been giving to all things Lo and Landon for the past two years, it's probably ridiculous to care about an extra hundred bucks here or there.

Books, flights, hotels, private investigators . . . all of it adds up.

But no one ever said obsession was cheap.

The fact that *this* book exists, though, that you're now holding it in your hands?

That makes every penny spent worth it. I tumbled down this rabbit hole two years ago trying to solve a mystery, trying to answer questions I hadn't known I needed to ask.

What I found was something deeper, stranger, and far more twisted than I ever could have guessed. St. Medard's Bay wasn't a town with one mystery—there were many, coiled around one another like the inside of a nautilus shell.

And at the heart of those mysteries, a place: the Rosalie Inn, that pink building that had achieved damn near mythic status in St. Medard's Bay, the one structure always left standing no matter how fierce the wind and waves.

And in that place—four women. Four women also left standing in the wake of destruction, four women who somehow managed to be as blessed as the Rosalie Inn, and as cursed as St. Medard's Bay.

The Mother.

The Loner.

The Liar.

The Murderer.

And which was which?

Pages of unfinished manuscript titled
"Be a Good Girl: Lo Bailey, Landon Fitzroy, and
the Scandal That Brought Down a Dynasty."
Found among possessions of August Fletcher, 8/3/2025

CHAPTER TWELVE

July 28, 2025

6 Days Left

It's just past seven when I knock on August's door the next morning.

I can hear him in there, the clatter of his keyboard, but it still takes a second knock and then a third before he comes to the door.

When he does, I see this week has done just as much of a number on him as it has on me. Between Edie, the revelation about Landon being my father, and the storm slowly making its way up from the Caribbean, I feel beyond shattered, and I look it, too. My skin is pale, my eyes red, the circles beneath them so dark they look bruised.

August is the same, his stubble thick and dark against his grayish skin, and as he frowns at me, deep parentheses appear on either side of his mouth.

"What's up, Geneva?" he asks, standing in the doorway. Over his shoulder, his laptop glows, and I see the still-unmade bed, smell the faint odor of burnt coffee and unwashed man. Gone is the charming, smiling guy who first stepped into the Rosalie just a few weeks ago, and as he looks at me with barely suppressed irritation, I wonder if this is some kind of writer thing. Like he's "in the zone" now and can't be bothered by my interruption.

In any case, he can get over it.

Pointing into his room, I say, "I wanted to get that box back from you."

I don't figure I need to specify which box, but his frown only deepens, and at first, I think it must be confusion.

"The . . . box? Of my mom's? With the articles and stuff in it?"

Rubbing the back of his neck, August glances over his shoulder briefly before turning back to me and asking, "Why?"

I blink at that, unsure of how to reply. It didn't occur to me he might not want to give the box back, and I suddenly feel awkward standing there, the memory of our kiss still lingering between us.

A few excuses flit through my brain—*There's something I need to double-check* or *I want to make sure it's safe when the storm comes*—but then I think, *Fuck that*, and go with the simple truth. "Because it's mine?"

There's no real argument to that, although I can see August looking for one before he finally sighs and heads into his room, pushing the door slightly closed as he does.

When he returns, he's got the box in his arms, but I swear it doesn't look as full as it did the last time I saw it.

But I let that go for now, giving him a terse "Thanks" before turning away.

I'm only a few steps from his door when I hear the keyboard clicking away again, and an uneasy, sour feeling settles in my stomach.

He's writing so much because now his story has an actual angle, a real scoop.

Me.

I push that thought away and carry the box up to the second floor, shifting it onto my hip as I reach up to pull down the attic stairs.

As they thump onto the carpet hallway, heat rolls down from the attic, and I grimace but start climbing up anyway.

The heat and humidity are a physical thing, a crushing weight as I flail around for the light switch that turns on a bare bulb overhead.

I hardly ever come up here anymore. I look around, taking in the broken deck chairs, the covered pieces of Grammy's old furniture from the '70s, a giant console stereo with a turntable, extra sandbags, all the flotsam and jetsam of a building that's both a business and a family home.

I let the box thump to my feet, sending up a cloud of dust, and even though it's hot as hell and I'm sweating everywhere a person can sweat, I sit down and start digging through the box yet again.

This time, though, I'm not looking for anything about Lo.

I'm looking for Landon.

And holy shit, do I find him.

Looking at this collection now, knowing what I know, I understand why there's nothing really about the trial, or even the investigation.

This was never meant to be a record of Gloria Bailey—Mom's old friend who became infamous overnight and who, *possibly*, committed murder.

No. Instead, it's a memorial to a man she loved—and lost.

I see it now, in the creases of every glossy magazine page that has Landon's face on it. I see it in the way the articles aren't just about him, but about his family. His wife, his father.

And yes, his sister, Camile. Her engagement announcement is buried toward the bottom of the box, something I'd overlooked the first time I'd gone through it because a small column of newsprint with no pictures didn't warrant a second glance.

I now see what August, with his keen and skeptical journalist's eye, must have seen when he reviewed everything my mother had saved, and it breaks my fucking heart.

Somehow, even with the picture of Camile, even with the "L" bracelet on Mom's wrist, I still wanted to believe it couldn't be possible.

Yet it is, the truth so undeniable that it's now slapping me in the face. Landon and my mother slept together. And Landon is my father.

But why did she hold on to all of this, for her entire life? Given the pains she went to in getting her affairs in order after she received her diagnosis, why didn't she destroy the box and its damning contents? Was she saving it for me to discover one day?

Was that what this was all about?

I wipe sweat from my forehead with the hem of my T-shirt, then paw through the box all over again, like I'm missing something, like there will be some hidden message from Mom explaining everything, or a hidden diary that I somehow missed but was tucked inside a glossy magazine all along.

Of course there isn't. Of course it's just the same magazine pages as always, but then something catches my eye.

It's a black-and-white shot of Landon standing by a lake, majestic mountains rising in the distance. He's wearing a short-sleeved button-down and aviator sunglasses, his grin wide as he poses with his hands in his back pockets, one foot resting on a rock in front of him.

I get it, looking at that picture, why my mom and Lo both would've gone so crazy for this guy. He's good-looking, sure, but it's more than that. He radiates a kind of confidence and ease that would draw anyone in, and his smile looks so . . . kind. It's a good smile.

It's my smile.

And then I see the caption beneath the photo.

Fitzroy in 1976, while studying in Geneva, Switzerland.

My name has always been a bit of a weird one, even in the South, where people are routinely named things like Hilliard or Sterling. I asked Dad where they got it from once, and he said he thought Mom had read it in a book. But when I asked her, she said, *A friend of mine said Lake Geneva was the prettiest place he'd ever seen, and I thought it was the prettiest* name *I'd ever heard.*

I think back on that moment now, trying to remember it clearly, trying to visualize Mom's face as she uttered those words. I know that whatever my brain is conjuring—a wistfulness in her tone, a dreamy look into the middle distance—is just my imagination, not an actual memory.

But if I needed any more proof, this does it for me.

By the time I come down from the attic, I'm sweaty and red, my eyes stinging from the crying jag I had as I slid the box on top of an old chifforobe up there, the highest place I could find, just in case.

The lobby is empty, the Rosalie feeling eerily quiet, and I jump when my phone abruptly trills from my back pocket.

When I see the caller is the hospital, my stomach fills with ice.

I answer only to learn that nothing has changed, that Edie is still in her coma but "doing as well as can be expected," and that they'll be in touch soon should anything new develop.

I've just ended the call when I hear August ask, "Any news?"

Startled, I turn to see him standing in the hallway just behind me, his shoulder against the doorjamb, his arms folded over his chest.

I shake my head, shoving my sweaty hair back from my face. "Not really. Edie is still with us at least, but no telling when she'll wake up."

"And no telling what she'll say when she does," he replies. "I wonder if she'll even remember Lo attacking her."

"We don't know that's what happened," I say, my voice nearly a whisper, but August only looks at me, his expression unreadable.

"If it wasn't her, Geneva, then *who* was it?" he asks, and I suddenly realize why I've been trying so hard to focus only on Edie's recovery, not on what happened to her.

Because August is right. If it wasn't an accident—which, based on the severity of Edie's injuries, seems increasingly likely—it had to be Lo.

But *if* it wasn't Lo . . .

I watch as August retreats back down the hall to his book, and for the first time, I wonder if I've put my trust in the wrong person.

CHAPTER THIRTEEN

August 3, 2025

1 Day Left

By the last day of July, there's no doubt Hurricane Lizzie is headed straight for us. The TV in the lobby, the computer in the office, the app on my phone—all of them show her getting bigger and bigger, her turn almost graceful as she bypasses Cuba, her gaze instead focused on the Gulf Coast of Alabama.

On St. Medard's Bay.

Edie, still unconscious in her hospital bed, would've already left town by now. And she would've told me to do the same.

But I stay.

August, Lo, and I are the only people left at the Rosalie. All the other guests have checked out or canceled their stays, so there was no reason to ask any other staff to come in until after the storm had passed. There's barely any reason for *me* to be at the inn, but I don't know what to do with myself except show up every morning, so that's what I continue to do.

I make Walmart runs, stocking up on more bottled water,

batteries, and an extra first aid kit. Our handyman, Ray, comes by to help me move some of the outdoor furniture to the storage shed, and I take down all the hanging plants. I even do my best to secure the Airstream because if—*when*—the storm hits, I'll ride it out at the inn.

I tell myself that these are just smart precautions, that nothing may even happen, that hurricanes are notoriously unpredictable once they hit the warmer waters of the Gulf.

But I know.

It's like a steady thrumming behind my eyes as the pressure gets lower, the air thicker, and I wonder if it's some innate sixth sense I have, as a native of this town. Or could it be genetics, a spooky kind of inheritance? My rational mind knows that Lo and Edie and my mom were just little girls being silly when they called themselves the Witches of St. Medard's Bay, but maybe there was more to it. Or could it be that my real father is sending me a message from beyond the grave, urging me to take every possible precaution so I don't suffer the same fate?

My real father.

I try not to let myself indulge that line of thinking too often because I can already feel something giving way inside of me, some bulwark I hadn't even realized was keeping my sanity intact, despite everything.

But it's getting harder.

In the days leading up to the storm, I don't see that much of August or Lo, but I sense them constantly, almost like they're ghosts, haunting the place.

I hear August's laptop keyboard clicking away whenever I pass his room, and it's a reminder that he's potentially prepping a nuclear bomb to drop into my life. And maybe he understands that, because he's kept his distance ever since that morning in my office. The only real conversation we've had since was a few days ago, when I asked if he and Lo were going to leave.

He'd actually looked surprised, his eyebrows shooting up. "Are you kidding? And miss the chance to experience one of St. Medard's Bay's famous storms firsthand? I couldn't live with myself if that wasn't in the book."

"You won't be able to live with yourself *literally* if you *drown*," I'd replied. My tone was aiming for playful, trying to recapture whatever banter we'd had before, but he only looked at me with serious, dark eyes and said, "I didn't do all this not to take a few risks, Geneva."

All this? I'd thought, mentally rolling my eyes. *What have you done except come to a beach hotel and work on a laptop sixteen hours a day?*

But there was something about the gravity with which he'd said it that bothered me, even hours later, something I felt like I was missing. I kept remembering how terrible he'd looked when he came into the office with that picture of Camile Fitzroy on his phone, how . . . *consumed* he seemed by the fact that Landon could very well have been my father. I chalked it up to writers being writers—obsessive, consumed by the story they're weaving. Or maybe the falling air pressure alongside the almost unbearable tension that seemed to be rising inside the inn was making August as crazy as it was me.

I thought Lo might leave even if August wanted to stay, but when I'd asked, she'd given me that sweet-as-pie smile and said, "Baby, I'm one of the Witches of St. Medard's Bay, remember? I can't abandon it in its hour of need!"

And we were back to the witches.

I can't help but notice that she's writing, too.

Lo.

As I go about the inn, trying to find things to do, small

projects to keep me from spiraling into panic and madness, I see her perched on the sofa in the lobby or sitting in one of the rocking chairs on the porch, a yellow legal pad in hand, her pen scrawling so fast I wonder if later she'll even be able to read anything she's written.

It adds to the unreality of all of it, the idea of Lo and August in their separate corners, telling different versions of the same story. A story that might involve me far, far more than I ever could have guessed.

THAT NIGHT, I get two calls.

One is from the hospital, where Edie is still in critical condition. They brought her out of the induced coma, and while she's far from out of the woods, the prognosis is, as her doctor put it, "tentatively hopeful." Tonight, the call is to let me know that patients will not be evacuated unless they lose power, which would mean that all of their backup generators had gone out. The doctor assures me it isn't likely—St. Medard's Memorial is prepared for storms. "We've never lost power, not even during Marie, and that was a *doozy*," he tells me, chuckling, and I fight the urge to scream and laugh all at the same time.

Yup, sure was a fucking doozy, Doc.

The second call is from Hope House. They *are* evacuating a handful of patients, the ones who, like Mom, don't require intensive medical care. "She'll be at Magnolia Manor in Montgomery," Opal tells me. "Say *that* three times fast. I'll keep a close eye on her."

"I know you will," I say, but my voice is thin and tired.

We tell each other to stay safe, and I hang up, resting my phone against my chest as I study the ceiling over my bed. It's late, almost midnight, and from the little TV on my kitchen counter, I hear newscasters say things like "Landfall within the next thirty-six hours" and "Check generators and batteries" and "Not since Marie in eighty-four . . ."

Marie in '84.

Landon.

Lo.

My mom.

And now, more than forty years later, there's another hurricane, and instead of Mom, there's me.

Instead of Landon, there's August.

But in both cases, there's Lo, right back in the center of things—the eye of the storm itself.

The past feels like a wave, retreating for a while only to rush back in.

Which of us will be left standing when it slides back out to sea?

I lie there in the dark, my thoughts churning, my heart pounding, and then suddenly I'm on my feet and headed to the door.

The wind has started, and while it's not nearly as strong as it's going to get, it's enough to wrench the trailer door out of my hand as I open it. I can't see the ocean over the rise of the beach, but I can hear the surf pounding. The air itself feels heavy with moisture, and my lips are salty when I lick them.

I make my way to the inn, squinting against the wind and the fine bits of sand swirling in the air. With every step, I tell myself the same thing, the thought I had while I was lying there in my bed.

I'll make them leave. I can do that. I don't care that it's the middle of the night, I don't care that I'll be alone when that fucking bitch Lizzie slams into the Rosalie, I'm not doing this, I'm not reenacting this fucked-up story, I'm not offering up my life, my mom's *life for fucking* content, *I'm making them leave, I'm making them leave, I'm making them leave.*

I go to August's room, knock hard, and he answers almost immediately.

"Is it here?"

I blink at him, confused, but then I see his open laptop on the desk behind him, a document pulled up. An unusually sober Ray boarded up the windows this afternoon, so August has been shut away in here with his writing. I bet he hasn't even checked the weather in the past few hours. He told me that he can get completely absorbed in his work, but that's not what has me confused.

It's how . . . excited he seems. Eager, almost. Like he can't wait for waves and wind to pummel us.

That's good, though. It's the fuel I need to push into his room before turning to face him.

He leaves the door open, and there's a wariness to his expression, the way he's studying me.

"Geneva, I know you're stressed and scared, but the other night was . . . well, it was a mistake, I get that now. Really unprofessional of me, and now that you may end up being a much bigger part of all this—"

I hold up a hand. "For fuck's sake, August, I didn't come in here looking for some kind of hurricane hookup."

It's insulting how relieved he suddenly looks, but I ignore that and press on. "I want you and Lo out. Now."

Silence lands heavy between us, the wind outside muffled by all the boards.

"Now," August repeats slowly. "In the middle of a hurricane."

"It's not here yet," I tell him. "You can be in Montgomery before dawn, and there, the worst that might happen is you'll get rained on."

"Geneva," he says, and I don't like his tone, like he's trying to placate a pissed-off horse. "You don't want us to go. You don't want to go through this alone. You'll need help, or at least company. Don't make decisions when you're this freaked out."

"Here's a fun fact, August—the story of my life is going through shit alone. I very rarely have help, and I *definitely* don't have much company, and I am always—*always*—making decisions while freaked out. So yeah, I want you to leave. I'll deal with this like I've dealt with everything else."

"What's going on here?" August asks, stepping a little closer. He hasn't shaved in days now, his beard dark against his skin, which has gotten paler thanks to all his time locked in here with the book. He looks like he's lost a little weight, too, and I try to remember if I've seen him leaving to eat or get groceries in the last few days.

I turn away from him, clutching the back of the desk chair, trying to gather my thoughts as the wind keeps pounding against the inn, as the lights start to flicker. "It's just too much," I say. "Lo and my mom, and my . . . and Landon, and you, and this book."

I gesture to the computer screen, glancing at it as I do, and my eye snags on my name.

Leaning in closer, I read, *And Geneva. In the end, she was the one I felt the most sorry for, the only one who didn't, in some way, bring her own doom down on her head. But maybe it was natural that my sympathies would lie with her given*

It stops there, and I whirl around.

August is still standing near the door, his hands held out at hip level, knees bent like he might bolt. "What is this?" I ask, slashing a hand toward the screen, but before he can answer, there's a massive crash from the lobby, shaking the floorboards.

I move without thinking, my mind picturing a million and

one disasters, some of which make sense (a heavy planter I forgot to move from the side porch falling over), some of which are nonsensical (a piece of the wrecked *Rosalie* trying to beach itself at the door), but all of which fill me with a terror I hadn't known I could feel.

Not for me or my safety, but for the Rosalie Inn itself.

My home.

The one thing left from a family that might not have been what I thought it was, but that was still *mine*, was still *real*.

And under that terror there's a fierce need to protect this place, to do whatever it takes to keep it standing.

Which is why it knocks the breath out of me to come into the lobby and discover one of the sheets of plywood pulled from the big window facing the sea. That's what I'd heard, the board hitting the ground. And standing there, looking out at the raging sea and driving rain, is Lo.

She's got a hammer in her hand. Where she found it, I have no idea, but the only question right now is the one I scream.

"What the fuck are you doing?"

"You wanted to see a storm!" she calls back without turning around. With her back to us and her hair down, her slim body clad in a long pink silk nightgown, Lo could be the girl in those pictures from four decades ago.

For a dizzying, maddening moment, I wonder if she *is* that girl, if being here has somehow turned back the years and when she turns around, she won't be sixty anymore, but nineteen again.

Beautiful and young and deadly.

"And you just *had* to see it," she goes on, raising her voice along with the wind.

She turns then, and I'm relieved to see that no, she's not some vengeful ghost, not some unnatural creature made young again, but the same Lo who showed up here a little more than a month ago.

No longer young, but still beautiful.

And now, I realize, still deadly.

"If you want to understand what happened the night your daddy died, you have to understand the storm, baby."

She knew.

The thought eats into my stomach like acid, a sour taste at the back of my throat.

She knew, she knew, she knew. She talked to me like we were friends, and all the time, she knew who my real father was, and that's why she killed him, because she knew, she—

And then, through the blur of tears, through my own fury and betrayal, I realize she's not talking to me.

She's talking to August.

MARIE

August 3, 1985

I learned my mama was a murderer after Hurricane Audrey.

Frieda would never believe me, but the guilt damn near ate me up inside after her family was killed. That's what it felt like, a hollowness in the center of my belly, a gnawing sickness that never went away. If I hadn't come up with that plan to camp out, to lie to all our parents, Frieda's family wouldn't have been out looking for her, wouldn't have driven their car straight into rising waters.

I tried not to let it show, how bad I felt. It sounds crazy, but I thought if I just acted like nothing was wrong, then maybe it *wouldn't* be. I think they call that "magical thinking," and oh, Lord, I've engaged in a lot of that over the course of my life. I used to tell myself that it was a good quality, the power of positivity and all that bullshit.

Now I see it for what it was. Hell, what it *is*, because I'm sixty fucking years old and still doing it—playing pretend. Tell yourself the world is one way, and boom, presto chango, that's reality. Making yourself feel better with pretty, silly lies, like a little kid who has to be told that thunder is actually angels bowling.

I think if I make it out of this next storm, this Hurricane Lizzie bearing down on all of us right now, I'm gonna try to stop doing that. Maybe it's time to see things clear-eyed for once, live out the next four or five decades (a girl can dream!) in a state of Maximum Reality.

Maybe that's why I'm writing this for the book. The whole story, for the first time.

Crazy thing is, I bet August won't even believe it. He'll think it's another one of my "experiments in personal mythmaking." That's what he wrote in that little journal of his. That every interview he tried to do with me failed to dig below the surface because, what? I was too self-absorbed? Too obsessed with the image of Lo Bailey, Teenage Temptress?

What August doesn't get is that it's always been *other* people who made the myths. Even my own mother.

All I've *ever* wanted was the truth.

Maybe Mama understood that, or maybe she could just see how miserable I was after Hurricane Audrey because, good as I was at hiding things, you really can't hide much from your mama.

It was six months after Audrey hit—six months after Frieda's family drowned. Mama and I were on the couch one night, watching the tail end of an episode of *The Love Boat*. Mama was stroking my hair as I rested my head on her knee, and then she said, almost like it was nothing, "Your father wasn't a very nice man."

Mama had hardly ever talked about Daddy, certainly never called him "your father," so I'd perked up from my drowsy state at those words.

It came out slowly, the story of their disaster of a marriage, of his thousand cruelties, big and small, her unrelenting misery. She told it all like she was talking about someone else, but pain still lined every word, like those fancy Bibles you see with the gold and bright colors swirling around the top of the page.

That's how I learned that on the night Hurricane Delphine hit St. Medard's Bay, Daddy wasn't just unlucky. He made it into that tree after all, and Mama's foot saw him right the fuck back out of it and into the nasty waters Delphine splashed everywhere.

And I'll tell you what. After she told me, I wasn't horrified or shocked or traumatized or whatever else you probably think I should've been.

I was . . . *glad*. Proud, even. I loved my mama, but until that night, she'd always seemed so boring to me, so simple in her wants and needs, so dull in her dreams.

Now I knew that all that might still be true, but deep inside her, there was something fierce and deadly and unexpected, just like the hurricane itself, and for the first time, I understood not just her but *myself* a little better.

That it lived inside me, too, that storm.

We never talked about it again. The only thing that changed in our little house was that the next morning, the few pictures of Daddy that Mama had kept on display had disappeared. It was a lie neither of us needed anymore.

And honestly—you're not going to believe me, but like I said, we're all about truth right now, baby—I never thought much about it after that.

Not until Hurricane Marie.

Not until the storm that lived inside me decided to break.

People don't talk much about Marie herself anymore, the actual storm, and I think they've forgotten what an unusual one she was. How fast she moved, how quickly she came in. We'd been getting the warnings for days, but until that last afternoon, she was still just a Category 1, looking like she'd go overland in central Florida. We expected rain, thought we'd probably lose power and all that, but no one knew that she'd swell up out of nowhere and make a hard left for St. Medard's.

I wanted to say that at the trial. How could I have plotted to use the storm to cover up my crime when none of us even knew how bad the storm would be until *after* Landon was dead?

But of course, I couldn't say that because it would only lead to questions about *how* I knew exactly when Landon died.

I'm getting ahead of myself, shoot.

Let me back up.

I think if he had chosen anyone else—anyone in St. Medard's, anyone in the *world*—other than Ellen, I might have survived it.

I knew there were other girls occasionally. Yes, yes, I lied to the cops when I insisted that Landon was faithful to me (well, in his fashion). I said that I never suspected he was with anyone else besides his wife, but that wasn't true. I was nineteen and naïve as all get-out, but I wasn't *stupid*, and Landon wasn't always careful. There was the time I caught him talking on his car phone at two in the morning, parked outside the bungalow. "International stuff," he'd said, but I'd seen the way he'd been smiling in the dome light before he'd noticed me standing in front of the hood of the car.

And there were the random weeks of silence, the mysterious trips he was always vague about, even the clichéd lipstick on the collar once, a rich ruby red that was nothing like my hot pinks or Alison's tasteful dusty rose.

I knew, and I ignored it because, like I said, I believed that I didn't get to be jealous.

But Ellen . . .

Even now I'm shocked that he pulled it off for as long as he did, seeing us both. More than that, I'm shocked that Ellen never gave it away. Not with a guilty look or a teary moment as I waxed rhapsodic about Landon, not with an agonized confession over drinks at The Line. Do you know, she even spent the night at the bungalow with me once when Landon wasn't there, the two of us having a slumber party like we were still in seventh grade? She lay next to me in the bed I shared with the man she was also in love with, and she slept like a goddamn baby.

Looking back on it now, I feel some of that same pride and admiration I felt when Mama first told me what she'd done to Daddy. Sounds crazy, I know, but it must've been so hard keeping all that in, and she did it without flinching. Maybe you'll say that makes her a bad person, but I don't see it that way. I think it made her strong. Loyal, even.

I sure as hell couldn't have done it.

She had him first, you see. In a way.

Years before he walked into The Line, he'd met little Ellen Chambers at the Rosalie, and they'd become friends. Pen pals, you could say, writing back and forth. And as she got older, the letters got longer, the yearning in them more explicit, but she was a good girl, the kind who felt guilty for simply being in love with a married man, so she'd ended it before it had ever really begun.

And then he found me, and that was good, I guess.

For a while.

He never stopped writing her, though. Not the entire time we were together.

That's actually how I found out.

The prosecution were right about a few things. I *did* call Landon the day before Marie landed, telling him I wanted to talk to him. I had to leave a message with his secretary (always a huge bitch to me, but fair enough, Linda, fair enough). And I *was* upset when I made that phone call.

But you'd be upset, too, if you'd just found a letter from your best friend to your lover telling him that she regretted sleeping with him just a few months before, that it had been a "beautiful mistake, but a mistake all the same," that she was moving on with her life, that she hoped he was happy—"with Lo or Alison or both or neither."

Mama had wanted me to help out at the store, and I had, but that had taken us only until lunch, so after that, I'd gone to the bungalow with some half-assed idea of storm prepping only to realize I had no idea what to actually *do*. I'd seen people board up windows, but where did you even get those boards? (Cut me some slack, I was nineteen.)

So instead of doing anything sensible, I started cleaning the place. Shit you not. Making up the bed, washing the two wineglasses we'd left in the sink. Outside, it had started to rain, and the wind was picking up, but it wasn't anything scary, not yet. I'd had the radio on, and I remember it was playing "Gloria" by Laura Branigan. That was *my* song even though no one ever called me Gloria, and I was singing along as I scooped up the few things in the little bathroom hamper, just one of my negligees, a damp bathing suit, and a hopelessly wrinkled linen jacket of Landon's.

I've thought about it a million times, how none of it would've happened if he hadn't left that flimsy white jacket behind on his last visit. Or if I hadn't gone to the bungalow, or just picked a different useless chore to do. So many tiny little things like that, our whole lives hinging on them.

But I did pick up the coat, and I could feel something in the inside pocket, paper crinkling slightly.

I wasn't even suspicious, that's what kills me. I reached into that jacket still singing along with Laura, just sort of mildly curious, wondering if it might be an envelope of cash since Landon always seemed to have twenties and hundreds flowing from his fingers, but instead, it was a letter.

There were no names on it. Not his—the letter was just addressed to "L"—and no signature.

But Ellen Chambers had been my best friend since kindergarten. I had seen her handwriting in yearbooks, on raggedy pieces of notebook paper pushed secretly from hand to hand, on Frieda's cast in eighth grade, on the letters she'd sent me that one summer her parents made her go to Bible Camp up near the Tennessee line.

And it was that same neat, looping handwriting now telling Landon that the night they'd shared was "lovely" but "could never happen again, for too many reasons to list." That "seeing Lo every day is too hard because I want to tell her so much," but "is the truth worth telling if all it can do is hurt someone you love?"

I've thought about that question so many times over the last forty years, and I still don't know the answer.

But what I do know is that in that moment, the truth didn't just *hurt*.

It obliterated.

Of course I hadn't been enough for Landon. Of course I wasn't special. Of course this wasn't some grand love story. It was just two stupid teenage girls falling for the lies of an older man, a man who wasn't content having every toy known to man but had to make *people* into toys, too.

So yeah. There's some truth for you.

I decided to murder Landon Fitzroy right then and there, standing in the middle of the bungalow he'd bought for me, the little house just down the beach from the *other* other woman. And there was no plot to use the storm to cover it up because, baby, I am *not* a planner, and to be honest, in that moment, I didn't give a fuck if I got away with it or not.

The only thing I cared about was seeing his blood on my hands.

And baby, I got that in spades.

CHAPTER FOURTEEN

August 3, 2025

2:33 AM

The Day Of

I turn away from the wide-open window, with its clear view of the churning waves, to look at August. I expect to see the same shock and confusion on his face that must be on mine, but he's watching Lo with an expression I've never seen before. Not from him, not from *anyone*. His jaw is clenched, his hands in fists, but he's almost . . . blank.

Until you look at his eyes.

Dark, dark eyes—the same dark as mine, I suddenly realize.

The same as Landon Fitzroy.

In an instant, my stomach roils, and bile is pushing up my throat, gagging me.

"You don't look much like your daddy, until you do," Lo tells August over the sound of the storm. "I didn't see it at first."

Then she points at me. "This one, I was shocked no one had

figured it out over the years. She looks just like Camile, and her smile?"

Lo flashes one of her signature bright grins, but it wobbles slightly. "That's Landon's smile. Hits me right here every time I see it."

She thumps one hand against her chest as outside, the wind seems to keep rising and rising, the sound somewhere between a whistle and a scream. Through the window, all I can see is darkness and chaos. Fitting, because that's all I can see inside, too.

"But you?" Lo takes a step closer to August. "I don't think you got anything worth having from him. Other than his hair."

August laughs, a brittle, broken sound. "Don't you think I might have gotten a lot more from him if you hadn't smashed his fucking head in forty years ago, Lo? Like, I don't know, his name?"

"And his money?" Lo counters, and August shakes his head. There are tears in his eyes, but he's still got that funny little half smile on his face.

"You *would* think that's what this is about," he tells her. "You think that I spit into a tube in December 2022 and found out my father was Landon Fitzroy, and suddenly I saw dollar signs? That I had some big fantasy about prodigal son–ing my ass into the lap of luxury? That's not what I saw, Lo. You know what I saw?"

He takes a big step toward her, startling me, but Lo doesn't move as he lowers his face inches from hers to shout, "I saw that I was the son of a fucking *murder victim*, Lo. Do you know how surreal that is? To learn that hey, not only is your real dad dead, but he was also pretty famously killed, and oh, bonus! The selfish little bitch that did it got off scot-free, zero consequences."

"Zero consequences?" Lo laughs at that. "Oh God, only a

man would think the goddamn *electric chair* is the only conse-
quence that matters."

"It's what you deserved," August says, straightening up. He
turns toward me then, his hands stacked on top of his head as
he looks up at the ceiling. "I got that stupid ancestry kit thing
as a Christmas present from a girl I was dating. Just this . . . this
dumb little gift, with no real purpose, just, 'Hey, find out how
Irish you are, how Italian,' what-the-fuck-ever."

He gives that weird laugh again, the one that makes my skin
itch, then turns back to Lo, his expression almost bewildered. "I
never even suspected. Not for a second. Do you know what it
did to me to confront my mother? To sit there and listen while
she cried and told me her biggest shame? Do you know that I
still haven't managed to look my father—the man who raised
me—in the eye since I found out?"

August's gaze swings back to me. "Do you know what it felt
like to see that picture of Camile Fitzroy and realize I nearly
slept with my own *sister*?"

Nausea rises up again, and I make a slight choking sound as
I step away from him, from Lo, from all of this. "This isn't happening," I hear myself say.

"Your mama said that, too," Lo says softly—so softly that at
first I think I've misheard her. But then she adds, "When Marie
came. When Landon was dead. She kept saying that. 'This isn't
happening.'"

Moving forward, the wind blowing her nightgown tight
to her body, Lo looks like a ghost again, and outside, I hear a
mighty crack somewhere in the distance.

The Witches of St. Medard's Bay, I think, nearly hysterical
now, a laugh or maybe a sob trapped in my throat.

"But honey, I'm gonna tell you the same thing I told Ellen

that night—this *is* happening. And you'll be on the other side of it soon."

The howling seems to be inside me now, echoing through my skull, and I have this almost overwhelming urge to run outside into the storm, let it overwhelm me.

"My mom," I say, and Lo nods.

"Yes, your mom. Ellen. She was there that night."

"Of course she was," August says as the inn creaks and groans around us. "That's why you killed him. Because you found out Ellen was pregnant with his baby. With Geneva."

"And somewhere in . . . what? Ohio? Your mama was pregnant with you."

"New Orleans," August corrects. "That's where she was living when she met him. Some cotillion thing. She was engaged to my dad, but she was only twenty, and she said Landon was . . ."

He trails off, at a loss for words, but Lo nods, understanding. "Oh, he was," she says, almost sad. Then she looks up. "August. Your name. Because—"

"Because that's the month he died, yeah. She couldn't give me his name, so this was her own little secret tribute to him, passed on to the son he never got to have."

He gestures at me. "There's probably a similar story for you, Geneva. It's an unusual name, and I'm guessing not a family one."

A friend of mine said Lake Geneva was the prettiest place he'd ever seen, and I thought it was the prettiest name *I'd ever heard.*

"So, what?" I ask August now, my voice little more than a croak. "You found out your dad was murdered—allegedly, *possibly* murdered—and you became obsessed with getting revenge on Lo?"

August stares at me with those black eyes, his hands limp at his sides. "I got obsessed with the *truth*, Geneva. I'm a writer, a . . . a journalist, it's what I do. It was *my story*. Hell, it's *your* story. Don't we deserve to know it? To *tell* it?"

I can feel it again, that sense that something inside me is threatening to break in a way that can never be fixed, and I see in August's eyes that the same thing inside him *has* broken, and broken for good.

"Because of her, both of us have lived a lie," August goes on, pointing at Lo. "When she killed my—*our*—father, she killed any chance either of us had of lives not . . . *infested* with secrets. Landon wanted kids, Geneva. Lo told me that herself, several times. Alison couldn't have them, and . . . and if he had lived, who's to say he wouldn't have wanted us?"

August reaches out and grabs my shoulders, his hands clammy, and I grit my teeth against the instinct to wrench out of his grasp. "We could've been a family, but she took that from us."

There's a new sound outside, a rushing, wet sound, and again, that urge to run strikes so powerfully that my legs actually twitch.

But I stand there in August's grip and shake my head. "That's insane, August. He—he was married! Besides, neither of our mothers would've just—what, given us up?"

"But we don't know!" he shouts, his voice catching on a sob before it's quickly drowned out by the storm. The wind is nearly deafening now, and I can feel water against the soles of my feet. It's seeping in under the doors, pushing against the walls and windows, and somehow, I know that this is finally it.

That the storm that will take the Rosalie has arrived, and it's going to take me with it. Me, and these two people I've been orbiting my entire life without ever knowing. It'll take us, and all the twisted secrets that have woven the three of us together.

Is that why Lo tore the boards off the window? Does she want all of us to die here? Some fucked-up idea of atonement or retribution?

"You know, August, there's just one little problem with your happy family dreams," Lo says, and when I open my eyes to look at her in the dim glow of the emergency lighting, she looks older than her sixty years for the first time.

"You're so quick to blame me, just like everyone else was. Because it's easy, because it feels good—fuck if I know why, but damn, do y'all love to do it. But no one ever seems to blame Landon. Oh, sure—they'll say he was a playboy or a philanderer, but those are awfully pretty words for a man who screwed anything that crossed his path. So, when you're wallowing in your self-pity, maybe ask yourself why Landon Fitzroy had *evvvvery-thing* he could've ever fucking wanted, and it *still* wasn't enough. Maybe ask yourself if all the secrets, all the bullshit, are actually the fault of the man who fathered the two of you, and *not* the girl who eventually decided the world could do without Landon Fitzroy."

The inn seems to be breathing along with the storm, the walls alive as they shudder under the force of the wind and rain, and Lo stands in front of us, eerily lit and grinning.

"So, there you go, Auggie," Lo says. "Here is your big ending for your big book. I called Landon down here from his fancy event in Birmingham because I found out about Ellen, found out she was knocked up, and that the baby was his. And when he got here, I took a piece of an old anchor that had washed up on the shore, and I slammed it into the back of his head until he was dead, and I have never, *ever* felt bad about doing it. Not for *one. Goddamn. Second.*"

August's hands on my arms tighten to the point of pain, and then three things happen at once.

I see Lo reach for the hammer at her feet.

I hear August roar with rage.

And I watch as a tree limb thicker than my body slams into the front window, bringing rain, broken glass, and what feels like a tornado with it.

Hurricane Lizzie sweeps into the Rosalie, and death follows.

MARIE

August 5, 1984

This is how it happened.

I woke up on what turned out to be the last day of my life—my old life, my normal life, the life where I thought I knew what kind of person I was—and decided to tell Landon about the baby.

I'd known myself for only a little while, maybe a couple of weeks, and there were still times I tried to pretend it wasn't real. It didn't feel real in a lot of ways, not that early. I was nauseous, a kind of motion sickness that struck even when I was standing still, and my breasts ached the way they did just before I got my period, but those things were fairly easy to ignore.

Still, it was there, like a sore tooth, a persistent throb of worry in the back of my mind, and at night, I'd lie awake, considering my options.

The first and most obvious option was that I would go to Mobile and, as ladies around here euphemistically put it, "get things taken care of."

That was the most sensible one, but I wasn't sure I was brave enough to go by myself, and who could I tell? My mother was a kind and good woman, but our relationship had always been a little formal, a little distant, and the thought of telling her—of the shame in her face—was scarier even than the thought of going alone.

I could tell Tim, of course. We'd slept together a handful of times by then, and he'd assume it was his. But Tim was too sweet, too honest, and the thought of lying to him about something like that—of putting that weight on his heart when he'd done nothing but love me—was too much to bear.

Lo and Frieda . . .

They would have been with me, no question. They would've assumed it was Tim's, and I wouldn't have to lie, just not correct them, but something about that felt just as bad as lying, and the plain truth was I wasn't good at lying.

It almost makes me laugh to think about it now. How in the end, all I could think was something you usually saw stitched onto samplers in old ladies' houses or posted on a kindergarten bulletin board: Honesty Is the Best Policy.

Funny—in trying to be honest, I only ended up committing myself to a lifetime of lies.

So that morning, the morning before Marie, I woke up knowing that the only thing to do was tell Landon the truth and see where the chips fell.

So much of that day still feels like a dream. It had started too early, with the shrill ringing of the phone. My brother had been at camp that summer, the same one Mama and Daddy had sent me to, right on the Tennessee line in Ardmore, and for whatever reason, he and some of his bunkmates had gone out the night before to do . . . I don't know, whatever stupid things young boys do when they're teenagers and trying to prove their masculinity. In Adam's case, it had ended in a broken leg and a concussion, and Mama had been frantic to reach him.

He'd always been her favorite.

She wanted to go to him, but she didn't drive—do you know, I never asked her why that was?—so it would have to be Daddy behind the wheel, but she couldn't stay behind, not when Adam needed her.

It probably sounds awful, my parents leaving me alone with a storm headed our way, but I was the one who urged them to go. Marie wasn't really supposed to be all that bad, truth be told. A Cat 1 that might fizzle into a tropical storm before she even got to us. And I promised them that, should things turn, I'd go stay with Frieda and her aunt. They had a storm shelter, and I'd be safe there. It was much more likely that I'd lose power for a bit, and they'd be back by the next night anyway.

And I craved the solitude, storm or no storm. With the inn empty of guests and my parents gone, it might be easier to listen to my own thoughts, my own soul, and decide what to do about the baby.

So after they drove off in our sensible station wagon, I, almost without realizing it, found myself making my way down the beach to the little house Landon had gotten for Lo.

She wouldn't be there that day; I knew she would be at her mama's store instead, helping Miss Beth-Anne prepare for the storm. She'd mentioned it the night before on the phone, her sigh so loud I was surprised my hair didn't blow back.

"Honestly, the best thing that could happen to Beth-Anne *and* me would be all that plastic shit getting washed out to sea, but I guess that's bad for, like, dolphins or whatever," she'd said, and I'd laughed. It must have sounded weird, though, because Lo suddenly asked, "Are you okay?"

I almost told her then. Part of me wishes I had. Who knows what might have happened if I'd just spilled the whole story, then and there. It would've been awful, I know that. For all I know, it might even have been deadly, too. But it would've been different, and that's all I have ever been able to think about. That surely, there had to be some other outcome, some other fate than the one headed to us on Marie's back.

But that had been another thing I wasn't brave enough for, so I'd just told her I was worried about the storm, and then we'd moved on to other topics.

She didn't talk much about Landon at that point, but then he barely ever mentioned her, so I never really knew where they stood with each other, and honestly, even if I'd asked, I'm not sure either would've told the truth.

Lo always liked to act like things with them were perfect, a fairy tale, while Landon seemed to think that as long as he never brought her up, I might forget about the two of them altogether.

It had killed me at first, the two of them. I hadn't had any claim to Landon, not really, but those letters between us, the stolen conversations when he was in town, the way he'd always find some way to touch my hand or rest his warm palm on my shoulder . . . I'd held all of it so close to my heart for so long. And I'd felt so guilty about his wife, which is why I'd never let it go any further.

But Lo hadn't had the same compunction, and I think I hated her for that. At least for a little while.

For taking what I was too afraid—too *good*—to reach for.

Until that last letter arrived from Landon, asking me to meet him on Memorial Day.

I can admit it now: I was flattered that he still wanted to see *me*, even though he had Lo—the most fun, the most dazzling, the most gorgeous girl St. Medard's Bay had ever seen.

Just this once, I'd told myself, and it had been only that once—well, that one night, at least—and look what it had led to.

In any case, I knew Lo's place was empty that morning, and for whatever reason, that's where my feet took me, and that's where I found myself picking up the phone and dialing his office.

I want to be clear—I didn't ask him to come to St. Medard's Bay.

At least that's not on my conscience.

I can still remember the warmth in his voice when he realized it was me calling. I'd told his secretary I was Lo, doing, I thought, a pretty good imitation of her careless and casual drawl.

When Landon answered, his voice sounded tense, the words clipped as he said, "Dad wants me in Birmingham for that donor thing tonight, Lo, I have a five-hour drive ahead of me, so whatever it is, make it fast."

I didn't know what any of that meant, but later I found out he'd been meant to attend some political dinner with Beau Fitzroy's wealthiest donors, glad-handing the right people to support his na-scent political career.

So, yes—it's true that I never *asked* him to come to St. Medard's Bay. But it's also true that he would've been far away from Marie that night if it weren't for me.

"It's Ellen," I replied, and I could hear the squeak of leather as he sat down. I pictured him there, in the office I'd never seen, handsome in his suit and tie. And even though I'd sworn I'd put us behind me, in that moment, my hand found its way to my stomach. I remembered that no matter what, this baby had been created out of love on a beautiful night in moonlit waters.

I think I knew then that I was keeping it.

Her. I was keeping *her.* Somehow I knew that, too.

"Oh my God," he breathed. "Hi. Hi. Um. God. Okay. Are you all right? I've been watching this storm, and—"

"I need to talk to you."

"The most terrifying words a man can hear," he joked, but I'd heard the sudden wariness.

"I mean . . . in person," I continued, as I stood there in the house he'd bought for another woman.

It was pretty, very Lo in its hot pink and floral, and I could see my reflection in a seashell-framed mirror that hung over the bed as I stood there, pale and sweaty in my T-shirt and shorts, the phone cord twisted around my finger.

"Not today, obviously, you're busy, and the weather—"

"Ellen, if it's important—" he started, but I shook my head like he could see me through the phone.

"No, it's . . . it can wait a few days. I just . . . I miss you."

I hadn't intended to say that, but the words tripped out of my mouth all the same, and I was surprised to find I really meant them.

I did miss him, and while I cared about Tim—loved him—it wasn't anything like what I'd felt with Landon. Tim was steady and honest and *good* in his bones, and I knew even then that Landon could never be any of those things, but something had happened that night we'd sat in the back pantry of the Rosalie, something as alchemical and primal as the hurricane itself, and it still had me in its grip.

What else did we say after that? I don't remember. I wish I could because those were some of the last words we'd ever exchange, the last time it would ever be good between us, even if it was just for a moment over the phone.

But it's the *I miss you* that has snagged in my memory. It was that unspoken plea, I think, that doomed him in the end.

When I went to sleep on the night of August 4, Marie was still miles and miles away, still sending only wind and rain.

That's what I thought I heard on my window at first, the rain, but somewhere in my fitful dozing, I realized there was a pattern to it, a rhythm, and I sat up, my heart pounding in the darkness.

It was Landon, standing outside in the rain, his fist still raised to the glass.

He looked young, I remember that, younger than usual, the rain plastering his dark hair to his face, his grin wide as he took in my shocked expression.

The bright green numbers on my clock radio said it was just after midnight, and I padded quietly out of my room, down the hall, through the lobby of the inn. We hadn't even boarded up the windows, and the porch light illuminated the steady rain and, in the distance, the pounding surf.

Just as I stepped outside, Landon came around the corner of the inn, still wearing a tuxedo, one that probably cost more than all the clothes in my closet—maybe all the clothes in St. Medard's Bay put together—only now it was soaking wet, ruined.

Even then, that was wildly romantic to me, him turning up like a groom caring more about seeing me than about his fancy dinner, his expensive suit.

Landon stepped onto the porch, and without thinking, I reached out both my hands. He took them, his skin cold, and he said something. "I've missed you, too."

That's what I've always told myself he said, but truthfully, I was so surprised to see him, so in love and confused and relieved, that I might have imagined it.

I do know what I said in response.

"Landon, I'm pregnant."

I had to raise my voice to be heard over the rain and the wind and the sea, and the words felt too loud, too abrupt, and I watched as his grin—that beautiful, beautiful grin—slowly faded from his face.

"What?" he asked, the word flat, and before I could repeat myself, he turned away, one hand on the back of his head.

For a long moment, we both stood there, frozen in this weird tableau with the rain streaming off the porch roof and thunder rumbling somewhere far out over the ocean.

The air felt thick, mist and salt seeming to settle on my skin, but when Landon turned back around, he was smiling again.

This smile wasn't right, though. It was a little too tight, a little too . . . shiny, I remember thinking. "Hey," he said, and then he stepped forward, one hand on my cheek.

"This is going to be fine," he said, and it was the first time he'd ever said something I didn't believe.

"*We're* going to be fine," he went on, and then his other hand came to rest on my stomach, not unlike how my own had done earlier that afternoon.

But I didn't like the way it felt there. It was too heavy, too firm, and I stepped back, but he followed, keeping his palm just below the waistline of my nightgown.

"This kid is going to be so loved, Ellie," Landon said. "And that's the most important thing, right?"

I nodded even as I heard myself say, "I haven't decided what to do yet, but I wanted you to know. You—you deserved to know, I thought."

The wind was a little stronger now, blowing my hair back, bringing the scent of rain and salt and Landon's cologne.

"There's nothing to decide," Landon replied, and those words felt as heavy as his hand on my stomach. "This baby is a Fitzroy, Ellie. It has a destiny, just like its dad."

She, I thought again. *Her.*

But to Landon, I said, "But it can't be a Fitzroy, Landon. You're married."

His hand finally dropped from my body, and he stood up straighter. "*I'm* a Fitzroy, and any child of mine is going to be one. We can . . . we can make this work."

He turned away again, pacing, that hand going to the back of his head again, his fingers tightening in his hair. "I'll find a place, a really nice place where you can stay. You'll tell your parents you . . . you got accepted to some kind of program, some study abroad thing, all expenses paid."

I felt like he had suddenly started speaking in another language, and I could only stare at him as he went on. "You'll have the baby, and I can adopt it. Alison and I will."

A cold that had nothing to do with the rain began to seep through me. "No," I said.

He didn't hear me, or maybe he just ignored me because his eyes were brighter as he stopped pacing to stand in front of me. "No, no, this will work." Landon laughed then, a high, almost disbelieving sound, like he was shocked at his own brilliance. "We'll raise it, we'll wait for all this political shit to get settled—Dad's election, mine—mayor, senator next, maybe, who knows, and then—then!—it'll finally be safe to divorce Alison, and we—" He took both my hands in his again, but now his skin just felt clammy and dead to me. "We can get married. We can be a family."

He squeezed my hands, and I looked into his smiling face and had a sudden memory of Adam when he was about seven and I was five.

Christmas morning. He came down early, way before anyone else woke up, and when the rest of us found him, he'd opened every present under the tree. His, mine, even the ones Mama and Daddy had gotten for each other.

"These are mine!" he had shouted, so excited he was practically vibrating. He was holding as much as he could, a bizarre assortment of G. I. Joes and Barbies and slippers and a box of Jean Naté and a tie and God knows what else, things he didn't want, things for girls or grown-ups. But it didn't matter because he had *decided* that they were his.

That's what Landon reminded me of standing there on the porch that night, his dark eyes bright as stars. A little boy clutching as much as he could to his chest, whether he wanted it all or not.

I pictured me, Lo, Alison, and now this child inside of me all gathered up in his arms as he crowed, "These are mine!"

Shaking my head, I backed away. "No, Landon," I said. Other words were there, waiting to spill out. How I couldn't stay hidden from my own family for nine months. How Alison might have something to say about all this. How the idea of waiting to be able to raise my own child filled me with a horror I could barely articulate, but in the end, I let those two words—*No, Landon*—stand alone, because they were the only ones I should have needed.

And like Adam when Mama and Daddy had very firmly told him all those things were *not* his, and he was in fact in big trouble, Landon's face crumpled—first in confusion, and then in anger.

Unlike Adam, Landon covered it quickly, that shiny, fake smile sliding back into place. "Okay," he said, reaching for me again.

I stepped back, and that anger flashed, harder to conceal this time.

"It's a lot," he said. "I know that. But Ellie, what other choice do we have?"

A shocked sort of sound burst out of me. "So many!" I cried. "I could—I could go to Mobile, to the clinic there, or I c-could marry Tim, or—"

"Unacceptable," Landon said. For the first time, I saw the man others must have seen, the scion, the governor's son. The man who always got his way. "I told you, Ellie, that baby is a Fitzroy, and he'll be raised like one."

"She!" I burst out, tears stinging my eyes, burning my throat, and then there was a flurry of movement from the corner of my eye, and suddenly Lo was there, shoving Landon so hard he stumbled back, his arm hitting my hip.

"Baby?" she shrieked. "Baby?"

"Lo," Landon said, but she was all motion, all swinging fists and wet blond hair and fury like nothing I'd ever seen.

"Son of a bitch!" she screamed, and her nails went for his eyes.

"Stop!" I remember crying out, but it was chaos, and the rain was coming down harder now, the waves crashing seemed louder, and one of the smaller potted plants on the porch railing crashed over the side.

Landon caught her hands before she could gouge out his eyes— and she would have, I had no doubt—and shoved her back, her Keds sliding across the wet floor.

"Goddammit, Lo, we don't need this shit right now," Landon said, still holding her as she tried to kick him.

"Lo, please," I said, and she turned to me then, her green eyes blazing.

But there wasn't any anger there, or at least not for me. Instead, there were tears mixing with the rain, and she shook her head. "Why you?" she shouted.

I've thought about those plaintive words a million times. Did she mean why had Landon chosen me when he had her? Or why was I the one having his baby and not her?

I don't know the answer, and I guess I never will.

"I'm sorry," I told her, and now tears were spilling down my own face, hot against the cool rain. "I . . . none of this . . . if I . . ."

Words burbled out, tripping over one another because what could I say? What would make any of this okay? If only I'd told her before, if only she knew that Landon had been mine *first*, if not in body, then in soul . . .

"Ellen and I are having a baby, Lo," Landon said, "and I need you to be mature about that."

She swung back to him.

"Mature?" Lo laughed, the sound high and jagged. "If you want 'mature' women, Landon, maybe don't fuck nineteen-year-olds."

And with that, she spit in his face.

The anger Landon had tried so hard to hide from me came flaring back now as he shoved her roughly away again, wiping at his cheek. He looked back and forth between us, pissed off, yes, but also . . . bewildered. Like he just couldn't believe this was happening to him, Landon Fitzroy. Whatever Landon thought his destiny was, it wasn't *this*, two women, one raging, the other suddenly not as biddable as he'd thought.

"Go home, Landon," I said, suddenly exhausted, wanting nothing more than to curl up in my bed and let the storm come, let it tear down everything if it wanted to.

"I will, but you're coming with me," he said, and I shook my head.

"I said no, and I meant it. Whatever I decide to do, I'll let you know, but I'm not hiding away and then handing my baby over to another woman."

Lo made a disgusted sound. "Was that your big plan? Stick her in a convent like it's 1890 or something and then give her baby to your frigid-ass wife?"

"Enough, Lo," Landon said again, but this time, there was more than just annoyance under it. There was something serious, something real, and it made the hair on the back of my neck stand up.

"Lo," I said, reaching for her, but Lo Bailey was never going to heed someone telling her "enough."

There *was* no enough for Lo.

"You piece of shit," she went on, venom dripping from every word. "Do you know what I'm going to do? I'm going to go to every paper I can think of, and I'm gonna tell them about all this. About how the governor's precious son is running around some trash beach town with not one but *two* girls, girls a lot younger than him, and hey! He's even knocked up one of them. And then you can kiss your career, and certainly your asshole *daddy's* career, a *very* final goodb—"

He moved so fast I barely had time to register it before he was on Lo, his hands gripping her biceps so hard his knuckles went white. "You are never gonna fucking learn, are you?" he shouted over the storm, and then he was pushing her against the porch railing, his face close to hers. "You are nothing, you hear me? You're a pretty girl in a cheap town, and there are millions just like you, Lo, trust me. The idea that someone like you can hurt me? Fucking laughable, truly."

"Let her go!" I yelled, tugging at the back of his suit jacket, but he gripped Lo even tighter, his face so close to hers I had the crazed thought he might bite her.

"You are nothing!" he shouted again, and Lo struggled in his grasp.

"Fuck you!" I heard her say, but her eyes were scared.

I'd known Lo almost all my life, and the only thing I'd ever seen scare her was a hurricane.

So maybe it was that, the fear in her eyes, the real terror as Landon screamed at her, or maybe it was him calling her "nothing," and knowing, deep inside, that I was nothing to him, too. A distraction, a fun way to pass time, and now, at last, the bearer of something he actually wanted, but me? Ellen?

Nothing.

I tugged at his jacket again, feeling something give, but he didn't let her go, and I turned, my bare feet sliding on the wet porch, my eyes scanning for anything, anything I could think of that would make him let go of Lo.

There was this wooden pelican we kept outside the door, and that's what I think I was reaching for. It was hollow, not that heavy, but it would have gotten his attention.

I reached blindly, panicked and forgetting that Mama had moved that silly statue that morning, my hands closing around something cold and metal and much heavier than the pelican, heavy enough that I almost lost my balance, and without thinking, I swung.

The sound is something I've never forgotten even though I have tried and tried and tried.

When I reached for that stupid bird, I grabbed the anchor for the inn's rowboat. A twenty-pound anchor with sharp points and rust on its edges. Daddy had been meaning to replace its chain, and it had sat there by the back door for nearly a month as other chores took precedence.

Or maybe it was always meant to be there, waiting for me when I reached.

Destiny.

I think Lo screamed, or maybe it was me, and everything dissolved into a liquid horror.

Blood, spraying on Lo's face, mixing with rain and tears.

Blood, running out of Landon's dark hair like a river.

Blood, slicking my hands as I tugged the anchor free from his skull and watched as he staggered toward the steps before turning to me.

Landon's eyes were wide, and his mouth was open, a string of saliva dripping from his lower lip as his mouth moved with no sounds.

A step backward, then another, and then he was falling into the sand at the bottom of the steps, his torso convulsing, rattling gasps in his chest, like a fish thrown onto the deck of a boat, and then Lo was moving past me, the anchor dangling heavily at her side as she lurched down the steps.

She rolled him over, I remember that, his face pressed into the wet sand, and then the anchor was coming down on the back of his head again, the sound heavier and thicker this time, and finally, Landon was still.

My legs went out from underneath me, my skin numb, and I sat down heavily on the top porch step, rainwater soaking into my night-gown.

Lo dropped the bloody anchor on the sand, the wind so strong now that she seemed to be staggering against it as she made her way up the steps to drop to her knees in front of me.

"It was both of us!" she yelled, pressing her palms to my cheeks. Her hands were bloody, and the copper-penny smell made bile flood my mouth, but I reached up anyway, my fingers over hers. "It was both of us," she said again, and then lowered her forehead to mine. "Not just you, Ellen. Not you. Us."

It was a gift, the greatest one anyone ever could have given me, but I couldn't see that right then. All I could see was Landon's body on the sand and the bloody anchor that I had wielded.

"Oh God," I said weakly. "Oh God."

I'd killed the first man—maybe the only man—I'd ever loved.

I'd killed my baby's father.

I'd killed the governor's son.

Big Yellow Mama, that's what they called Alabama's electric chair, and I knew that's where I'd go, my arms and legs strapped to painted wood, a steel cap on my shaved head, and my baby . . . my *daughter* . . .

"Listen to me," Lo said, her grip getting tighter like she knew where my thoughts were going. "You have to be strong a little longer. We have to get him to the water, okay?"

The water.

My eyes landed on the surging seas, and I nodded, making myself stand on trembling legs as rain and wind cocooned us both in this nightmare.

Landon was not a large man, but we were two teenage girls, one of whom was pregnant, the other maybe a hundred pounds on a good day. We tried dragging him to the water, but he was too heavy, we were too weak, and the sand was too wet, Landon's body sinking into it like it wanted to hold him there forever.

With a low moan, I dropped his arm and sank to the sand. "We can't!" I shouted over the storm. "We can't, we can't, we can't."

Standing there in her David Bowie T-shirt and cutoff shorts, her hair wet and sticking to her face, Lo faced the ocean, her bloody hands on her hips.

"The storm!" she said, and when I only stared up at her in confusion, she said, "The storm. It'll be here in just a few hours."

"I don't care," I told her, but she shook her head, picking up the anchor.

"My daddy didn't die in Hurricane Delphine, did you know that?"

"Yes, he did," I replied, wondering if she'd lost her mind like I thought I might be doing.

"My mama killed him and let people think it was the storm," she said, and I shook my head, the idea of Miss Beth-Anne killing anyone so impossible to believe that I was sure Lo had gone crazy.

But all I said to her was, "It won't work, it's not like that hurricane, it's weak, and we're . . ."

"We're the Witches of St. Medard's Bay," she said, the look on her face both fierce and calm all at once. And as she stood there in the wind and rain, her red hands and her weapon—*our* weapon—at her side, I almost believed she was some kind of sorceress or ancient goddess.

She turned and walked toward the surf, and I followed, wading out after her until we were up to our thighs, the waves buffeting us, our feet sliding on the sandy bottom as Lo dragged the anchor through the dark water, Landon's blood washing away. Later, once Marie was over, the anchor would wash up onshore, but of course there was no sign of the wreckage it had wrought that night. Just another piece of storm debris.

That's what I felt like myself, standing there in the water with Lo. Something sucked away by the tide, returned to shore battered and twisted.

I tipped my head back, rain in my face, stinging my eyes as I looked up at the black sky.

Lo's hand found mine, our fingers intertwining, seawater and blood.

Were we witches?

I don't know, but we sure as hell called a storm that night. What was supposed to be a Cat 1 that merely grazed us instead became a Cat 3 that roared directly over us, turning and getting stronger in a way that the meteorologists on TV the next day called "completely baffling."

A once-in-a-lifetime storm, they said.

Sometimes I think the storm never ended.

LIZZIE

August 3, 2025

I feel like the world has exploded around me.

Wind and rain pour in the broken window, and I hear glass crunching as August makes his way to Lo, watch through squinting eyes as she stumbles on the edge of her nightgown, inadvertently kicking the hammer farther away from her.

That's good, I think, dazed. *She won't hit August with the hammer, that's a good thing*, but for some reason, I'm crouching down, wrapping my own fingers around the handle and holding the hammer close to my chest, its weight weirdly comforting as August grabs Lo, shoving her backward toward the window.

"You took everything from me!" he screams, but Lo only laughs.

"You never had anything, baby boy," she says, and he reaches for her again.

"Stop!" I hear myself yell, but am I talking to August or to Lo? To both of them?

I don't know, but I'm moving toward them even as water stings my eyes.

Lo is near the busted window now, her bare feet moving over the broken glass. Blood mingles with water, but she doesn't seem to notice, her shoulders thrown back, her eyes blazing as she smiles at August. "Is this what you pictured?" she asks him. "Is this what you saw when you imagined your daddy dying?"

"Shut up!" he yells, and this time, he shoves her hard enough to send her sprawling to the floor.

She looks small in her wet nightgown, her bedraggled hair covering her face, her feet covered in blood, and then August is on her, over her, yanking her up by one arm and moving her toward the broken window, jagged shards of glass sticking up from the frame like teeth.

To my horror, Lo grabs one of those shards as she tries to steady herself, and we both cry out when the glass tears a gash across her palm, thick droplets of blood splashing to the floor.

"August, stop!" I scream, but he only grabs both of her arms, hauling her to her feet.

"She killed our father, Geneva. She attacked Edie. Tell me she doesn't have this coming."

The hammer is suddenly heavier in my hand as I think about all those pictures of Landon my mom saved for years, of Edie bleeding. I look at the water currently pouring into the inn thanks to her and consider all the damage this one woman seems to have wrought in every aspect of my life.

"Bullshit!" Lo spits, struggling against him even though she has to be in pain. "I killed your daddy, you're damn right about that, but I didn't touch Frieda."

She looks at me then, tossing her hair out of her face with a flick of her head, her eyes boring into me. "I hurt her enough in 1977. I'd never hurt her again. You believe me, Geneva."

It's not a question. It's a demand.

Or maybe it's a plea.

I don't know.

I don't know anything anymore except that the storm is here, and the inn won't survive it, and maybe that means none of us are going to survive it, either.

Maybe none of us should.

That's all I'm thinking as August pushes Lo steadily back against the broken window, as she slips in her own blood, as I find myself walking toward them like a sleepwalker, the hammer still in my hands, now gripped in a fist, now raised.

Lo sees me over August's shoulder, and the fight seems to go out of her all of a sudden, her body slumping into his hold, unbalancing him, and he grips her harder, making her cry out again.

"Hit her, Geneva!" August yells, seeing me and the hammer now. "Hit her!"

I swing.

It's an inelegant, clumsy thing, nowhere near hard enough to kill or even knock someone out.

But it clearly hurts if the shocked grunt of pain that August makes is any indication.

I catch him on the shoulder blade, and he immediately lets go of Lo, whirling around on me with wide eyes, his mouth twisted with fury.

"You need to stop!" I say, because that had been the only thought in my head as I swung at him, that he was hurting her and he needed to stop because no matter what she'd done, she didn't deserve this, and what does it matter when the storm is going to kill us all anyway?

But then August grabs the hammer from my hand, sending me staggering back, and he turns back to Lo, who is trying to hobble away from the window.

And then everything feels too fast and too slow all at the same time.

Lo is moving too slowly; she's not going to get away.

I'm moving too quickly, stumbling over my feet, trying to get to August before he gets to her.

The wind is howling through the inn, the water is sloshing around my ankles, and I hear a crack from upstairs that reverberates through my bones. I think about all the things it could be—a tree branch hitting the roof, a piece of glass breaking, a dresser tipping over. Then my hands are out in front of me, and I'm pushing, my hands against August's wet shirt, and suddenly Lo is on her feet again, her bloody hand pressed alongside mine.

August tips backward, toward the window, and I want to shut my eyes against the sight of his body falling, and the water splashing down on my feet is warm.

And dark.

Because it's not water after all. It's blood.

Blood, because as he fell backward, August hit one of those nasty pieces of glass, and it sliced his throat. I shut my eyes again, but not before I see his body jerking violently, and Lo's hand is on my back, and the world is nothing but rain and wind and broken glass and blood. Upstairs, there's another crack, louder this time, and I clutch Lo because I don't know what else to do.

The wind seems to be trying to pull the inn apart at the seams, and *me* apart at the seams, too. I think of my mother, and Edie, and feel a small sliver of gratitude that they're not here to see this. For if there ever were Witches of St. Medard's Bay, their magic is now gone, because this storm has come to take the inn, and to take Lo and August and me with it.

Then, there's a creaking from upstairs that turns into a roar, a sound like someone ripping a hole in the very fabric of the universe, and I—

Journalist, Author August Fletcher, 40, Dies in Freak Storm Accident

August 6, 2025

Columbus native and noted journalist August Fletcher has died in St. Medard's Bay, Alabama, as a result of injuries sustained during last week's Hurricane Lizzie. Fletcher was staying at the Rosalie Inn in St. Medard's Bay while working on a book with local woman Gloria "Lo" Bailey. In a tragic twist of fate, Bailey became a tabloid darling in 1984 after she was accused of the murder of her lover during another storm, Hurricane Marie, also in St. Medard's Bay.

According to coroner Robert Byrd, Jr., Mr. Fletcher was killed by debris while riding out the storm in the Rosalie Inn.

The inn itself sustained significant damage as well, losing its roof, and authorities are unsure if it will be reopened in the future.

While hurricanes in the area have frequently been serious and often deadly, Mr. Fletcher was one of only two deaths reported in Hurricane Lizzie.

The Columbus Dispatch

CHAPTER FIFTEEN

December 20, 2025

139 Days After

The morning Lo Bailey comes back to St. Medard's Bay, the sun is shining.

I've been expecting her, but it's still something of a shock to come out of the inn and see her sitting in one of the Rosalie's pink beach chairs, her bare toes pointed toward the water even though it's only in the fifties.

There's still an ugly ridge of scars along the arch of one foot, the result of the surgery she'd needed to repair a tendon after Lizzie, but other than that, there's little sign of the ordeal we went through together almost five months ago.

The same can't be said for the Rosalie. The picture window in the lobby has been replaced, and we've got new carpeting downstairs, but the first floor is still bare of furniture, and parts of the roof are still covered in blue tarp. Soon, I'll hear the cacophony of hammers as the workmen get here, slowly but surely bringing the Rosalie back to life, but for now the morning is quiet save for the surf and the gulls.

Lo is the only person on the beach this morning. Cap didn't make it through Lizzie, dying not from the storm but from a heart attack as he loaded up his car to get out of town. He was the only other person this storm claimed, and for St. Medard's Bay, that's considered a relief.

"Morning, sugar!" Lo calls out as I drag two chairs down next to hers and flop into one, burying my hands in the sleeves of my oversize hoodie.

"You are too chipper for this early, Lo," I tell her, and she smiles at me, her head lolling to one side.

"I'm always chipper," Lo says. "It's one of my many gifts."

I snort in response, but I can't really argue with her. After Lizzie, after August, I was a wreck. Nightmares, panic attacks, all of it. Later, I learned that those harrowing moments—August attacking Lo, me hitting August, him slicing his neck on the window, the storm peeling the roof off the inn—all happened in less than ten minutes.

That's still hard for me to believe. I felt like Lo and I spent an eternity huddled in the chaos, but the roof was Lizzie's big finale, turns out, one last *fuck you* as her power drained away and the seas and the wind calmed.

For weeks, I was too paralyzed to even think about the inn. My trailer was gone, the heavy limb of a live oak taking care of that, and I stayed at Hope House of all places, sleeping on a rollaway cot they found for me. Every night, I moved it next to Mom's bed so that I could take her hand before falling asleep. It was the most physical contact we'd ever had, and I think I might have stayed there forever had Lo not come for a visit.

She looked rough, her hand bandaged in thick gauze, a pair of crutches shoved under her arms as she hobbled into Mom's room, but she also looked like . . . Lo. Beautiful still, sassy in her bright green linen dress, sparkly earrings dangling from her ears.

"Girl, you can't *move in here*," she'd said. "Or everything we went through won't be worth a damn thing."

I didn't need to ask if she was talking about August or Landon because I was pretty sure she was talking about both.

We sat there in plastic chairs on either side of Mom's recliner, and then, with a gusty sigh, Lo said, "I guess it's time you finally learn what really happened to Landon."

And she told me.

Sitting there in Mom's room, the afternoon sunlight spreading slowly across the linoleum floor, Lo told me about finding the letter from my mom in Landon's pocket, about going to the Rosalie to confront Mom first only to find both her and Landon on the porch. Then there was shouting and fighting, then Landon's hands were on her, the storm howling. I listened, I nodded, I tried to follow along. But in my mind, I wasn't seeing Landon—I was seeing August. And when Lo told me about Mom picking up that anchor, I saw my own hands clutching the hammer, my clumsy strike to August's back.

Memories, echoes, time circling back on itself. A ritual that had to be performed every few decades, another one of the sacrifices demanded of St. Medard's Bay.

That's when I knew that Lo was right—I couldn't hide at Hope House forever. And I couldn't abandon the Rosalie, not when it had somehow, miraculously, withstood yet another storm.

There was damage, certainly. The crack that turned into a roar that became the last thing I heard before blacking out—that was the roof coming off. Five windows on the second floor blew out; all the carpet and hardwood had to be torn out on the first floor. The porch was almost completely washed out to sea.

But she was still standing—weary and battered, but not done for yet.

The next day, I called the number on the card that FEMA had given me, and a few days after that, a crew arrived at the Rosalie to begin bringing her back to life.

I look back over my shoulder at her now, still glowing her soft pink in the early morning light.

Still holding our secrets.

"They called again," I say to Lo as a wave crashes hard against the wet sand, sending up spray that splashes the toes of my sneakers. "The Fitzroys."

The calls started shortly after Lizzie receded, after the whole story started to break. The police had believed me when I'd told them that August's death had been a freak accident. The board falling from the window, the broken glass, the hammer. All of it helped shore up my version of events, one where August was heroically trying to cover the window when the tree limb broke, that he was tragically caught off guard and slipped. That Lo's cut hand and feet were testament to her equally heroic attempt to save him, but it had been too late.

Lo's involvement in yet another storm death had barely rated a mention in the local press—that is, until someone leaked what had been found on August's laptop.

He'd been smart, shoving it into the room safe that I didn't think anyone ever used and so never thought to check. It was still there when the police started gathering his effects. The story of August's real parentage, his obsession with Lo, and his theory that she'd killed Landon.

His horror at realizing that he and I were half-siblings.

It started small, a local reporter doing a couple of stories on how bizarre and gothic the whole thing was, but then it got picked up by the AP, and after that . . .

It was everywhere. *We* were everywhere.

The police never came calling again, thank God, but the tabloids and podcasts sure as hell did. So did *People* magazine. Even dueling Reddit communities emerged, r/RosalieInn and r/AugustFletcher.

So I wasn't surprised the first time I got a call on my cell phone with the name *Fitzroy* flashing on the screen.

If anything, I was surprised it took them until November or so to reach out.

I didn't take the first call, or the second.

The third had come just last night, and I confess that I'd been tempted to answer.

Instead, I let it ring, hoping this time whoever it was might leave a message, but they didn't. The next time they call, I'm not so sure I'll let it go to voicemail. The curiosity might be too much, and then what?

Whoever is calling, they know where to find me, and if they show up at the Rosalie one day . . . well, I can burn that bridge when I come to it.

I don't mention any of this to Lo, even though I think she'd understand. Instead, I say lightly, "I wonder which one of them it is?"

Lo looks out over the water, her face hidden by a huge pair of sunglasses. "Beau died in 2000, so at least you know it's not that old bastard," she replies. "My money is on Camile."

"Have any of them tried to contact—" I start, but she cuts me off.

"Nah. They had their way with me already. Although once I film this *Dateline* thing, they might come back for more."

Yup, we even got our very own *Dateline* episode. Or we will in the spring, apparently. A crew is coming down next month to interview Lo and shoot footage around the Rosalie. They wanted to talk to me, too, but I'm not sure I'm ready for that, not even for my beloved Keith Morrison. If there's one thing I've learned in this ordeal, it's that I'm more like Mom than I ever realized, more content to keep my feelings—and my secrets— close to my chest.

And besides, Lo is a natural at this. Aside from the injuries she sustained during Hurricane Lizzie, she seems to have de-aged a decade overnight. I wonder if finally sharing the truth with someone is the reason why.

Although, so far, I'm the only one she's shared that truth with. In every interview, Lo has stuck to her original story: she never saw Landon that night; it had to be the storm that killed him; what—or who—else could it have been? When the reporters inevitably ask her about me, about August's claims, she always demurs.

"Honey, that's not my business," she said to the Mobile anchor lady in her first interview.

"I didn't know a thing about that, so I don't know what I *could* say." That was in *People*.

"Honestly, I think August's mind just started unraveling, holed up in that room every day," she told the hosts of *Two Girls, One Murder*. "Geneva might have a passing resemblance to Camile Fitzroy, but do you know how many shiny-haired brunettes with sweet little majorette faces there are in the South, baby? Lord, I've seen more girls that look like Geneva in a Target in Mountain Brook than I can *count*."

It's a kindness I didn't ask for, but one I'm grateful for nonetheless. Still, I can't help but tell her now, "You know, if you want to tell the whole story on *Dateline*, I wouldn't blame you. It's your story, and it can't hurt Mom. Not anymore. Not now."

"And betray my fellow witches? Uh-uh." She shakes her head.

"Besides, I wouldn't want to give any of them the satisfaction of having me proven a liar."

She reaches over and squeezes my hand, flashes that big smile. "And I like my version better anyway."

Then she looks past me back at the inn and raises her voice to add, "It's a better version, isn't it, Frieda?"

Edie grimaces as she makes her way over to us. She's slow and unsteady on the sand, but she makes it to the third chair I'd set up and grips my upraised hand to settle into it.

"If you're fishing for another apology, you won't get it," Edie grumbles, but Lo only shakes her head before reaching across me to pat Edie's thigh.

"No, the one was all I needed."

Edie woke up two days after Lizzie and, to the shock of her doctors, remembered exactly what had happened—maybe not the moment of the attack itself, but definitely what had led up to it.

While I'd been at Hope House that night and Lo had been in her room, Edie had come across one of August's journals that he'd left behind in the lobby. She had been curious, wondering what the angle of the book was, wondering what Lo may have said about her and her testimony, wondering if August had figured out who she was.

Instead, she'd found page after page of accusations and grievances and rage, and—most alarming to Edie—sections that talked about Lo in the past tense, like she was dead.

When August came looking for the journal a few minutes later, she confronted him about it.

"My mouth has gotten away from me before," she'd confessed, almost sheepishly, and I could picture her, face red, hands planted on her hips, asking August what the heck this book was all about.

He'd calmed her, of course, all easy charm and smiles, and then suggested they talk about it outside, less chance of being overheard by Lo.

August had opened the back door and gestured for Edie to walk in front of him.

It was the last thing she remembered, but it wasn't too hard to follow those particular breadcrumbs.

Had he meant to kill her? Or was he merely trying to pin something else on Lo, bring me even more fully onto his side?

No way of knowing now, of course. Still, it was a relief to confirm that Lo hadn't been involved. After hearing Edie's full story, the nightmares I'd been having about August's body pinned in the window—his eyes staring and unseeing, the way a flash of lightning gleamed off the shard of glass poking through his neck—finally began to dissipate.

Edie doesn't work for me anymore—after what August had done, she'll never be as strong as she'd once been, and her balance is still pretty bad—but she came home to the Rosalie nonetheless. It was one of the first things I'd had the repair crews work on, getting two bedrooms on the first floor ready for me and Edie.

She keeps making noise about finding her own place, about not wanting to be a "freeloader," but we both know she's here for good, and I wouldn't have it any other way.

Neither would Lo. After Edie came back to the inn, she and Lo sat down on what was left of the porch and talked long into one evening. I don't know what they said, but when they came back in, there was a peace in both of them that I hadn't seen before, an ease that reminded me that once upon a time, they'd been as close as sisters.

With my mom right alongside them.

I think of her now as I sit between these two women, think of all the secrets they've kept, of all the women they've been.

Of all the women *I've* been.

The press had always wanted Lo to be one thing—a Teenage Temptress or a Vulnerable Victim—but she'd been both, sometimes simultaneously. Mom had been a Good Girl from a respectable home—but she'd also fallen in love with a married man, lied about the child he fathered, and, in the process, turned my life and my dad's into a lie, too. And Edie had been the Tough Broad, the strong girl with the big voice, who'd also been so scared and hurt and traumatized that when an opportunity had come along to punish the woman she blamed for her family's death, she'd grabbed it with both hands.

And me? Well, I'd been the Small-town Girl Running Off to the Big City, then the Small-town Girl Returned. A discarded girlfriend, a frustrated and broke innkeeper, a betrayed daughter, a sucker taken in by a charming smile.

But now? I've found a new side of myself. A woman who is embracing her family business, her legacy. A woman who is happier outside of the limelight.

And a woman who can keep secrets of her own.

The three of us sit there for a long time, long enough to hear the hammers start up and the distant whine of a buzz saw.

"It was for Ellen," Edie says, causing both me and Lo to turn in our chairs.

She's staring out at the ocean, her hand trembling slightly where it rests on her thigh, and a pelican swoops into the water and back up into the sky before she speaks again.

"I don't know if that makes it better or worse, Lo, but that's why I did it. Why I lied about seeing you with Landon. Because I knew. I knew what happened that night. The night of Marie."

She pauses to take a deep breath, as if she's steadying herself. "Because I was there."

It shouldn't shock me that there's still more to uncover about what really transpired that night, but my mouth drops open. I think it shocks Lo, too, an emotion I've never seen her wear before, because she takes off her sunglasses and peers more closely at Edie, her green eyes bright.

Edie nods. "I came by to check on her. I was worried about her being alone in the storm."

"You went out in the storm?" Lo asks, her eyebrows raised. "But Frieda, after . . . after . . . well, you were scared if it so much as rained."

"I wanted to be sure Ellen was okay," Edie replies quietly, and there's something in the way she says it—the things implied but unsaid, the sudden shyness of her voice—that lands on me and Lo at the same time.

"Oh," Lo says, nearly as softly as Edie, and Edie gives her a wry smile.

"Oh," she confirms, then sighs. "Not that Ellen ever knew it. From the time she met Landon Fitzroy, she was just as crazy about him as you were, Lo, and I knew it would end badly. I knew Ellen wasn't the type to be okay in that kind of situation for long. No offense," she adds to Lo, who only shrugs.

"But I didn't know about the baby until that night. That's what y'all were yelling about when I got here. You didn't even see me, and I stayed hidden around the side of the porch." She gestures back toward the inn. "But I saw. I saw Ellen hit him first, then you. I saw you try to drag him to the surf, but you couldn't, probably because both of you looked like a stiff wind would blow you over." She gives a snort, then her expression sobers.

"After y'all went back inside, I didn't want you to know I

had been there, but I also didn't want you to leave Landon's body so close to the inn. I thought the authorities would figure it out for sure, that you'd both get the dang chair if he wasn't moved, so I tried my darndest to get him out to the ocean. Figured I was stronger than both of you put together, and I was, to be honest. I got him a good ways down the beach, but then the storm started picking up, and I . . . I got scared. I hoped it would be enough, and I ran."

We're all quiet for a moment until Lo says, "So you were there in the end. It was all three of us."

"All three," Edie agrees. "But then the police started asking questions, and I was so afraid they'd find out about Ellen, about the baby, about all of it, and . . ."

She blows out a long breath and lets three waves crash against the shore before saying, "I thought if I gave them you, Lo, it would all go away. You always sucked up all the oxygen in the room, and if people were looking at you, they couldn't look at anything else. And I—I told myself it wasn't a lie, not really, because you sure as heck were the one to deliver the last blow, and, well . . . the rest of it is what I told you when I got back from the hospital. I was still angry about my family, still blaming you in some corner of my heart, and I admit, it felt good. Seeing you suffer consequences for once. It felt good—until it didn't, but by then it was too late."

Another long silence descends, and I watch Lo as she takes it all in. Then, with another one of those very Lo waves of her hand, she declares, "Well, it's a good thing you sucked so bad on the stand, else I'd have scorch marks on my backside right about now."

It's such a Lo thing to say that Edie and I both begin to laugh uncontrollably, big honking laughs that send a flock of sand plovers scurrying farther down the beach.

Once I've caught my breath, I stand, reaching into the pouch of my hoodie, my fingers closing around cold metal. Mom's bracelet, the one with the "L," sparkles in the sun as I pull it out and twist it this way and that.

I'd picked it up the last time I'd visited Hope House. Mom hadn't been wearing it—it had been sitting on top of the TV, and when I asked Opal about it, she said, "I guess she's lost a little weight because that dang thing will *not* stay on her wrist. I keep finding it on the floor every time I put it on her."

It's probably that. A few pounds lost, the cold weather always making jewelry looser.

Probably.

But what if it's not?

Maybe whatever hold Landon once had on my mother is gone. Maybe, somewhere in her locked brain, she understands that I know the truth now, and she's ready to be free from it.

I know I fucking am.

Walking toward the surf, I wind my arm back and then throw as hard as I can, the bracelet flashing against the blue sky and the green water, and then, with a faint *plop*, it vanishes beneath the waves. I imagine it drifting to the wreck of the *Rosalie*, settling into her shattered hull.

A piece of buried treasure, or maybe a curse, but no longer mine to carry.

"What was that?" Lo asks, and I settle back into my chair as behind me, the Rosalie Inn stands like it plans on being there for another hundred years.

"An offering," I tell her. "To St. Medard."

She smiles and takes my hand. After a moment, Edie takes my other one.

"We'll make a witch of you yet, Ellen Chambers's Little Girl," Lo murmurs, and I think of Landon with his demands and August with his grievances, and both their blood seeping into the boards of the inn, of my home.

I squeeze both their hands, these women who knew and loved my mother, these women who know and love *me*.

"You already have."

ACKNOWLEDGMENTS

Writing this book occasionally felt like being in a hurricane of my own making, so I am so grateful, as always, to work with such a seaworthy crew as everyone at St. Martin's Press. My editor, Sarah Cantin, deserves her own beach vacation—possibly her own private island!—for getting me through this one, and I am so thankful for her patience, her discerning eye, and her firm kindness. Likewise, Drue VanDuker remains a gift of an editor in her own right, and an absolute delight to work with.

Thank you to the entire team behind the Ladies Who Murder (Aspirational) Brand at SMP for all that you do, and also to everyone at Root Literary and CAA.

Of course, none of this is possible *or* fun without my family, both the one I came from and the one I created, and I love all of you for never once being as dysfunctional as the characters in my books! (Okay, maybe not NEVER once . . .)

And thank you thank you THANK YOU to you, my readers. You waited a bit for this one, and I hope it was worth it!

ABOUT THE AUTHOR

John Hawkins

Rachel Hawkins is the *New York Times* bestselling author of *The Wife Upstairs*, *Reckless Girls*, *The Villa*, and *The Heiress*, as well as multiple books for young readers. Her work has been translated into more than a dozen languages. She studied gender and sexuality in Victorian literature at Auburn University and currently lives in Alabama.